THIS

A Simple, Complex Love Story

NAOMI RIVERS

Cover Design: TLK Graphic Solutions

ISBN 979-8-9873297-0-2 (paperback)
ISBN 979-8-9873297-1-9 (ebook)

www.naomiriversbooks.com

For all who believe in fairy tales.

CONTENTS

ACKNOWLEDGMENTS

This book is a twenty-year labor of love, and I am eternally grateful for everyone who provided encouragement to "finish the story." I greatly appreciate Shellie Blackson and Keith Butler, early readers who reinforced my belief that our stories need to be shared. Pamela Dell's outside perspective and inside expertise were immeasurable. Support received from established authors Elizabeth Andre and Siera London was invaluable in helping me with the business of writing. And Nila Curry's review, sage advice, and friendship helped me make this story that much better.

{ONE}

T

Summer 2002

Despite Baltimore's brutal weather this summer—filled with long days of intense heat and high humidity smothering us like a wet, weighted blanket—I wasn't going to let a little sweat and discomfort get in the way of my slight obsession with maintaining my athletic body. I was getting my weekly run in around the Inner Harbor, listening to Nelly's latest hit "Hot in Herre" on my iPod, and trying not to let the pain from the pounding pavement interfere with beating my run time. I'd seen her before, just a passing glance, walking a little white dog. I wasn't a dog person and didn't recognize the breed, but it was cute, and she was even cuter. She generally smiled. I smiled and kept running.

"Coco noooo!" I heard her screaming. Oh no, the little mutt was loose. *Damn it!* I ran faster, the dog ran faster, and she ran after the dog. Are dogs supposed to nip at your ankles? "Hey, stop running!" she called out, "she thinks you're playing with her." Playing with her? How could the dog get that impression? I was minding my own business. But I slowed down anyway and eventually stopped as the woman caught up to us and apologized for the interruption. Which was the exact moment I became more aware of the throbbing pain in my right thigh. Since I couldn't run anymore, I walked gingerly along and she and Coco—apparently that was the dog's name—fell in step without so much as a proper introduction.

"I've seen you running around here before, you have a nice pace," she said. "I'm so sorry for the inconvenience, obviously Coco likes to run too. I believe she finds the leash a nuisance."

"Yeah? Thanks. I do okay. Running is better than trying to keep up with the latest grapefruit, protein, smoothie celebrity fad diets. And Coco and I may be kindred free spirits," I said, smiling.

"Hah, you're funny," she replied.

"Nice scarf, it's very intricate. Of course, it's eight hundred degrees, the extra layer might be overkill," I joked with her, wanting to keep the conversation going and recognizing the scarf didn't look like traditional, earthy kente cloth, it had richer red and purple tones.

She playfully took a swing at me, "Hey! Take that back. It's lightweight and it's one of my favorites."

"I will do no such thing, it is hot as hell out here," I replied with a smile.

"Well, I travel a lot," she explained.

"For work?" I asked.

"No, I wish someone else could foot the bill. But I recently returned from three weeks in Ghana, which is where the scarf came from," she said.

"Nice!"

She continued, "Even though it can be a headache to navigate customs, visas, and whatnot, there is nothing like experiencing a culture that is both familiar and distant you know?"

"Wow, that's amazing. It sounds like you had a nice time. Did you travel solo? With friends?"

"I did have a great time. It was both profound and peaceful. I spent time learning history at places like Cape Coast Castle and the 'Door of No Return.' But did you know Ghana has beaches that rival any in Florida? Palm trees, sandy beaches, delicious seafood...," my new friend said, ignoring my nosy questions about travel partners.

"I did not know that. So can I thank your vacation for the glow or is your skin always so smooth?" I asked.

"Excuse me?"

"I'm sorry." *Oops*, hopefully I didn't offend her. "It's just that your skin reminds me of the chocolate mocha, with a hint of latte, that I had yesterday."

"Are you always this forward?" she asked quizzically, making direct eye contact.

"No, not always," I replied and looked away. *But can you blame me? You're gorgeous in a natural, I-don't-know-I'm-gorgeous sort of way. Your dark brown eyes light up when you laugh, and your supple lips confirm your ancestors are from the motherland.* I interrupted my own train of thought, "So what kind of dog is Coco?"

"She's a Bichon Frisé."

"A what?"

She laughed, "a Bi-chon Fri-sé, they're very friendly and have never met a stranger."

"Oh, well, that explains a lot."

"Indeed. Not to mention she's spoiled rotten, prone to seasonal allergies, fiercely protective, and oh by the way loves walks and car rides."

"How long have you had her?" I smiled because she smiled easily talking about her dog.

"Almost five years now, I got her when she was only seven months old."

"Wow! So do you have kids, like the two-legged kind?" I asked, laughing.

"No, how about you?" she replied.

"No ma'am, I have enough kids at school?"

"You're a teacher?"

"Yep, I teach art." I shared that I was an art teacher by day and an artist by night, albeit at times a starving one that opposed her parents' wishes, but it made me happy. I liked to crank up the music in the studio and leave my thoughts and dreams on canvas. It was cheap therapy. And, despite teaching at a summer camp or two, I enjoyed my summers off.

"Where do you find inspiration?" she wanted to know.

"All over, people, my surroundings, nature, being here near water. The soothing sound helps me sort through questions and provides calm when there's chaos. There's also a sense of humility when I consider an ocean's enormity."

"That's deep, I hear you. Water can be unforgiving if it's not respected. I'm not a fan of working out, but walking near water is therapeutic," she added.

Considering I started running around five-thirty after painting all day and it was only six o'clock when the damn dog started chasing me, I realized that I had talked to a stranger for two hours. About what? Everything and nothing in particular. I found out we shared a profession, somewhat. She was a social worker in a past life and now taught adult education to psychiatric patients—against her mother's pleas to pick a profession to be paid her worth without the aggravation—and she loved dogs.

Our conversation was familiar, comfortable, like we were old friends, not two strangers that had just met. It was different, unlike the countless, boring ones I've had with women in this area since I moved here. We sat on a non-descript bench in downtown Baltimore and talked until the sunset turned the clear, cloudless blue sky a rich shade of yellow-orange. When the conversation paused, I stood to leave; my thigh pain had dissipated to a minor ache.

"Hey, I apologize again about Coco chasing you," she said as we stood to leave. "When are you planning to run again?"

"Now who's being forward?" I kidded her but her directness was refreshing. "I don't know, two, three days depending on the swelling and pain."

"Well, I hope to see you again soon."

"Me too," I said honestly.

That was my cue to ask for more information, but I didn't. I was still trying to figure out my current situation and didn't want any additional complications. She looked a little puzzled when I turned to walk away, then I heard a faint "see you later." I stopped for a minute wondering if I had missed an opportunity. I would see her again right? No one talks for two hours without having some kind of connection. I got the sense that she was interested; I was too. That I knew for sure. She passed me driving from the lot in an older black Volvo that appeared to have seen better days, taking the long way around to ensure I saw her leave. She waved, Coco barked. I smiled and quickly jumped back since the damn dog was hanging out the window.

I took the scenic route back to my Bolton Hill neighborhood, replaying the conversation over the past two hours in my head. I turned the corner sprinting the last leg of my mental marathon. Shit! Sheila's car was here. I instantly tensed up, causing the thigh pain to start again. Although I liked the refreshing contrast of my new friend's casual calmness, that didn't matter now. Sheila was a walking, talking, one-woman theater production.

I was hoping for a moment of peace when I got home. You know, time to stretch and unwind, think about the wonderful conversation I just experienced while soaking my aches and pains away in a nice, hot bath. But THAT shit won't happen—as I unlocked the door, I was immediately greeted with, "Where have you been sweetie? It's date night!"

Fridays had become the designated day when Sheila and I made a point of spending time together despite whatever was going on in our lives. The ritual had gone on now for the two years we'd been seeing each other. Sheila's way of keeping the relationship fresh. And unless one of us was out of town or extremely ill, Friday was "date night."

***

I met Sheila von Doran at Nordstrom. I was shopping for an outfit to wear to a social function and apparently the fact that I abhor shopping was written all over my face. She shooed away another customer, came up to me, and winked. Sheila said that shopping should be a pleasurable experience and proceeded to pick out several combinations for me. Her keen eye for knowing what I would like and my exact sizes in different clothing lines was impressive. Since she was so kind in helping a desperate sistah out, I offered to repay her with dinner. We went out and she never went away. The pretense of a relationship has worked for us.

We've had ebbs and flows where we've gone weeks with very little communication except seeing each other on Fridays or times when we had fun going to various social events. Our relationship was transactional at best. I bought meals and baubles, and she graced me with her presence. I stuck around because she provided some consistent companionship even though the arrangement often came with heavy doses of irritation. It wasn't unusual for me to be on the receiving end of her verbal assaults, usually a result of her feeling she wasn't getting enough attention. I could thank her folks—who came from old money—for spoiling her so freely.

However, the financial spigot went dry about four years ago when her parents decided to pay a surprise visit to Baltimore and discovered her roommate was more than a roommate. On Sheila's twenty-fifth birthday, her parents drove down from Philly to take her out for dinner—after church of course—but all hell broke loose. Dr. and Mrs. von Doran let themselves into her condo with their extra key at ten o'clock in the morning and witnessed Sheila and her roommate naked and asleep in each other's arms on the leather sofa. As Sheila and the woman scrambled about the living room trying to find something to cover themselves with, they couldn't explain the aroma of hours of uninhibited passion mixed with aromatherapy candle scents, an empty bottle of Asti Spumante, and clothes strewn about.

Her parents fussed and fumed and had everything they had ever purchased for Sheila packed into a moving van within hours. They were kind enough to offer not to sell her over-priced condominium and let her assume the mortgage. Aside from the standard exchange of routine birthday and Christmas cards, Sheila was completely excommunicated from the comfortable life she took for granted while growing up in an affluent Philly suburb.

When she met me, she concluded I was "The One." Although my earnings weren't much to brag about compared to Daddy von Doran's, they were respectable. Sheila figured my artwork was on the verge of exploding in a big way and therefore accepting less now would pay off in the future. But she was too impatient for the future to get here and in the interim had done a good job of getting on my last nerve.

The ever-present voices in my head proceeded to have their own conversation. 'Hello, how are you? I'm fine thank you, my day was great! Mr. Arman, you remember him right? The wealthy art collector? He really liked my portfolio and is seriously considering offering me a commission...' Instead "Hey, I was out runnin'," came out of my mouth.

So much for honesty being the best policy. My high school geometry teacher would say that before every test to discourage dumb jocks from cheating. It didn't work. Anyway, I found that it was easier to say what women wanted to hear versus what I was really thinking. Technically, I wasn't lying, I just omitted things. Most of the women, most people for that matter, accepted that. When they asked, I suspected they really didn't want to know what was on my mind, how I was doing, or how my momma was doin'? Those were all rhetorical questions to fill in the time to get to "Let me tell you about me, me, me." And for someone that didn't care much for talking about myself—I was more observational than conversational—the combination was an acceptable symbiosis for me and Sheila.

"I was hoping you were home when I got here so we could go out to eat." As per usual, Sheila interrupted my train of thought. I suddenly regretted that she had a key.

"Let me take a quick bath, it's only eight-fifteen, neither of us has to work tomorrow, although I was going to spend a little time in the studio, so I don't see what the issue is."

She retorted, "You said you would be home!"

"I'm here, damn!"

At that moment I realized two things. One, I needed some Star Trek type of shit to beam myself back to that bench and my newfound friend. And two, I didn't even know her name.

{TWO}

Jasmine

I stepped into the foyer and immediately smelled grease from frying chicken. *How the hell am I going to say no to that?* "Hey baby," I said, greeting Toni, my girlfriend for the past decade, with feigned enthusiasm. Peaks and valleys are common in all relationships. Unfortunately, we had been monotonously settled in a valley for the past five or six years.

"Hey yourself," Toni said, switching from one of those mindless talk shows where everyone ends up throwing chairs to the evening news. Toni started taking chicken out of the heavy iron pan. "I only made a few since you said you were having salad," Toni said.

"I thought *we* were having salad for dinner," I replied.

"Uh, uhn, I ain't on no damn diet! How come every time you go on a diet, me and Coco gotta suffer?" Toni sarcastically commented. "Besides, I don't have a problem, I'm fine already," she boasted as she slid her hands over her athletic torso.

I just sighed. "Thanks for the support," I mumbled as I left the kitchen. Coco stayed behind, hoping something would fall from the kitchen counter. I walked to the bedroom to change. I paused, looked out the hall window and saw the neighborhood children getting started early on summer fireworks. The red, orange, and yellow glow reminded me of the colors of the sunset at the harbor.

When I got to the bedroom, I slowly took off my sweaty clothes, took a shower, and changed into an oversized T-shirt and pajama bottoms giving me time to think about my new friend and our conversation. Hmmm, she was slightly taller than me, toned body, medium brown complexion, dreads—which I don't usually care for, but she wore them well—very nice smile until she became conscious that she was smiling, and an ass for life. And those eyes, those piercing eyes, were a shade of brown, not hazel, but not brown brown, or dark brown either. As the sun and clouds transitioned across the sky while I sat next to her, I swore her eyes changed colors, but I couldn't be certain. The conversation had definitely generated a spark, and that made me giggle.

Wait! What was her name? I wondered and smiled.

{THREE}

T

To keep our date night from crashing, I took Sheila to T.K.'s, my favorite dinner and jazz club. Friday nights were always packed because of the live sets. It was a nice, quaint spot. Not really Sheila's kind of place though. She very much preferred the glitter and glam of Baltimore's high society balls. But she accompanied me here every now and then. I knew I was biased about the venue. The food was superb without a lot of grease and cholesterol. There wasn't a bad seat in the house. I loved the easy-going atmosphere with top of the line, nouveau riche styling like the comfortable easy chairs with soft cushions and wide armrests. And the staff knew me and treated me well, it didn't hurt that my favorite cousin, Kevin, was a co-owner.

Twelve years ago, Kevin Johnson migrated from Savannah a few years before I did and was largely the reason I moved to Charm City—he thought it would be a good idea to put a little distance between me and a ghost of my past. He and his life partner Terrance not only owned T.K.'s Jazz Club, but an art gallery on North Charles Street called Gallery 54 as well. Both Kevin and Terrence were great friends and advocates helping to keep Baltimore's art and social scenes alive. Their standing as a Baltimore power couple somehow transcended societal norms. Having contributed nice sums of money to various causes may have had something to do with that.

The club occupied the top floor of an old 1915 warehouse in Fells Point. Rustic brick walls acted as perfect backdrops for local artisan's work and beautifully restored mortise and tenon wood trusses were reminders of a time when carpentry was considered a fine art. Large arched windows provided a perfect lens through which to peer down at the boats bobbing in Baltimore's idyllic harbor. Individuals, couples, and groups were enjoying themselves on the first night of the weekend. Niches on the perimeter provided opportunities for more semi-personal interaction and spots out in the open were generally occupied by those with larger-than-life personalities.

Unlike Sheila, other women I brought here enjoyed it. They could see and be seen. I, on the other hand, liked to sit in my favorite corner on the mezzanine with fresh flowers and candles adorning the table and absorbing the positive energy. The staff knew I wanted either slightly chilled apple juice or more often than not a Tequila Sunrise. And when there was a new woman with me, a bowl of fresh strawberries. Who said customer service was a dying art?

We were quickly seated, ahead of many on the reservations list. As soon as we settled into a booth, Sheila whined, "Baby I want us to do more things together."

Damn it! I hadn't even looked at the specials. "Like what?" I reluctantly asked but stayed focused on the menu.

"Like dancing, going to the opera, horseback riding. We haven't been riding in a long time. J and Dee invited us on a night ride next Friday. I wanna go. We haven't gone to a house party in a while either! Sometimes I feel like you'd rather be alone than spend time with me?! Baby? Baby, are you listening to me?" Sheila continued to whine.

Sheila was once again going on and on about who knows what? The woman talked a mile a minute without taking a breath. It reminded me of a *My Wife and Kids* episode with Damon Wayans and Tisha Campbell-Martin where neither was listening to the other. You saw their mouths moving, but only Mandarin Chinese was coming out. That was how I felt now. I was immersed in thought but decided to answer before starting a scene here in public.

"Yes, of course I'm listening to you. I'm going to pass on the horseback-riding thing though. The last time we went, I was on my back for a week. And not engaged in pleasures I usually associate with being in that position. Why don't you go and have a nice time?"

Sheila snapped, "Because I want to be with you!"

All I could muster to prevent opening Pandora's Box and ruining my night was, "we'll see."

{FOUR}

Jasmine

"Is it Monday already?" Paula, my co-worker, asked coming in the door with an armload of patient charts. "Where did my weekend go?" Paula continued to moan as she threw herself in her chair. I really liked my new office mate. She started at Crownspring Hospital Center about three months ago and there had not been a dull moment since.

I had worked at Crownspring for almost five years. It was built in the early 1900's and the campus building aesthetic conjured up images of black and white asylum movies. As for building conditions, they had seen better days. I'd been on the community transitioning unit for the past three years working with chronically mentally ill adults. This unit was the best, in my opinion, because these patients had some hope of leaving the hospital. They previously lived in group homes but were sent back to the hospital after a potentially serious incident left the community concerned about patients residing in residential neighborhoods.

I taught them life skills—resumé writing, reading recipes, and navigating bus schedules—those sorts of things. Ultimately, my goal was to get patients to see themselves as more than their diagnoses and help them understand that all of their actions had consequences. Done correctly, I walked a fine line between teaching, occupational therapy, and social work.

Paula's outlook for our patients was a mixture of acerbic wit and tough love that she freely showered on both the patients and treatment teams who made decisions during patient hospitalizations.

Paula pushed the teams to listen to patients when they talked about their personal goals and not blindly implement what the treatment teams always wanted. Team expectations and patient goals were almost always different. For example, one day out of the blue a patient emphatically declared that he wanted a girlfriend. Paula asked the staff if any of them had ever considered that patients may have companionship needs? Crickets, complete silence, no response. You would have thought she asked for a million dollars. What Paula highlighted that day was that none of them saw patients holistically as people with needs beyond their mental health diagnoses.

I secretly wished that I could be more like Paula. However, since she came aboard, I frequently ended up being a peacemaker when tensions escalated to the point of eruption in many morning meetings. Mainly, Paula challenged treatment teams about their antiquated ideas of patient care. Deep down, I believed the psychologists, psychiatrists, and nurses liked Paula but only in small doses. I also appreciated her, as she was the first ever co-worker that knew anything about my personal life other than my fictitious boyfriend's name. Paula discovered the real "Todd" after bumping into me and Toni at a club while she was out with a lesbian cousin. A *cute* lesbian cousin might I add.

"Anything exciting happen with you over the weekend?" Paula asked me. My thoughts immediately turned to my extended talk with the lady runner. I couldn't tell Paula, my newfound confidant, that I had met someone just yet.

"Oh nothing, same ole, same ole. It was a quiet weekend," I answered.

"That smile tells me otherwise," Paula slyly said, "but you'll tell me when you're ready."

There's nothing to tell, yet.

{FIVE}

T

Much to my dismay, it took longer than usual to recover from my sore muscles. Then with consecutive days of oppressive heat with indices above hundred degrees, it was two weeks before I attempted to run again. I was looking forward to running on a day with lower humidity and blue sky, free of afternoon storm clouds. More people were out and about walking, rollerblading, biking, and jogging. The fair-weather athletes I called them, clogging trails and sidewalks, either not understanding or not caring about sharing the width of paths.

I turned east towards the Rusty Scupper Restaurant to continue running along the waterfront. As I picked up my stride leaving the crowded area behind, my train of thought was starting on another tangent when I spotted a dog in full gallop—as much as a little dog can gallop—dragging a leash and coming towards me. Wait, I think I know that dog, is that? What was her name?

Just then, I heard someone yelling. "Coco! Coco! Get back here!" Why do people talk to their dogs like children? "Coco! You know you hear me!"

I mumbled, "Yeah, she may have heard you, but she damn sure isn't listening." I was getting nervous. The dog picked up speed. I ran full speed and cut over into a grassy area. I needed to find something to defend myself, dog bites are the worst. I dodged a little kid but then tripped over a rock and stumbled and bumbled my way to the turf. I didn't land gracefully.

"Coco no!" Just then, the beloved Coco commenced to licking my face as I wiggled and rolled around on the ground, hating that I had altered my route today.

"Coco, you heard me!" I looked up to see an embarrassed, yet coy upside-down smile.

"I told you she likes you and thinks you're playing."

"Yeah well," I said as I jumped up, brushing the grass off my legs and dog slobber off my face. "I'm not too fond of being chased and licked." Now that I had my wits about me to get a good look at my tormentor's owner right side up, I immediately wished I could strike that last comment from the record. It was the mystery woman.

{SIX}

Jasmine

Oh, my god!! It's her! I thought I saw her from a distance but wouldn't believe it was her until I got closer. That damn Coco! This woman was going to think I'm some kind of nut who can't control her dog. I swear, that dog insisted on saying 'hello' to everybody and made me look foolish. She just took off running... again. I couldn't have caught her if I tried, and Lord knows I did. Who knows why Coco was chasing her but whatever the reason, Coco was as close to her as I wanted to be.

Damn! I felt an intense tingling sensation radiating down my spine. Breathe, Jasmine, speak slowly and clearly. "Enunciate your words," I heard my aunt saying in my head. I tried to be cool, I didn't want to seem too interested and I certainly didn't want her to think I was desperate for attention.

"Well, hello?! I would say funny running into you again, but somehow the look on your face doesn't make me believe this reunion has been pleasurable," I said, trying unsuccessfully not to laugh as the look of fear slowly disappeared from her face. Was she really that afraid of dogs? This might not be a good thing. I thought the three of us had established a nice rapport the first time we met. But dogs can really sense good and not so good people. I have tried hard to give most people the benefit of the doubt, but dogs can tell. I have always trusted Coco's instincts and because of that, she's kept me out of a few situations that I would rather not think about.

Coco patiently waited for her head to be rubbed or at least some acknowledgement from my mystery woman. She slowly reached out to rub Coco, but Coco, who was so impatient, jumped up at her. "Hey!" She screamed—lost her mack and everything—and jumped back.

"She didn't do so well in obedience class... the instructor said she anticipated the commands," I rambled, trying to explain my dog's excitement.

"You don't say?" she said sarcastically, seeming not to notice that I cared that Coco and I were not making a good impression.

I decided to stop talking, smiled, and attempted to gracefully walk away. I had lost every cool point that I was born with, so I pulled Coco and turned to leave. Why was I getting so worked up, and why did her opinion matter? I didn't know this woman from Eve, but she had certainly been on my mind these last few weeks. The voices in my head were having a good laugh. This scene looked like something from a bad romantic comedy. Oh, what the hell.

"Since first impressions, or second impressions in our case, are lasting unfortunately, at least tell me your name. That way I can refer to you correctly as the one who got away," I said laughing.

{SEVEN}

T

Smiling with a hint of apprehension and looking her square in the eyes, I extended my right hand. "Hi again, my name is Teresa, but my friends call me 'T.'" She reached for my hand and asked with a slight grin and one raised eyebrow, "So what shall I call you?" As I made a mental note to self about the softness of her hands I replied, "Well if your dog's instincts are correct, you'll fall into the friend category in no time."

"Hmmm... so you think you know a little something something about dogs?"

"No, not really, I know very little about dogs, but I hope he..."

"She," the dog owner interjected emphatically.

"Excuuuse me, I hope *she* likes me since this is the second time she's attacked me."

"Come on now, attacked is kind of melodramatic don't you think?"

"Attacked, knocked to the ground, jumped on...," I said, I knew what I experienced.

She interrupted impatiently, "Okay, okay, this is not how I imagined our second meeting."

"Sooo, you've been thinking about me?" I asked, unable to wipe the silly grin off my face and curious as to why my stomach was fluttering.

Coco barked before she could respond. "I didn't say that."

"Maybe not explicitly, but you just admitted you imagined meeting me again and," I said, singing like a schoolgirl, "your dog confirmed it." I gave her a sly grin.

"Whatever!" she exclaimed and rolled her eyes.

"Testy, aren't we? Alright look, let's start over. I'm 'T'," I said extending my hand primarily to touch her again. "What's your name?"

"Jasmine, and this is Coco."

"Hi Coco," I said and scratched her head, "haven't we met somewhere before?" Her tail wagged feverishly, and she barked in reply.

"Hmmm, Jasmine? I should have known, you've been blowing through my mind like a summer breeze…"

"What?"

"Nothing," I said, surprised that I'd even said that thought aloud. "You come to the Harbor often?"

"Not as much as I should," she answered.

"What do you mean?"

"I mean I should move my body more often. You know, at least walk more and consistently do strength training. Every time I start lifting weights, I wake up sore the next day. So, I stop."

"Hmmmm," I mumbled, the imagery of Jasmine's body moving and me feeling Jasmine's body moving and rubbing her sore muscles lodged in my mind. Though she mentioned she wasn't very satisfied with her current body build, I personally appreciated it. The ample curves on a five and a half foot frame were in all the right places and I imagined how pleasurable it would be to cuddle up next to such a warm, inviting creature. She interrupted my lustful thoughts as we walked slowly together.

"You seem to like running."

"I don't know that I like the act of running so much as I like how it makes me look and feel."

It was Jasmine's turn to be inarticulate, "Hmmmm" I couldn't help but smile. She found her words again and asked, "So what else do you like to do for fun?"

"I read, I paint, listen to music, take pictures," I said.

"What kind of music do you like?"

"My taste is quite eclectic," I responded.

"Really?"

"Yeah, really. Why do you sound surprised," I wanted to know.

"No reason really. I guess I just wasn't expecting that. So, R&B?"

"Of course," I said.

"Classical?" she continued.

"Yes."

"Pop?"

"Some," I responded, amused by her interest in my musical taste.

"Hard Rock?"

"Not so much. But here's one for you..."

"What?" Jasmine wanted to know.

"I love country music," I said with a smile.

"Country? Like Hee-Haw, Merle Haggard country?" she asked while laughing.

"No silly," I said, bumping her gently with my shoulder, "More like Shania Twain, Rascal Flats, Martina McBride, Trisha Yearwood country."

"Oh, you were serious?"

"Of course I was."

"Interesting," she said. I didn't know what quite to make of that but left it alone. She continued her inquiries, "I have at least twenty questions..." *Oh no!* "If money were not a factor, what would you be doing with your life?"

"I'm actually doing it," I replied.

"Really?" she asked with more surprise in her voice.

I smiled, "Yes, really. You find that hard to believe?"

"I just don't meet many people that say they're actually doing their life's work."

"I love making art and I enjoy teaching, most days that is. I would make art even if I didn't get paid for it."

"Wow!" Jasmine seemed impressed.

"And if I could teach without being subjected to administrative nonsense like countless unnecessary meetings, grumpy parents, and new requirements stemming from the president's new 'No Child Left Behind Act,' it would be ideal. That aside, I guess I am kind of lucky to do what I like and get paid for it."

"You're right about that."

"What about you? What would you be doing given the chance?" I asked.

"Well, I like what I do but, if money were no object, I would be a florist."

"A florist?" It was my turn to be surprised.

"Yeah, there are so many possibilities and varieties and colors and combinations of flowers and plants," Jasmine rattled off.

"Hmmmm, that sounds a lot like painting," I observed.

"Yeah, I guess it kind of does, doesn't it?"

"Something else we have in common, I guess. Creative energy!" Not that I needed another reason to adore Ms. Jasmine, but that little nugget added icing on the cake.

"Change of subject," she exclaimed.

"Oooh-kay…"

"How long have you been growing your locs?"

"Ummmm, about four years now. Why?" I asked.

"I thought about loc'ing my hair once but when I found out they are just as much maintenance as getting my hair permed, that idea quickly faded."

That made me laugh. "I hear you, I don't think of them as a lot of work though. I have a great loctician who doesn't take all day to do what she needs to do."

"Hmmmm, that's a blessing. Do you always wear them up?"

"I do when I'm running or when it's bloody hot. The extra weight and heat are too much on my neck," I replied.

For the next hour and a half Jasmine and I walked along the sidewalk talking like we were old friends again. Her attentiveness, apparent interest, and our commonalities were refreshing, a much-needed change of pace from the normal blah, blah, blah. Before I knew it, we were standing near her car, and it seemed like neither one of us was in a hurry to leave.

"Hey!" we both said after a pregnant pause.

"You first," I said.

"No, you," Jasmine countered.

"I was, um, it's just that we seem to enjoy each other's company and all and, um, if you're not busy…"

"Teresa?" she said, ending my obvious clambering.

"Yes?" I was extremely embarrassed.

"Just spit it out."

"Okay." I took a deep breath. "There's an art exhibit next Friday downtown, I was wondering if you'd like to go? Maybe have dinner afterwards?"

"I'd love to," Jasmine said smiling and without hesitation.

"Really? Great!" I said feeling relieved and excited at the same time. "What time should I pick you up?" At the mention of time, she looked down at her watch.

"Oh shit! Excuse my language." Suddenly, she was in a hurry. "Uh, that won't be necessary," she said nervously while putting the dog in the backseat on the passenger side of the car and dashing over to the driver's side all in one fluid motion. She quickly handed me a card as if that were planned. "Here's my cell number, call and leave the address and I'll meet you there. What time?"

"Seven, seven o'clock is fine," I said, trying to read her hurried thoughts. "So, I look forward to seeing you then."

"Yeah, same here!" She shouted as she started her engine, not waiting for the car to warm up, and pulled away. And with that, all that lingered of Jasmine was the nicely printed business card in my hand and rampant thoughts of the next time I'd see her.

{EIGHT}

Jasmine

Argh! How could I have been so careless and let time slip away?
I knew Toni would be pacing and cussing because I was late,
especially since we had to drive nearly two hours to get to Fort
Washington and Lord only knows what Friday evening traffic would
yield.

During the WNBA basketball season, a group of friends took
turns hosting parties to watch Washington Mystics away games,
those that are televised anyway, but that is a different story for
another day. This gave them a chance to stay connected with the
Mystics while they were on the road and an excuse to get together.
West coast away games usually started later in the day which gave
everyone time to get settled, eat, and relax before tipoff. But it
wasn't like Toni's friends were ever prepared to start anything on
time. Most of them had a distant relationship with punctuality. But
Toni ALWAYS had to be at so and so's house on or before the
designated time.

Because of my girlfriend's proclivity to be on time, necessary in
her line of work managing an HIV/AIDS advocacy organization,
but unhelpful for me personally, I didn't know how many times I
ended up helping with last minute preparations at other people's
houses. Hell, I was tired! I'd been working all week and didn't feel
like helping cook, arrange snacks, or set food out. When I got a
chance to rest, the last place I wanted to be was sitting in a thick,
smoke-filled basement watching people drink, "party," and laugh at
nothing particularly funny.

I didn't travel in the same social circle since the D.C. lesbian scene was much different from Baltimore's. In the same vein, my interests were vastly different than Toni's friends. If it wasn't for her, I probably wouldn't have crossed paths with them. Truthfully, I really didn't like most of them and therefore, most of our interaction was superficial. "Partying" was their euphemism for smoking weed or if you asked them, it was their way of releasing creativity or managing chronic pain. I was skeptical to say the least and suspected that the more private parties included extra-curricular shenanigans involving scantily clad women dancing for dollars. What damn affinity Toni had with any of it, I will never know. Dear God, I shouldn't have to lie. I simply didn't want to go!

I pulled into the driveway and the front door was already open. *Ugh,* this was not going to be good. I opened the car door and immediately heard Toni yell, "I thought you were going for a quick walk. You've been gone a long time, I started to leave!"

I should have stayed longer then, I was having a better time there anyway.

"We are going to be late… I'm driving." All said without taking a breath. I knew at that point I definitely didn't want to go, and I damn sure didn't want to be in the passenger seat strapped into what was about to become a low flying aircraft. I got motion sickness riding that erratically.

I took a deep breath and tried to count to ten, but I responded at seven. "Leave for what? The game? The nonsense? What are you so interested in getting to?" I demanded to know a little louder than I meant to.

"We are supposed to be there at seven. Are you ready?" Toni responded.

"I will be in ten minutes," I ignored her sucking her teeth as I walked past. If I didn't ignore the sound, we would have kept arguing. I was still fuming as I brushed my teeth and washed my face. I kept thinking, why am I doing this?

***

Just as I thought, when we arrived the basement was already filled with smoke and the lights were dim. The only people here yet were the core group of party animals. Some rapper was bragging about his bitches and hoes on the stereo and an unwanted uneasiness in the pit of my stomach that I had come to associate with hanging out with Toni and her friends took hold. More and more, I despised this whole scene. I could think of twenty different things I would rather do on a Friday night, including watching paint peel, but Toni wanted me with her.

At least that was what she always said although we were usually not in close proximity at these functions. Besides, if I could avoid smelling like a chimney from my hair down to my beautifully pedicured toes, I did. More often than not, I felt like a showpiece. She liked me to accompany her so the doms knew that I was off limits and to make them jealous. Sad, in the most objectifying way possible I know. But I tried to make myself useful and help in the kitchen with the other "good wives." It's funny, growing up watching my mother take care of my father and brothers hand and foot, I said I'd never be that submissive to a man. Guess I should have considered the same gender in the equation as well.

At first, these parties were tolerable; at least that's what I remember. I was so in love with Toni that my judgment, looking back now almost ten years later, was probably skewed. We used to dance, play cards and dominoes, gossip about who broke up, and who was sleeping with whom this week. Some of her friends changed girlfriends like some of us changed panties—and not the expensive ones—so it always made for interesting comic relief.

I saw Toni differently then. She seemed to be more settled and stable than her friends. We prided ourselves on our solid relationship. Two college educated, professional women that had a lot going on other than trying to screw half of the female population in Baltimore or D.C., lesbian or not. Little by little though, the draw of the parties became more about smoking weed and drinking rather than truly enjoying each other's company. My gut sensed that T's idea of a Friday night was different.

"Hey girl!" Stephanie, the only friend I had amidst this crowd, interrupted my trip down memory lane and perhaps into my future.

"Hey," I said with a warm smile.

"I thought you were supposed to put the finishing touches on the crab salad. You over here deep in thought. And judging by the size of that smile, it's more than you being happy to see me."

"No, I'm not deep in thought and what smile?" I lied, trying to hide the physical manifestation of joy that the thought of T brought.

"Well, whatever it is, we can talk about it in a few minutes, but we need to finish the food before the natives in the basement get restless," Stephanie reminded me.

"Girl, it's nothin', just listenin' to the activity that's all."

"Uh huh…you can't fool me. We've been through too much shit together. I've been able to read you like a book since eleventh grade." Stephanie didn't wait for my response. Instead, she grabbed the bowl of crab salad, placed it on a serving tray with crackers and headed downstairs. "I'll be right back," she called over her shoulder.

Shit! I was not in the mood for one of her therapy sessions tonight. Stephanie was a clinical psychologist with specialties in educational and counseling psychology. She was the only person I knew that was more adept than me to get people to talk about themselves to divert the focus from herself. We had been analyzing each other since high school when I complimented her on an extraordinarily short mini skirt with matching pumps. The girl had a fabulous sense of style even then and I adored her strong self-assuredness.

"Jazzy! Jazz? Baby come here for a minute," Toni screamed from the basement stairs.

"God, I hate when she calls me that," I mumbled.

"Jazzy?" The footsteps were getting louder as she reached what I assumed was the top landing. "Jazz! I know you heard me girl. Come here for a second."

"What is it Toni?" I said disgusted, but still moving in her direction. She grabbed me around the waist, pulled me to her, and planted a kiss on my lips. A few years ago, I would have been instantly turned on by her cockiness, but right now I was trying to ignore the taste of Corona and burnt ash.

"What's the matter baby?"

"It's…" I started.

Toni continued without waiting for an answer. "Pat and Peaches invited us down to watch the Mystics' game next Friday, the season's heating up you know."

"I thought the game was in Indiana," I said trying to choose my words carefully knowing full well that by the time they were all drunk out of their minds this time next week, I'd be otherwise engaged. I hoped I would be staring into someone else's eyes and doing my best to prolong time spent with that fine, intelligent life form.

"It is, they're having some people over to watch it on digital. They have the sports package."

"Oh." Damn satellite has been the source of many of my problems.

"Yeah baby!" she exclaimed trotting back down into Satan's den, "It'll be fun!"

Goddamnit! See that's what I was talking about. We used to discuss these things. At what point did she stop soliciting my opinion and start being my social coordinator?

***

Without too much of a Stephanie inquisition, although she sensed something was different, I managed to have a little fun. My inner diva was in full effect tonight and the "family" couldn't keep their eyes off me. The doms were drooling, and the femmes were jealous. Don't hate me because I can still send the "children" into a frenzy.

But even worse than going to these damn parties was the drive home and impending request for sex. Like usual, Toni was high and drunk and foolishly wanted to drive home. And like clockwork, she got loud and irritated in the process of us fighting for her car keys. Finally winning the battle, I got in the driver's seat, took a long, deep breath, and put the key in the ignition. "Phew…I survived another Friday night," I whispered.

"What's that Jazzy?" Toni slurred, having reclined the passenger seat all the way back so she could sleep on the way home.

"Nothing."

***

As I came into the kitchen the next morning Toni asked, "What did you say about going to Pat and Peaches' house on Friday for the game?" I hesitated, knowing that I would need to come up with a plausible excuse for why I wasn't going with her. At least with me not there, Toni didn't have to worry about how many beers she drank or joints she smoked. But my excuse had to be good. I stalled, "Remember I told you I have a seminar, and a couple of us are going for drinks afterwards?"

"How come you can drink with everyone but me?" she asked. I smiled before I replied, but the voices in my head screamed, "BECAUSE I ALWAYS HAVE TO WORRY ABOUT DRIVING AND THERE'S NO REASON FOR BOTH OF US TO BE DRUNK." I verbally replied, "I try to have a good time with you too."

Hmmm… The house smelled like a wonderful blend of basil, rosemary, and oregano. Toni was making the best smelling spaghetti for what I assumed would be tomorrow's dinner. One thing I couldn't complain about though? She did most of the cooking, and her damn spaghetti was so good that when my mother asked, 'who made the spaghetti' and I replied 'Toni,' she was at our house within minutes with plastic bowls like she ordered take out.

***

When I walked in the office Wednesday morning, I must have been smiling absentmindedly because Paula said, "You sure can tell it's 'Hump Day', people just look more relaxed and pleased for no reason at all. Or do we have a reason for smiling?"

"Nope, just happy the weekend is almost here," I responded.

"You and Toni have plans?" she asked trying to get into my business.

"No," I said as my face fell slightly, the gravity of what I may be contemplating coming into sharp focus. An old saying went something like, 'don't start what you don't plan to finish,' but elders imparting that wisdom didn't take into account that "life" happens.

Even though I swore my relationship with Toni would be different, it seemed to be going the way of others before it. While I mentally understood that all relationships needed maintenance, our relationship had grown tired, and I had grown tired of trying. I may as well be honest with myself; I wasn't happy and had not been for a long time. I could have easily blamed it on Toni, but truth be told, I had just as much weight to bear for the relationship's degraded state.

As our relationship matured, I just didn't feel like dressing up in lingerie and setting the mood to have a little sex. Of course, it wasn't all about sex, but sometimes I didn't want to have to entice Toni. I wanted to be wanted... Was that the beginning of the relationship's end? A thousand revelations came to mind. I stopped trying to pick out the right outfit. I wasn't beating my face to look 'natural', cool, fresh, or sexy. Our walks stopped. I slacked on cleaning the house. She stopped bringing home "just because flowers." I no longer received mid-day "Hi, I was thinking about you" phone calls. Her extracurricular activities—smoking and drinking—eventually made her unattractive to me. The accumulation of all these things cracked open the door of new possibilities; like the possibility there may be someone better out there for me.

Even when Toni and I had those god-awful heart-to-heart talks, things only changed for a few days, or weeks, at best and then it was back to business as usual. In my formative years, I routinely heard that you had to work just as hard at a relationship as a full-time job. Toni's retort to that usually was, "Yeah, but no one wants to do hard labor." I didn't particularly like what I was planning to do Friday, but weirdly I felt both powerless to stop it and empowered to discover what comes next. I mean really, T was hot, and she had definitely sparked an interest and energy that I long thought was dead. Apparently, it was simply dormant. But do I let smoldering kindling progress into the slow burn that I suspect may follow? *What the hell was I doing?*

{NINE}

T

Man! The old Heinz Ketchup jingle, "Anticipation Is Making Me Wait," was a good theme for this week. It seemed like it had been six months, not seven days since I saw Jasmine. And although it was a pleasant surprise talking to her briefly yesterday when I called to leave the gallery's address, the fact that she had been on my mind quite a bit was something different for me. I was used to providing attention to whomever was occupying my space on any given day. But since meeting Jasmine, the anticipation of what's yet to come was making me crazy, yet excited.

Sheila was still reeling from me not going horseback riding last Friday and pitched a bigger fit when I told her I had a show downtown tonight. She gave me the silent treatment all week since I was going to miss two consecutive date nights. Oh well. Thank goodness she had never been too interested in my artwork—beyond the money it garnered—or the whole art scene in general. Otherwise, I wouldn't have had as much flexibility in using it as an excuse to dabble a bit. Like last night, I was trying to pose a preemptive strike since I knew I wouldn't be available tonight and invited her to join me to visit the galleries on North Charles Street for 'First Thursday.'

Every first Thursday of the month galleries open their doors for cocktails and an open house of sorts. I bemoan the social aspect since I'm a loner by nature but being out there was good for business. Sheila wanted no part of it. She said although the people were eccentric and talented, they were boring. At times I think she regarded me the same way. But that's okay, Ms. Thing may be on her way out.

Thank goodness it was Friday. Not only because I was excited to see Jasmine, but I swore the kids in the weeklong summer art camp that I ran made a pact with the devil to drive me nuts. One decided to stick clay in his friend's hair, another was inclined to paint on his arm and not the provided canvas, and yet another was determined to load test the weight limit of several light fixtures by swinging on them like they were monkey bars. After I described his unsuccessful trapeze act to the principal and his mother, I was spent. Thankfully, I had been assigned an intern, a talented young artist from the Baltimore School of the Arts that I mentored. She had natural artistic talent and after speaking with her mother, I somehow agreed to continue encouraging her work. She had been a huge help all week and I was still worn out. But not enough to dampen my excitement about seeing Jasmine.

***

That evening, I was a nervous ball of anxiety. To calm down, I danced around the house to the *15 Greatest Hits of Marvin Gaye* and slid on my hardwood floors in sock-clad feet while trying different combinations on. You'd swear I was sixteen years old going out on my first date. I looked in the full-length mirror for the hundredth time and finally settled on a simple all black outfit; slacks with pleats that fell just right and a silk short-sleeve shirt that gently caressed my defined biceps.

Would the eclectic group of artists and art collectors in the gallery repulse Jasmine? I didn't tell her this was *my* exhibit opening tonight and that these were my peeps. I wanted it to be a surprise just to see her reaction. I realized I was taking a chance on getting my feelings hurt, but I was certain to find out if she was a keeper. Oh well, what will be, will be. I needed to mingle and act like I had a mortgage to pay.

***

"Teresa, hi."

"Cousin Kev, aren't we being formal? How are you tonight?" I teased and gave him a hug. But he was all business.

"I'm fine, I want to introduce you to Nia. Teresa, this is Nia Bostic. She's interested in the piece you called *Two Faced*."

"Hi Nia, it's a pleasure meeting you," I said, extending my hand to and making eye contact with the beautiful caramel-colored sistah. She had a cute, short pixie cut and her makeup was flawless. Her almond-shaped eyes were seductively inviting, and thanks be to God for the little black dress that clung to her petite, but toned body.

"Hi," she said with a warm smile and feathery soft handshake, "the pleasure is mine since I've met the mastermind behind such incredible work."

"I don't know about the mastermind part, but the work is mine," I said.

"Talented and modest, I like that," Nia said coyly.

Kevin noticed I was getting terribly embarrassed and volunteered to escort Nia to the office to make purchase and delivery arrangements. But not before she winked and placed her business card in my hand, which she held longer than necessary.

With impeccable timing, John Bonaparte, my personal critic and brutally honest best friend emerged gracefully from behind a partition. "T baby, how are you? I see you're still working the ladies. As usual, you have out done yourself in this show. I particularly like the pallet of colors you're working with these days. Bold, primary colors always make a statement." John had a knack for chatting, which is why I always invited him to these things. He also kept me out of trouble.

"Hey sweetheart, how are you?" I asked, giving him a hug, and ignoring his comment about 'the ladies.'

"I'm fine. If you don't pocket at least five grand tonight, I'd be shocked!"

"You're just saying that to make me feel good," I said while looking around.

"Chile please, I have never had to boost that oversized ego of yours and I'm not going to start now. Really, they're good, I'm telling you, you need to stop dealing with them little rug rats and spend more time in the studio." John was scanning the gallery too.

"Who you lookin' for trick?" I asked.

"Hell, I'm looking for whoever you're lookin' for," he answered with a raised eyebrow and sly smile.

"I'm just seeing who's here that's all," I said trying to sound nonchalant.

"Bullshit! You may be able to fool these little girls that pine over you, but not me honey, I…"

Just as John was beginning another diatribe, Jasmine virtually floated in the front door.

"Damn! Who is that?" John questioned.

"Her name is Jasmine Charles. Someone I'm trying to get to know and who I hope is interested," I blurted out.

"In what?" John asked singing the question as I walked away from him and towards the door.

"Time will tell," I countered with a smile and wave over my shoulder.

{TEN}

Jasmine

Wow, it was really crowded in here, I thought as I walked into Gallery 54. The crowd was mixed... black, white, straight, gay, and those not quite sure. I used to go to art shows, though not many in the past few years. These shows brought out those who wanted to be seen. There were people posturing, the cultured children, and those desperately trying to figure out the art scene. I picked up a handcard with the night's artwork on it, dropped it in my clutch, and scanned the room.

Finally, I caught T's eye. She smiled and walked towards me. I took a breath, whispered a quick "thank you Jesus" to the universe and a subsequent, "damn, she's hot!" to myself. I met her halfway and gave her my best Colgate smile. We embraced briefly, but long enough for me to realize that her body felt as toned as it looked.

She knew a lot of people, as evidenced by the continuous "hellos" from people milling around. We made small talk. She asked if I had visited the Charles Street galleries before and if I had trouble finding parking. The positive energy was flowing; her hand was on the small of my back directing me around and then... *Damn it!*

"Teresa," some woman purred, "I just finished making my purchase." Oh, hell no! No, this little pixie ass fairy didn't just push me aside to get to T, practically drooling, batting her eyes, and gushing about some art she just bought. She wanted T to personally come and hang it in her Evergreen home, which I imagined was as ostentatious as she was.

I had taken all I could before cursing out that little Halle Berry look-a-like when a guy stepped in to help avert the catfight that was about to take place. I didn't usually do the violence thing, Rodney King asked America, "Can we all get along?" So, I tried not to show my ass. But size two women always seemed to think those of us with a few more curves should just step aside... I didn't think so. She was rude. It was on!

T stood there looking back and forth partially bewildered. That was the second time she lost her cool points. But the intercessor swooped in again and escorted me to the refreshment table. "Hi, I'm John," he said, extending his hand with perfectly manicured nails.

"Hi John, I'm Jasmine. I could have handled her myself thank you very much," I said defending my honor and returning his handshake.

"Perhaps, but that isn't necessary. I'm T's 'Ride or Die.'"

"Really?"

"Yes honey, we go waaay back. Look, don't pay no attention to T's fan club, they can be a bit much. Some people aren't happy with themselves and just need to be messy with a capital 'M'," he informed me.

"You don't say?" I sarcastically responded to the understatement of the evening.

"Now what we really need to focus on are the fashion faux pas that are all up in through here tonight. Like Mr. Man over there looking like Steve Urkel's twin brother. Chile..." he whispered. As John continued cracking on everyone in sight, another guy walked the pixie fairy out of the door.

John was trying his best to entertain me, but all I could think was, *I could be somewhere else not enjoying myself.* He did have a knack for humor though, kind of like the class clowns I grew up with here in Baltimore. Before long I was laughing at his stupid, outrageous remarks and impersonations.

We talked for a little while longer when I noticed an incredible painting that people were pointing to. The piece was an abstract, lots of intertwined figures I interpreted as black women—no one else had hips like us—in vivid hues of blue, yellow, and orange. I thought the painting would look nice in the living room but gasped at the price. "$2,500?" Not only no, but hell no!

"For you I'm sure it's negotiable." As if on cue, T slowly approached me from behind; gently placed her hands on my waist, leaned into me, and whispered in my right ear. I turned around and gave her one of my best "girl please" looks and sarcastically commented with more bite than necessary, "Oh, I guess you have some pull with the artist?"

She responded, "I might."

John chuckled. It was more of a cackle, but I thought it was a private joke and I was still kind of pissed to really care one way or the other.

"Don't think that you talking to the artist suffices as an apology," I said. "That woman was rude and disrespectful. I didn't appreciate Tinkerbell fluttering around at all."

"I thought you liked the painting?" she teased, totally ignoring my statements.

"It's amazing, but I don't think you have that much pull and I have lots of art in my basement by prominent artists that hasn't found its way to the walls yet," I responded.

She just smiled. As we stood there trying to figure out our next move, a couple walked up to T and congratulated her on the show. She graciously accepted their well wishes and turned to me as they walked away. It slowly dawned on me. I pulled the handcard back out and flipped it over. "Oh wow! You probably think I'm stuck on stupid huh? I just realized what's going on here. This is your work? Why didn't you say it was your show? Why didn't you tell me?" I asked question after question.

"I'm not so sure you would have come out if you knew it was my show. Plus, I wanted to see your unbiased, unadulterated reaction."

"I would have come even if you invited me to your school's art show, less known a professional exhibit."

"Oh really, that interested, are you?" T asked like she knew the answer to my question.

"I didn't exactly say that," I said slightly embarrassed.

"You didn't have to."

{ELEVEN}

T

Our eyes were fixed on each other and the internal warmth that seemed to be more frequent when I was around Jasmine made its return. Her eyes drew me into a comfortable place although at times it felt like she was trying to look through me. I wanted to pull her to me and kiss her supple, inviting lips right then and there. I knew she sensed the same thing because of the slight smile she tried to hide as she slowly shook her head, made an "umh, umh, umh" sound and looked away. Clearing his throat to interrupt our intrigue-induced trance, Kevin saved me. "Well you two, tonight was a resounding success. T, perhaps you should let our guests know you appreciate them before you get too distracted."

"You're right," I responded to Kevin with a little snark. I looked at Jasmine and gently touched her elbow, "Excuse me for a moment."

I stood near the exit, shaking hands and thanking the remaining patrons as they trickled out of the gallery with as much enthusiasm and sincerity I could muster. This was the part of business that I didn't care that much for. But Kevin was right, folks neither had to be here nor did they have to dispense with their hard-earned money.

After the last guest left, I walked up to Kevin and Jasmine who were already engaged in conversation. "Kev, I couldn't have done it without you really," I said referring more to him escorting Nia out than the exhibit opening itself. But he and his staff were, without question, responsible for this great affair. "It was my pleasure," he said.

"I was going to introduce you two, but I see you've met?" I inquired.

"Kind of, but why not do the honors any way T?" My cousin was being facetious.

I poked him in the side. "Well then smarty pants, I want you to meet a friend of mine. Jasmine, this is my cousin Kevin Johnson, Kevin, Jasmine." Jasmine extended her hand. "It's a pleasure to meet you, Kevin. So, you coordinate events, *and* you have to referee?" Ugh, now Jasmine was in on the ruse too.

"I guess you could say that. We do what we can to help talented artists like T," he responded with a smirk. "And I have been refereeing T's *events* for a long time."

"I'm sure you have. And you're also right. I had no idea Teresa was so talented since she chose not to tell me she was a local celebrity," Jasmine said rolling her eyes at me.

"Alright people, enough talking about me like I'm not standing here," I complained. Just then John walked up and placed his arm around me. "T honey, I understand your night has only begun. Kevin and I will take care of closing the gallery."

"I don't know what you're talking about Mr. Man, but are you sure? I'm in no hurry," I tried not to sound too eager to leave and get into a more intimate atmosphere to have Jasmine all to myself. Kevin said, "It's no trouble T, your work made us some money tonight, go have fun." I hugged them both, they both hugged Jasmine and after exchanging salutations, Jasmine and I stepped into the humid summer night air. Even though it was nine at night, it was still hot as hell.

"Well Ms. Charles, if it's okay with you, we're going to T.K.'s Jazz Club."

"How did you know my last name? Where's that? Should I follow you?" Jasmine asked.

"Geesh, that's a lot of questions. You gave me your card remember? It's in Fell's Point. And why don't I drive, your car will be fine. I'll make sure you get back safely," I said with a wink.

"How do I know you're not just trying to have the upper hand by separating me from my car?" she inquired.

"Don't be so skeptical, I was just trying to be considerate, parking can be limited down there. Trust me, I'm no psycho ax murderer, at least not yet," I joked.

"What?!" she asked, lips pursed, head cocked to the side.

"I'm joking, I'm joking, you need to lighten up a bit," I said.

"Ooookay…" Jasmine said hesitantly.

We walked to my car in relative silence though the energy between us was palpable. So many thoughts were running through my mind, I hoped I was making a favorable impression and that she wasn't completely bored out of her mind. As we approached what I call my chick magnet, a 1993 black limited-edition Mazda Miata with red leather interior, I unlocked the door with the keyless remote, opened the passenger side door for her, and closed it once she was comfortable. Going around to the driver's side, I did a little jig, happy that I survived the first part of the date.

"This is a surprise and you're in a good mood," Jasmine commented when I got in the car.

"Why do you say that?" I asked, unable to hide my smile.

"I would have thought you drove a larger vehicle to transport your art. Plus, this car has mirrors you know."

"So what, you're watching my every move?" I raised my eyebrows a few times. "I also have a cargo van that I use to carry my work. But that thing is not an appropriate carriage for a queen," I said.

"Why do you always manage to turn things around? I asked you a question," she said nudging my arm.

Turning to make eye contact I chided her, "You're just trying to touch me, aren't you?"

"See, another question in response to my question."

I gave in. "Okay fine. Yes, I'm in a good mood. The crowd in the gallery was thick, I can pay the mortgage for a few more months, and I'm spending the evening with a gorgeous woman."

"Stop. There you go again, turning the focus away from you," Jasmine said blushing.

"What? I was answering your question. That's what you wanted right?"

"I know," she said sucking her teeth, "Anyhoo…"

I just laughed and started the car. We drove south on St. Paul Street and turned east onto Pratt towards the thriving Inner Harbor. Jasmine mentioned how different downtown was now than it was twenty years ago when you dared not come down here after dark. I agreed without going into a long diatribe, which I'm subject to do about the city's urban planning and revitalization efforts. I pulled up to the T.K. valet.

"Good evening, ma'am," he said to Jasmine while smiling and opening her door. "Good evening," she responded.

"T! What up? What do we owe dis pleasure?"

"Jimmy, you know me, gotta make that paper. I had an opening tonight."

"Right right, I know da shit was slammin'!"

I smiled, "I did okay, take care of her okay?" I said tossing him the remote.

"You know how I do," he said with outstretched arms and flashing his latest platinum tooth.

"Yeah, I know how you do so… take care of her," I said laughing and opening the club's door for Jasmine.

The hostess greeted us warmly and escorted us up to my usual table in the corner with the flowers. Handing us our menus, she smiled, made longer than necessary eye contact and said, "Your server will be right with you T, enjoy your meal."

"Thanks Mariah," I said returning the smile.

"Is there anywhere you go that people don't know you?" my dinner companion asked while simultaneously kicking me under the table.

"Ouch! Of course," I said without looking up from the menu.

"It doesn't seem like it, the valet, the hostess…"

"T, I heard your show was absolutely fabulous." Terrance, the T half of T.K. and Kevin's partner, which I failed to tell Jasmine, helped himself and pulled a seat over to our table.

"Hey sweetie, how are you?" I asked leaning over to hug him and kiss him on the cheek. "It went well, I was pleased. Terrance this is my friend Jasmine, Jasmine, Terrance," I said introducing them.

"Nice to meet you," he said taking her hand and planting a soft kiss on it. "Any friend of T's is a friend of mine and is welcome at T.K.'s anytime. Is this your first time here?"

"Yes," she replied. "It's very nice, I'll definitely be back. The flowers are beautiful, who's your florist?" Jasmine asked pointing to the table centerpiece.

"Thank you, I have my man Kevin to thank. He's the creative one in our family. You may have met him?" Terrance asked Jasmine.

"I did. Wow! I didn't know I would meet so many movers and shakers tonight," Jasmine said giving me the side eye after making the connection between my cousin and Terrance.

"I don't know about moving and shaking, those days are probably over for us," Terrance said with a smile. "What can I get you to drink Jasmine?"

"Um, I'll have a glass of white zinfandel. Who's your florist?"

"White zinfandel coming up. Oh yes, our flowers, we use Pearson's Florist at North and Charles, his arrangements are gorgeous!" Turning to me, Terrance asked, "And honey do you want the usual?"

"That would be great, thank you," I said with a wink.

After he left to give our drink order to a server, Jasmine started again. "See what I mean?"

"This is just one of my favorite places that's all, they know me up in here."

"Yeah well, it seems like they know you quite well, especially Ms. Mariah?" she questioned with a neck roll, her lips pursed, and a chuckle.

"What? The woman was just doing her job." I tried to get Jasmine refocused, but took a second to reminisce about the brief moment Mariah and I dated. Anytime a sistah starts rolling her eyes and neck, there's going to be trouble in River City. "Uh huh...," she said. "By the way, what's your usual?" Jasmine asked smiling.

"A Tequila Sunrise without the tequila," I answered.

"Without the tequila?"

"Yep, without the tequila."

"Why?" Jasmine seemed determined to get to the bottom of this travesty. I was used to the line of questioning and couldn't help but laugh.

"I don't drink."

"At all?"

"Nope," I said matter-of-factly.

"Wow! Okay." She seemed very surprised. "I don't know that I've ever met such a creature." This made me smile and laugh even harder.

The server brought our drinks and a bowl of strawberries. "Excuse me," Jasmine quickly said to the server, "we didn't order these." She pointed at the bowl. Smiling at me and then turning his attention to her, he said, "They're courtesy of the owner ma'am. I'll return in just a moment to take your order."

Ah shit, preemptive strike time. "Okay look Jasmine, is it a crime to get great customer service? Especially since I'm related to one of the owners. Savor it when you can, like these flowers for instance," I said.

"You're changing the subject with flower talk? I'm just cautious by nature that's all. Often, good customer service is the exception rather than the rule. It also seems that people just gravitate to you, and they eat up your shy, 'I don't know I'm attractive as hell' demeanor," Jasmine said while looking around at the restaurant's clientele, starting to feel the sassy groove the band was playing. But then she stopped her smooth chair dance and turned back to me, realizing she had said more than she wanted to. Our eyes met again like they did at the gallery. She lowered her head with a slight tilt such that her shoulder-length hair, which I had only seen in a ponytail before tonight, cascaded beautifully over a portion of her face. She closed her eyes, sighed, slowly shook her head, and uttered "umh, umh, umh" again.

I couldn't help but smile.

"Hmmm, may I ask you a question?" Jasmine asked.

"Uh oh, that sounds serious... what's up?" I was a bit nervous.

"What color are your eyes?"

"Phew," I exhaled. "Is that why our eye contact has been so intense?" I asked her.

"I'm not sure what you mean." She tried to feign innocence.

"I mean, I've felt at times like you were looking into my soul or something. Never mind, I'm probably not making sense. I should be used to this question," I said, knowing full well that I wasn't articulating the warm, electrifying energy I felt when she looked at me. "I'm not really sure what color they are, I just say they're brown."

"Brown? My eyes are brown," Jasmine said. "Well, your eyes are brown but... they are... they are..." Jasmine couldn't quite pinpoint a color, nor could I for that matter. "I know!" she blurted out, "they're copper, like a penny... not a new shiny penny but an old penny... or bronze, yes, bronze."

"Did you just compare me to an old dusty penny? That's certainly a first," I replied, very amused.

"I didn't compare *you* to a penny, I said your eyes...," Jasmine tried to defend herself.

I could only laugh. She was right though. Depending on the lighting and how much my pupils dilated and shrank, the color of my eyes looked different. They definitely were not light brown hazel. Maybe they were dark brown hazel? Bronze was an apt description that I had not heard before.

What I did know however, was that they were an asset that helped attract suitors. And I have been known to rely on them to seduce a woman or two, a skill for which I had become quite adept. But when those same suitors talked about my eyes like they weren't actually attached to my body, it made me a bit uncomfortable.

Our server rescued me from Jasmine's gaze—and Jasmine from more embarrassment—and delivered our food with a flourish. "Wow, the portions are huge!" Jasmine said.

"I'm biased but I've never had a bad meal here," I responded.

I picked up my fork. Jasmine didn't. "Is everything okay? Is your order okay?" I asked.

Jasmine responded, "I'm sure it's fine. Are we going to say grace?"

"Oh," I bowed my head and waited.

Jasmine asked again, "No, are *you* going to say grace?"

"Me? What? Okay," I cleared my throat, "grace."

"T, are you serious?" Jasmine asked while reaching across the table to take a swipe at me.

"See, you're still trying to touch me."

"T, are you five years old?"

"I'm sorry, I'm sorry, I was joking. You caught me off guard. Would you like something a bit more formal?"

"Yes please, before they have to warm our food," Jasmine insisted.

"Wanna hear it? Here it go." Jasmine shot me a look. I laughed peeking out of one eye but stopped clowning around since Jasmine wasn't the least bit amused. I reached for her hand and blessed the food. "You were serious about praying huh?" I asked.

"I think we should give thanks," Jasmine said.

"Alright, that's a whole different conversation than I had anticipated. Where's religion on your importance scale?" I asked.

Jasmine responded, "I believe we need a little faith. What about you?"

"Is that like George Michael's 'Gotta Have Faith?' Or are you a bit deeper than that? Do you go to church?" I posed.

"I do," Jasmine responded, still not bowing to my silliness. So I asked, "And what does your church say about two women having dinner?"

"Women in the Bible eat," she said. It was my turn to shoot Jasmine a look this time. "Alright, alright… I attend church regularly, but I don't agree with every biblical passage, nor do I always agree with everything my pastor says. The practice, however, provides me with an assurance that there's a higher power working on my behalf. And Lord knows, we could all use a little divine intervention every now and again."

"Here, here," I said lifting my glass for a toast. We listened to the band and finished dinner in silence.

{TWELVE}

Jasmine

Thank God traffic on the Jones Falls Expressway, a.k.a. Interstate 83, was light because I was not completely paying attention to the few cars whizzing by. It didn't help that Magic 95.9 was in the midst of a Marvin Gaye triple play of "What's Going On," "Distant Lover," and my favorite, "Let's Get It On." I was in my own head as flashes of the evening also went by... the buzz of people in the gallery, my delicious dinner, live jazz music, our ride through Canton, and then our walk through Federal Hill. When we finally returned to the gallery and my car, we sat in her "magnet"—she seriously calls her car a chick magnet—for another hour.

We talked about God knows what. But the longer we talked, the closer we got to each other and the better *it* got. We were so close at one point that I could feel the fine hair on her cheek. I was certain that time stood still as I deeply inhaled the light nutty scent of shea butter emanating from T's skin. As we continued to talk, whisper really, she made circles with her finger on my thigh. The light pressure and sensual touch almost drove me outta my damn mind. She was comfortably in my personal space, taking charge, and I liked that. T didn't ask if she would see me again, she said that she *knew* she would.

It was a wonderful evening, well worth the erratic drive home at three in the morning. No use in messing up an enchanting evening by getting home after the "Mrs." Which would surely start an argument and spur questions and comparisons like why I didn't drink and have fun with her? How could I somehow stay out late when she wasn't around? And why I had this stupid, cheese-eating grin on my face.

For all of the evening's wonder, I really didn't appreciate that pixie fairy inserting her little narrow behind into our conversation and literally between me and T. T ignored my questions about it and tried to redirect the focus, which didn't work for me. I felt like I was being ignored. Plus, had I not picked up the handcard from the gallery, I still wouldn't have known her full name. Teresa Butler, the smooth-talking artist was going to be a force to reckon with.

I was not generally insecure, but I noticed the looks and attention she got from other women tonight. To me, those were bright red warning flags waving in a windstorm. We would need to talk about her women friends respecting boundaries, at least while we were hanging out together. Wait a minute. What was I thinking? For goodness' sake, it had only been three weeks since I met T, certainly my emotions couldn't be that invested... could they? Yeah, T could definitely be trouble.

However, I *felt* her body, both times were quick... hello and goodbye. But Lord knows I hoped to be that close to her again and soon. She had goals and plans. A lot of women had their public goals, ones that sounded good when they were trying to rap and impress, but I sensed that she said what she really believed. She was also good at blending humility with a healthy dose of self-confidence. Then again, how the hell would I know? A few weeks ago, she was a stranger I saw running at the Harbor. Now, I felt like a damn schoolgirl after a first big date.

What did she see in me? Oh well, no time to be self-conscious, the impression had already been made. But what did she think? I guess if she called again, it was positive. But what if she didn't? She would. *She liked me.* "Argh, I hated this already!" I screamed in the mirror, laughed, and instantly got sad. What the hell was I doing? What about Toni?

I turned into the driveway and didn't see Toni's car. Whew, made it in under the wire. Toni and I had a conversation two weeks ago about her needing to be respectful when she was out partying and bringing her ass home. So, needless to say, I didn't want to hear my own lecture about being considerate. Coco greeted me at the door, excited that someone was finally home. I let her out and picked up the phone to dial Toni's cell but stopped. I was not tracking her down; she was a grown ass woman. She knew to call if there was a problem. Coco relieved her bladder after sitting on the patio and surveying the yard for ten minutes like she was a first-time visitor. I let her in, filled a glass with water from the tap, and Coco and I went to my room in search of rest.

***

The jarring sound of the phone on the nightstand woke me abruptly. With my head pounding from the sudden rush of energy, I rolled over, glanced at the clock which read four forty-eight, and wondered who the hell was calling at such an ungodly hour and why.

"Baby, Jazzy," Toni's voice slurred. "It's me, I need to sleep a little while, the game was good, and I don't think I can drive yet. I'm going to rest and come home in a little while."

"You know this shit has gotten old, when did you realize that you had had enough?" I asked, instantly waking up and fuming.

"I'll see you in the morning," she continued to slur.

"IT'S MORNING NOW!" I yelled as I slammed the phone into its cradle.

Two hours later, Coco's whining woke me up, "Get your other mother," I moaned. Coco barked and I remembered her other mother wasn't home. An instant tightening and burning pulsated in the space where my heart usually was. I took a few deep breaths and considered my options. Jasmine, you could make this a good day or stay in a foul mood. Change your attitude now because Toni wasn't going to care either way.

***

Considering the rude awakening earlier, as the day progressed, my mood improved slightly. Being productive helped. I cleaned the house, started laundry, and was about to head out when Toni walked in.

"You leaving out early aren't you?" Toni questioned.

"No, nine is early. It's one-thirty in the afternoon, Saturday afternoon." Toni's eyes were bloodshot red, and she massaged her left temple. It was apparent that she had a headache, more reason for me to talk louder. But my pettiness was overcome by weariness. Why argue? "I'll be back later," I said over my shoulder.

"Fine," she said.

"Fine," I responded.

On the cell in the car, I called Leslie, one of my partners in crime. She and I used to be adjunct faculty at Baltimore City Community College. I taught an evening GED preparation course across the hall from her sewing class. She taught adults to fall in love with their abandoned sewing machines again by making easy home décor, children's patterns, and simple clothing repairs. Leslie picked up the phone on the second ring.

"Hey sistah, what's goin' on?" Leslie questioned.

"You, what are you doing, I need to run a few errands… come ride shotgun," I laughed.

"Can't, need to finish Portia's costume," Leslie remarked.

"Costume, for what? What show is your daughter performing in now?" I asked.

"Church play. What's wrong? You sound pissed," she countered.

"I'm fine," I lied.

"You aren't. Did she come home?"

"Nope, got home as I was leaving," I said shaking my head.

"You really need to deal with that," she said, stating what I knew to be true.

"I plan to, just need a little time." I wished that I actually had a viable plan or could snap my fingers and make my life make sense again.

{THIRTEEN}

T

To try and make up for having missed two date nights, I agreed to go shopping with Sheila, which equated to me spending way too much money on her. But one thing I had never understood, and most days downright detested, was the compulsion to shop. Of course, that was how I hooked up with Sheila in the first place right? But I was one of those people that went shopping for a specific purpose and I didn't linger for long. Trying on clothes? Who needed that? Clipping coupons? Took too much time. Going to several stores comparing prices for that perfect red sweater? It was not worth the effort. I had absolutely no desire to shop nor spend a beautiful Saturday in the overpriced tourist trap known as The Gallery at Harborplace. Many of the chain stores there were the same stores in other malls across the city. But because it was "The Gallery," prices were considerably more expensive.

Anyway, I survived the madness at the mall while pretty much trying to ignore Sheila's funky mood. But now, she and I were seated face-to-face at an outdoor garden café in Mount Vernon, arguably the gayest neighborhood in Baltimore. I people watched, Sheila, on the other hand, quickly became Perry fucking Mason.

"Sheila, I told you three times already, I was out with clients," I said slightly raising my voice, hoping she would hear my growing aggravation.

"Yeah, I heard you. I just want to know two things. Who were you with? Where did you go? And why did you have to stay out so late?" she inquired.

"That's three questions. You don't know them, the Inner Harbor, and we were having a good time."

"Just any ole' place at the Harbor? So why didn't you invite me?"

"Goddammit Sheila! How many times have I invited you to my shows? And how many times have you declined? You know you're only going to kick me in the teeth so many times before I learn to duck."

"How do you know I didn't want to go with you last night?" Sheila asked, clearly testing my patience.

"Did you?" I shot back.

"No, but that's beside the point."

"What the? We're arguing 'cause I didn't ask a question I knew the answer to? My crystal ball is broken Sheila and you're beginning to work my last nerve."

"And you don't think I get tired of not spending time with just you? I want to be with you not those quirky people you call business associates. It's always about either your art or your students. You have to give me the same dedication if you want this relationship to last."

"Yeah well, right now I'm questioning if I want that to happen." Shit! Did I just say that out loud?

"What? Did I hear what I think I just heard?" Sheila snapped.

"What did you hear?" I asked, trying to stall.

"T, don't play games with me," she said throwing her napkin at me.

"I'm not playing games." I looked around hoping she wasn't drawing too much attention but of course people were starting to whisper and point in our direction.

"Then answer my damn question!" Sheila exclaimed.

"Hell, I forgot what it was."

Her next question, punctuated with neck rolling, eye squinting, her own finger pointing, and deliberate annunciation, told me the day was going from bad to worse. "What – did – you – mean – by – your – last – statement – 'you're – questioning – if – you – want – to – be – with – me'?"

"Can we talk about this in private?" I asked, speaking through clinched teeth and hoping to diffuse the situation.

"Hell no! I want to talk about it now," she said loud enough for people at surrounding tables to hear.

"Sheila, there's no reason to make a scene," I all but begged.

"Oh, you haven't seen a scene yet," she said, this time whispering and standing to leave. "Teresa, I'm sick of your shit!" Just then Sheila lost her damn mind and poured her full glass of iced tea on my lap and began walking away.

"What the? Sheila that was so uncalled for," I yelled at her trying to wipe myself off and ignore stares from the other patrons. "Shit!" I cursed under my breath. This bitch just tried to ruin an expensive pair of linen pants. I had a good mind to run after her but didn't since I was already thoroughly embarrassed.

"Ma'am, here are some extra napkins," a waiter said to me rather apologetically.

"Thanks, I'm sorry about that, she can be a bit testy. May I have the check please?"

"Sure, I'll be right back." He was obviously glad that I was leaving too.

After paying the bill for a half-eaten lunch, minus the tea the restaurant was kind enough to deduct since I was wearing it, I found myself standing in the bright summer sun, $500 poorer from Sheila's shopping spree, wet, with no car since Sheila drove, and a big dent in my ego. One more Academy Award, drama queen performance and Ms. Thing was going to be a memory. I had too much going for me to put up with this kind of bullshit. This was so different from the wonderful time I had last night.

I'm sure that I looked plum crazy running through downtown in soaking wet, casual clothes leaving a trail a mile and a half long, but I didn't care. Fifteen minutes later, I was back in the safety of my insanity-free home. I showered, changed clothes, paced around, and replayed that madness with Sheila over and over in my head. I was so done with her.

I dabbled here and there with other women while seeing Sheila but it wasn't like I didn't ultimately want a strong, solid partnership—far from it. My parents provided a great example of what could be some day. But the one time early in my adult life I really gave it a serious go, my relationship ended in hundreds of pieces and my heart in thousands more.

We met in college and became permanent fixtures in each other's lives. It wasn't unusual for Imani to have Sunday dinner with me and my parents. I envisioned a future together and felt like I was deeply committed. She wasn't. John said that I cried until my tear ducts stopped producing water.

***

I needed a boost and picked up my phone to see who was home on a sunny Saturday afternoon. I scanned my cell's contacts to see who the lucky recipient would be. Hmmm, Jennifer, I hadn't hung out with her in a while. I hit number fifteen, for the fifteen months she and I had mind-blowing sex on a continuous basis. She was a freak from the jump. We spent entire weekends doing absolutely nothing except fucking, eating, and sleeping. Most certainly not the kind of girl you took home to momma.

"What's up? You've reached Jennifer's voice mail, do your thang."

"Hey Jennifer, it's T. What's up girl? Just callin' to see what you're up to. Give me a call when you can." I hung up. Okay, how about Tina? I flexed my bicep admiring the results of my workout routine waiting for her to answer the phone.

"Hello?"

"What's up Tina?"

"Hi T, what do I owe this honor?"

"I was just callin' to say 'hello,'" I said.

"You sure? Lately you've only called for a specific purpose, and you know what I mean."

"Come on now girl, can't a sistah' call a beautiful woman to feel some love?"

"Of course you can," she said as I heard her smile.

"That's better. So, what you up to?" I asked hoping I could stop by her house and temporarily forget all of my troubles in her bedroom. Tina and I met in a gym and although we found each other attractive, we figured out early that we didn't share a love connection. However, we kept in touch and maintained a hellified, freaky-deaky "friends with benefits" relationship.

"Well, I was on my way out to get my hair done," she said.

"I dare not get in the way of a Black woman and her hair. I guess I'll catch up with you later then."

"You promise?"

"What do you think?" I asked, not committing to anything.

"Okay, talk to you later."

"Later..."

"Bye."

With that, the dent in my ego was getting deeper. Third time's a charm, I thought hitting number twenty-six, the date Jasmine and I first spoke to one another at the Harbor. And since two plus six equals eight, the number of 'new beginnings,' I saw it as a sign. She picked up on the second ring.

{FOURTEEN}

Jasmine

The weatherman said it would be oppressively hot today, the perspiration forming on my forehead was confirmation. Nonetheless, I sat on a bench watching iridescent ducks swim and dabble at Columbia's Lake Kittamaqundi and listening to the songs of the cicadas. Shade from outstretched branches of mature oaks ensured I remained comfortable enough while I tried to figure out what I was doing with my life, my relationship with Toni, and whatever I was starting with T. Was I starting something with T? Just thinking that question made it more real. Hmmm... I needed a viable plan. But what should I do when I have no idea what to do. I had to do something? Didn't I?

Coming to no definitive conclusion or decision regarding anything substantive, I had made up my mind to engage in some retail therapy when my cellphone rang. Vaguely recognizing the number, I pressed the little green phone icon.

"Hello?" I said somewhat pensively.

"Hello yourself," T responded.

"Well, well," I said reflexively smiling for no good reason, "Didn't expect to hear from you today. Has it even been twelve hours since I last saw you?"

"Ummm... maybe not, but somebody had to call first, and since I didn't think you would," T laughed.

"I would have," I said. I wanted to earlier.

"Yeah okay, what are you up to?" T questioned.

"Nothing really, just running errands, I have to go check on a friend's house. She's out of town. Do you want to hook up?" I heard myself asking. "You could go to the house with me, it's nice. A huge house," I said.

"Have you eaten?" T asked.

"No, not yet," I replied.

"Where are you?" T questioned.

"I'm in Columbia right now, where are you?"

"At home. Want to meet in about an hour, say around four?" T inquired.

"Sure, where?" I responded.

"Sydney De Mars?"

"No, I'm not dressed for that place. How about Jillian's?"

"I don't think so, not on a Saturday afternoon, all those screaming kids," T said rather emphatically. "Where's the house?"

"Owings Mills. What about Red Robin, near the mall?" I questioned.

"Haven't been there, but I know where you're talking about. Meet you there in an hour?"

"Drive safe," I said.

"Yes ma'am," T replied.

***

Oh God! What have I done? I didn't have the same color on twice. I was so discombobulated when I left the house, that I threw on blue sweatpants, a yellow shirt, and a faded green hoodie that had seen better days and lots of washes. Well let's see, I'm close to my favorite pick me up store and I only have half an hour to shed my vagabond look before I need to head north.

Exactly twenty-eight minutes later, I emerged from Marshall's brand new from head to toe, and underneath just in case. Just in case what Jasmine? I stopped at Royal Car wash only because after riding in T's car, I wanted to make a good impression. Most days I could have cared less since I didn't obsess over cars. A clean car wasn't the same as a tidy living room, but since impressions are lasting, I purchased the premium wash.

T and I pulled up in front of Red Robin at the same time.

"Wow, is that how you dress to run errands? You look nice. We could have gone to Sydney's," T said as she gestured her hand up and down towards me.

"Thanks, didn't think I was dressed appropriately, they can be a little snooty there. You look nice too." I added.

We settled into a booth by a window and tried to keep the mood light but the energy between us was palpable. I wrote off last night as a one off, first date thing. How could something that started a short time ago, feel so good, so soon? It didn't make sense according to my logic.

"So, tell me about T," I said to harness my thoughts from wandering too much.

"What do you want to know?" T asked, doing that dodgy thing.

"I mean, what makes you tick? Tell me something about yourself beyond the surface, although I enjoy the surface." Oh no, did I say that out loud? Clearly, I did because T was trying unsuccessfully to hide her alluring smile. "You like the surface, do you?" T asked.

"Something like that," I said, having little dignity left. "Like, why don't you drink alcohol?"

"This is an issue for you huh?"

"No, not really an issue, it's just different I guess."

"Okay well, I used to. But I was at a house party about ten years ago and I had a really bad experience. I don't know if the bootleg bartender screwed up the mix or what. I seriously thought I was dying that night, or early in the morning as it were. It felt like the world was spinning but on a rotating axis like a gyroscope. My insides felt like they would spill out at any moment and I'm certain that I sweated out five pounds of water. It wasn't pretty," T confessed.

"Wow!"

"So, I promised the Creator that if I lived to see another day, I would never have another drink."

"Wow!" I couldn't think of another word. "And that was it?"

"Yep, that was it. I haven't had a drink since. Besides, I think my personality is pleasing enough without liquid courage. Don't you think?" T asked with a smirk on her face.

"Perhaps," I managed to answer.

T laughed, having given up her feeble attempts to mask her amusement and she cleared her throat, "Okay, here's something lighter—I like organization, probably almost to a fault."

I couldn't help myself, "Yeah, I kinda got that from the meticulousness of your car. Tell me something I don't know." She just smiled and didn't seem to mind my somewhat backhanded comment.

"That obvious huh? Hmmm, well here you go…," T said, snapping her fingers. "In spite of my skillfully crafted façade that my co-workers and most of my family would say exudes confidence—that teeters on cockiness—I'm extremely introverted."

"Really?" I asked, surprised because I had yet to experience that. Quite the opposite since it seemed people gravitated toward her.

"Yes, really, I find that other people's energy tires me out relatively quickly and I generally avoid crowds," T answered, "however, there are exceptions."

"Tell me about them," the psychology major in me wanted to know.

"Obviously when work dictates going outside my comfort zone, like last night's gallery opening and…," T trailed off.

"And what?" I asked more anxiously than necessary.

"And, and I find that I enjoy smaller, intimate settings with one, two people max." She was looking at me with those piercing, warm eyes with such intensity that I wanted to look away but thought if I did, I would miss something. A hint. A clue. An answer as to why I was so drawn to her.

"Intimate huh?" I asked.

"Yeah, intimate," T confidently replied, never dropping her gaze.

"Is that why you've talked my ear off since we met?" I kidded her.

"I most certainly have done no such thing, take that back," she said, nudging my knee with hers underneath the table, sending electricity to places in my body that I thought had short-circuited long ago. I didn't realize how much I missed laughing for the sake of laughter. I needed to laugh. My soul needed to laugh.

"Okay, your turn," T said with a smirk on her face.

"My turn for what?" I asked.

"Your turn to go beyond the surface. Tell me something about Jasmine Charles."

"I'm not sure there's much to tell," I said.

"I doubt that. Let's see… you said that you don't have kids?"

"Nope," I answered.

"Ever wanted kids?"

"Not really," I replied honestly.

"That's fair. What about a significant other? Surely, you've had one or two?" T asked.

"Yes, I have had one or two." Geesh, where did that come from? Did someone turn off the A/C? It was getting warm in here and I wasn't ready to talk about my relationship. "Here you go, I grew up in Baltimore in a very devout Pentecostal family. We went to church at least three times a week."

T took a deep breath and bit her bottom lip. I knew she wasn't stupid and was clearly aware of my evasiveness. "Ahhh, now your persistence to pray before eating last night makes sense. But you said, you like to have a *little* faith," T said holding her thumb and index finger a wee bit apart. "I'm exhausted just thinking about being in the same place other than home and work three times a week— drums, tambourines, speaking in tongues Pentecostal?" she asked. I was grateful she didn't press the girlfriend issue further.

"Yep, all of that," I responded. "How about you? Did you grow up in church?"

"Yeah, I did. A bit more conservative though. My family attended, and still attends for that matter, an A.M.E. church. I'm not so big on the whole religion thing myself but I suppose church was a good incubator for developing young people's public speaking and critical thinking skills," T offered. "You still go to the same church?"

"Absolutely not. The elders damned me to hell three times a week after I figured out that I liked girls and made the mistake of telling a friend, who told her cousin, who told her mother," I painfully recalled. "I tried a few non-denomination churches and spiritual centers where we were encouraged to focus on the Divine in ourselves and the essence of Spirit, but I needed a bit more grounding than that."

"Geesh!"

"Exactly. But the church I go to now isn't overtly condemning me to hell because of who I love," I shared nonchalantly.

"Right. They may not be overtly condemning you but you gotta watch out for covert operations though," T said with a smirk. She had a point. Hmmmm.

The server thankfully interrupted what was turning into a heavy conversation and set our food on the table. She also must have sensed the energy between T and I because she announced, "I brought all your condiments to the table, I'll only be back if you call me over. I don't want to interrupt anything." Then she laughed, turned on her heels, and left. That was perfectly fine with me. I had so much more I wanted to know about T. What made her tick? Where she was from cause her accent suggested she wasn't from Baltimore. All of it... I wanted to know her. Oh God, was that a Biblical reference?

While I had my internal conversation, T was staring out of the window. I playfully tapped her hand, "Penny for your thoughts." Instead of verbally responding and before I could withdraw my hand, she held it as gently as one would hold a baby chick. She rubbed her thumb across my skin like she was caressing a sleeping infant. I froze as the warmth of her hand transferred to my own and radiated throughout my body. Oh God, what is happening? Swallowing my nervous energy, I pulled my hand back to my side of the booth.

After that, I felt like my stomach did not need food on top of the knots that had formed in it, so I picked over my meal. I wasn't sure why T picked over her salad, but she did. What I did know was that we exchanged our fair share of non-verbal communication... subtle glances and knowing smiles that made my insides feel like the molten chocolate cake I saw on the menu.

"You aren't very hungry?" T asked.

"I was," I answered knowing full well my words just contradicted my actions.

"Then why aren't you eating?"

"I..." I was at a loss for words, so I switched the subject. "Hey listen, I still have to check on my friend's house. Do you mind if we move the party elsewhere?" Although I was loving every minute of our time together, I didn't want to stay out too late since Toni was already pissed.

There I went, concerned about what Toni thought despite not receiving reciprocal consideration. The ever-present yin and yang had been tugging away at me since I first noticed T running at the Harbor.

***

"These impatiens and hydrangeas are beautiful," I said pointing at the landscaping as we stood outside of the restaurant with takeout containers in hand.

"Huh?" T responded.

"The plants, they're beautiful."

"You're really into flowers huh?" T asked.

"You could say that."

"That's right, you want to be a florist in your next chapter."

"Yep."

"Tell me again, why?"

"It's simple, they're pretty and they don't talk back," I said, smiling.

"You're funny," T said laughing.

"Are you ready to go? I'll drive," I volunteered.

"I don't want to leave my car here," T replied.

"Why not?" I inquired.

"She's my baby."

"Uh, huh. It's a car and no one is going to bother it," I countered.

"Okay, okay but wait a second. You better be glad I'm digging you," T said.

"Oh really?" I asked.

"Yes, really," T shot back while getting in her car.

T put a club on her steering wheel, grabbed a small bag, and set the car's alarm before heading to my passenger side.

"You washed your car!?" T observed, settling into my car.

"How did you know?" I asked.

"I've seen your car before remember? You don't usually keep it this clean do you? And where's your hub cap?" T asked.

"No, but since I was having a guest…"

"How did you know I would agree to ride with you?" T asked.

I ignored her question. I would rather die than admit that I presumed I would have company. "I thought it could use a bath and I don't know. It disappeared a long time ago and I've never gone to the dealer to get another one. It's not a priority. Why do you ask?"

"You could get it detailed and bring the shine back a little, take the small scratches out," T said.

"Um yeah, that's right up there with washing my baseboards, just another something that won't get done anytime soon."

As we turned into my friend's driveway ten minutes later, T whistled. "They let Black folk live out here?"

"Few, very few. The association meets all prospective buyers," I answered.

"So, I *know* there are very few out here," T shook her head.

"'Chelle and Thomas have some very nice art pieces that I thought you might like," I said.

Standing in the two-story entryway filled with natural light from the oversized Palladian window overhead, I could feel T's hands on the small of my back. As I tried to step aside so T could see the tastefully decorated décor, she firmly held me still. She didn't have much to say about it, but I thought it was a nice house. T glanced down the hallway with walls covered with familiar black artist's work like Susan St. James and Jacob Lawrence that fed into a two-story living space.

Floor to ceiling windows on the back façade added grandeur to the space. Off to the right through an arched opening was a small sitting room with a baby grand piano. We could see numerous family photos from where we stood. I always thought the couple looked good together and looked genuinely happy. One in particular was a headshot of Michelle gazing at the photographer with deep piercing eyes that made me wonder what she was thinking at the moment the photo was taken. Was she telling her husband how much she loved him with those eyes? "Have you ever looked at anyone that way?" T asked. I shifted my weight. "Have you?" T asked again. I didn't answer. If I told her about Toni now, it would ruin this nice vibe we had. If I didn't, that could also end poorly. *Ugh!* I wondered if she was seeing anyone. I had been too chicken to ask. If she was, how did she have time for me?

She seemed to accept my non-answer. Her hands slowly moved down the front of my thighs, exploring my curves. As her hands traveled back up, she pulled me closer to her and whispered, "Am I being too forward?" I swallowed really hard to try and stimy the warmth radiating in my body that suddenly returned from earlier. But I managed to get a weak "No" out of my mouth. T spun me around, slipped one hand in my back jean pocket and gripped my ass like she had done this a hundred times before.

"Maybe we should go on a house tour first," I said scarcely getting the words out. "You can see more artwork."

{FIFTEEN}

T

Although I didn't get any love from my usual "friends," I was excited about seeing Jasmine two days in a row. I'm glad she agreed to meet me for an early dinner although neither of us ate very much. Because here I was standing alone with her, with nothing or no one else between us except the emanating energy drawing us together.

"I see a beautiful work of art right here," I said, "nothing could compare."

"Stop, you're embarrassing me," Jasmine said as she pulled away from me, grabbed my hand, and led me into the rear of the house. She opened the blinds to reveal several sets of French doors that led to the deck and backyard. We stepped onto the large wooden deck that stretched the length of the house. It overlooked a sloping, manicured lawn, which gently met a narrow creek.

Jasmine noticed me staring off into space again and leaned into my shoulder, "Penny for your thoughts... again," she said. I smiled and came out of my trance. "Sometimes I wonder why I stay in the city you know? The constant movement, sirens, people walking by all times of the night. Out here you can hear yourself think," I said, walking down the stairs onto the lawn with my camera bag slung over my shoulder.

"Yeah, that's why I moved a bit further out, too much going on for me in the heart of the city," Jasmine added, following me. "Where are you going?

"This place is perfect, and the sun has started to go down so shadows won't be as harsh," I said, knowing full well I probably wasn't making sense.

"Perfect for what? Please tell me what you're talking about," Jasmine wanted to know.

"Ever since I met you, I've wanted to take your picture."

"You just happen to have a camera in your car?" Jasmine was rightfully suspicious.

"Since I was going to see you, I grabbed it just in case," I said with a sly smile, "I hoped you would agree."

"Did you now?" Jasmine arched one eyebrow.

"Yes, yes, I did." I couldn't pretend like my carrying a camera was anything other than what it really was. I thought Jasmine was gorgeous and the artist in me wanted to capture that. "Since you got all gussied up, why not let me photograph you?" I asked while pulling my camera out of its case.

"Cause…" Jasmine said.

"Cause what?" I wanted to know.

"Cause I don't necessarily like taking pictures," she answered.

"I get that but you're beautiful," I said.

"You probably say that to all your girls."

"Not really," I gently responded, which was the absolute truth. I aimed the camera towards Jasmine, adjusted the lens, and pressed the shutter button. "You know what makes you beautiful?" I asked. Click.

"What?" Jasmine asked peeking out from behind the strands of hair that covered her face.

"You're smooth with it," I said, "like, you know you're beautiful, but you downplay it." Click. "Hey, go stand next to those trees." Click.

"T, you're a bit over the top don't you think?" Jasmine asked, trying to block the lens with her hand but she leaned against a tree anyway. Click. She stuck out her tongue. Click. Then frowned. Click, click. She did the look away, capture my profile thing. Click. She smiled. Click. She blushed. Click, click, click.

"You're not going to blackmail me with these photos are you?" she asked.

"Why would I do that?"

"I don't know. You know we're still in that 'getting to know you' stage. How do I know you're not going to do something malicious with them?"

"You don't. Does your intuition tell you I would?" I asked.

"No."

"What does it tell you?"

"You don't want to know," Jasmine said shyly.

"Yes, I do."

"Never mind."

"You can't just drop it like that," I said reaching for Jasmine's hand. "Tell me. What is your intuition telling you about me, about us being here, about our previously unspoken connection?"

"So, you sense it too?" she asked.

"How could I not?" I asked in return.

After a long silence, Jasmine said, "T?"

"Yeah?"

"It scares me," Jasmine said barely above a whisper and let my hand go. "The connection scares me. We've not known each other very long—a hot minute is being generous. I'm not supposed to think about you when I don't see you at the Harbor. I'm not supposed to count the days until I see you again or the minutes between our e-mails. I'm not supposed to get all warm inside when I do see you."

"Your intuition tells you to run like hell?"

"Yes and no, that's the scary part."

"What do you mean?"

"I shouldn't be telling you this," she said reluctantly.

"Why not?"

"Because if I speak it into the atmosphere, if I speak about us, as if there is an us, if I start wondering 'what if,' I believe it becomes closer to reality."

"I get that, and you don't want that reality?" I asked.

"I don't know T, I just don't know," Jasmine confessed, "My sensible, step-by-step approach to life says, 'get as far away from you as I possibly can.' On the other hand, I..." she abruptly interrupted her train of thought. "Come on, there's more to see." Jasmine grabbed my hand again and pulled me back towards the house. I really wasn't that interested in looking at this suburban, buppie house. What I really wanted to do was continue our conversation and just be next to her. I didn't have the urge to get her into bed, I just wanted to be near her, a departure from my norm. Was I getting soft or was Jasmine that special? Probably a little bit of both.

She led me back inside and up a curving staircase that meandered up to the second level. From the top landing we were across from the foyer window that framed the gorgeous view of Baltimore County's rolling hills and the orange glow of a setting sun. We saw the master suite which was two and a half times the size of my meager master bedroom. It was large enough to accommodate a king-sized bed, matching armoire and dresser, and fireplace with formal seating area. Gold, burgundy, and navy-blue colors gave the room a regal and elegant feel. The master bath was just as lavish. A sunken Jacuzzi tub in the center of the room was the focal point, outfitted with custom brass trim, knobs, and faucets. The bedroom's color pallet was repeated in here except the more dominant color was switched. It was obvious her friends had done well for themselves.

After seeing the other rooms on the second level, we made our way back downstairs into the huge eat-in kitchen where sleek stainless-steel appliances were a nice contrast to the natural maple cabinets and gray granite countertops.

But I had had enough of the home and garden tour, so I decided to break away for a minute. "Would your friends mind if I use the bathroom?" I asked. "I think I drank too much coffee at the Red Robin." "Not at all," Jasmine answered.

When I returned to the living room, I heard the Commodores' "Brick House" emanating in surround sound from a stereo and saw Jasmine dancing barefoot, watching her own reflection in the glass doors. I stood there for a minute enjoying the rhythmic sway of her hips and walked up behind her and placed my hands on her waist. "You like the song or are you just happy to be here with me?"

{SIXTEEN}

Jasmine

"Both," I said as I turned to face T. We stood there for what seemed like an eternity, warmth having turned to pure heat permeating throughout my core. Lionel, Diana Ross, and "Endless Love" were dangerous combinations. We danced long and slow and close, even when the music's tempo transitioned to something a bit more upbeat. Our bodies moved synchronously, like we had been dancing together for years. In addition to laughter, I also realized that I missed the feeling of being in sync with another human being, going in the same direction, with a common purpose. T broke into my thoughts and whispered in my ear, "What's next Ms. Charles?"

"I don't know, what do you want to do next?" I asked.

"How late can you stay out, or will you turn into a pumpkin in a few hours?" T responded with another question. "Oh, my goodness, we've been here for four hours?!" I gasped when I looked down at my watch, my heart racing for a different reason now. I lost myself in imagining what could be. T's tenderness and calm assuredness had a way of making time stand still. I enjoyed being with her, but I could kick myself right now. The intense burning in my core was now being fueled by my annoying need to 'do the right thing.' I had no intention of being here this long, and I certainly did not want to hear Toni's nagging and condescension.

"I didn't realize how long we've been here," I hurriedly said.

"Do you need to go?" T asked, both eyebrows raised.

"Yeah, I probably need to get home. Coco is probably sitting in the window."

"Is there anyone else to let the dog out?" T quizzed me.

"It's best for me to keep Coco on a regular schedule," I responded. As a master of side-stepping questions myself, I recognized an equally adept peer. T never answered tough questions. But that was the second time today she asked about my situation. I thought about the scene with me and Toni earlier and wondered for a minute if I *had* a situation.

That aside, I wished there was someone at home that I could count on. And I wished that I could flip a switch and soothe the bundle of knots that were building in my gut. Instead, I went through the house and turned off the lights and sound system, taking deep breaths in the process to stave off a full-on panic attack. But I also didn't want this goodness between me and T to end. "I'll be back on Wednesday to check the mail, want to meet here and hang out for a bit?"

"Sounds good. May I assume you'll be here in the evening?" T asked. "Yes," I answered, way to enthusiastically, thrilled that I would see T soon enough. "We can have dinner then. Do you cook or shall I pick something up?" T asked.

Ugh, the jumble of thoughts running through my head were interfering with my normally rational behavior. "Remember this as we get to know each other… bringing food is always a good thing," I said and laughed.

***

I dropped T back off at her car and we agreed on a time to meet on Wednesday. I was becoming quite comfortable with the feel of T's toned body, an extraordinary juxtaposition of muscles and softness that I could still feel on my fingertips. So, it didn't bother me at all when we hugged longer than generally socially acceptable for just friends. Was it too much to think so intimately about her and us so soon? *Ugh.*

Even though I lived less than twenty minutes away, it was a long, mentally taxing drive home. I thought about Toni and me. We had done the same dance for so long; I rehearsed the steps in my mind. But this time was going to be different, I wouldn't demand change.

I would just concede that Toni's priorities were different from my own and I didn't rank very high on her list.

I dropped the keys in the bowl at the door. The house was quiet, and I could hear Toni in the basement. I walked down the steps, crossed the room, and sat down. I looked at the TV to see what Toni was watching. In my periphery vision I saw her glance over at me briefly and shift.

"Where you been?" Toni asked but kept talking without a response. "I guess you upset, call yourself bein' mad huh?"

"I was upset this morning," I answered, solemnly, the room's heaviness closing in, sure to suffocate me at any moment. "Now I'm just...you know...not really feeling like this is working. We talk and it gets better for a minute, but not long. Let's do something different, let's actually agree that partying is important to you, and you would rather do that than be with me."

Toni countered, "You could have been with me when I got home, but you been out since early afternoon, it's ten-thirty at night, way after the damn malls have closed and you come home in a different outfit than what you left in?"

I looked down, oh SHIT. Busted! Don't stammer, keep an even voice and look her in the eye. "Yeah, I was feeling a little low and got an invite to go for dinner and drinks from Lynn."

"Lynn who?"

"A woman I used to work with."

"Yeah okay, whateva Jasmine, I'm not trippin' off you, you gonna do what you want whether I'm here or not. So, do yo' thang." Toni said with a half-ass shrug.

"Okay, you right, whateva," I parroted back at her as I got up from the loveseat. "Excuse you, I'm trying to hear the TV," Toni said raising her voice. My unnecessary stomping going back upstairs was apparently a bother.

Toni surprised me. That wasn't the fight I was expecting. Usually, our fights involved way more cursing and accusations. Oftentimes we said mean things that we later regretted. Most of the time I felt like strangling her. Now? That wasn't a fight at all... I took a deep breath. Our relationship felt like it was going from bad to worse. One thing was similar though, I was depleted, and I questioned my judgment to stay with Toni this long. I knew tears were going to come soon and I headed straight for the bedroom. There was no need to try and hold them back, first a trickle, then big droplets wet my thighs. I undressed slowly with a wounded spirit of sadness engulfing my soul.

I heard Toni come into the room but didn't acknowledge her. I didn't feel like talking, especially not with her. "Jazzy, I'm sorry, I was just worried about you. You weren't answering your phone; you didn't call. It's not like you to stay out so long without telling me where you are." That was an astute observation but silly me and my common courtesy. I inhaled deeply and exhaled very slowly to keep from cursing her out and providing more fuel to this conversation than necessary.

"Baby, I'm really sorry." Now her hand was on my shoulder, which she kissed softly. I still didn't say anything, so she continued kissing my shoulder, then my neck. The kisses turned to licking and her tongue caressed the length of my spine from my neck down to the small of my back. I just closed my eyes because I knew where this was going, but sex from Toni was the last thing I wanted right now.

{SEVENTEEN}

T

"Phew!" I plopped down on the couch, sweaty clothes and all, exhausted from my brutal, but necessary workout. I had eaten way too many crabs, potatoes, and corn on the cob at Kevin and Terrance's 4th of July cookout yesterday. I reached over and pressed play on my answering machine. The first message was from my principal, Ms. Sheldon, telling me about available space at Owings Mills Mall where artists could submit work for two-week exhibits. *Nice!* I wrote the information down since it could be good publicity. She also asked me about running next summer's art program. *Ugh!* This summer isn't even over. I knew Sheldon wasn't just being thoughtful. Delete.

The second message... the voice sounded syrupy sweet "T, baby we need to clear up our misunderstanding from the other day. Call me when you get home, it doesn't matter how late." Sheila must have bumped her head. The other day? It had been damn near three weeks since she threw her temper tantrum. She didn't even apologize about said misunderstanding, what the hell did she want? I turned the machine off; I didn't need to hear the rest of the messages. I resolved to call her later.

After showering and grabbing a bite to eat, I went upstairs where I kept my work and carefully thumbed through photos trying to think about an exhibit compilation. *Ahhh!* I came upon the latest batch that I developed in the school's photo lab. Despite having to buy my own chemicals, using the school's underutilized lab was still cheaper than getting them developed at Ritz Camera.

That was a beautiful day. Pleasant memories of me and Jasmine's impromptu dinner and photoshoot came flooding back. I realized I actually knew very little about Jasmine, who employed evasive tactics better than the average Army Special Forces grunt. I also realized that there was more I wanted to know. So, I picked up the phone and started dialing her number but hung up. Focus T, focus.

I pulled photographs out, figured I would keep the presentation simple; mat and frame some pieces, just frame others or not at all. I picked a couple from a vacation to Jamaica that Sheila and I took a year ago and a couple from her niece's birthday party; images of children with cake and ice cream on themselves and everywhere else were always fun. I threw in a couple of seasonal pictures, snow covered evergreens, breathtaking sunrises, and western Maryland's captivating fall foliage. Finally, I selected two photos of Jasmine. In the first one, she looked piercingly into the camera with an ever so slight grin, her hair blowing in the summer breeze. In the second, I captured her looking down at the ground, tucking her hair behind her left ear. It looked like she was deep in thought. Both made me smile.

***

"What are you up to?" I was having trouble not thinking about Jasmine, so I decided to call her the next day just to hear her voice. Lucky for my sanity, she answered.

"Well, this is a pleasant surprise," she said.

"I've been thinking about you," I confessed. I heard people in the background and wondered where she was.

"Really?"

I admitted my weakness and smiled, "Yes, really. Where are you? It sounds like you're outside."

"I decided to change my scenery. I'm walking around Druid Hill Park," she answered.

"Nice. I like the workout stations around the reservoir," I said.

"Of course you do. I like the benches, particularly the one I'm getting ready to sit on," she said while laughing at her own joke.

Smart and beautiful, I laughed too. "How was your holiday?"

"It was alright," she answered, less than enthused.

"Just alright?" I asked.

"Yeah, I hung out with a few friends, nothing special."

I wondered what kind of friends made her so melancholy but decided not to press the subject further. "Guess what?"

"What?" she perked up a bit.

"I developed the photos I took of you a few weeks back which transported my mind back to that day. A couple of them turned out really well."

"I would love to see them," she let me know.

"You will, I promise." I pivoted, I wanted the exhibit to be a surprise. "Something you said that day stuck with me."

"What's that?" Jasmine wanted to know.

"You said that our connection scared you."

"Yeah, I did," she confirmed.

"Now that it's been a few weeks and we haven't seen each other, is it still there?" I wanted to know, primarily because I couldn't shake the thought of her. And I wanted a little reassurance that I wasn't alone. She didn't answer. "Jasmine?"

"I'm here," she said and sighed.

"What are you thinking?"

"I'm thinking there is so much I want to tell you."

"And you're hesitant to do so because?"

"Because I have a lot going on in my life right now and I don't want to burden you with any of it. Because it feels good to be with you, to talk to you...," Jasmine's thoughts trailed off.

"Well, I don't want to be a burden, but I certainly would like to see you soon, maybe have dinner or lunch?" I asked.

"I'd like that," she said, "but I don't know when that will be. I have a few upcoming obligations."

"Fair enough... call me when you can?" I asked, sensing that Jasmine was ready to get off the phone.

"I will."

{EIGHTEEN}

Jasmine

This year's WNBA All-Star game was being played at MCI Center in D.C., which meant there were family parties, official and unofficial, all weekend leading up to the game on Monday. I agreed to join Toni for some of them but drove my own car so I would not be stranded and could leave whenever I damned well pleased. Don't get me wrong, I enjoyed being around the athletes, they provided plenty of eye candy. Dancing and mingling provided a much-needed distraction from what was happening on the day to day. And while Toni and I had a good time in general, T was constantly on my mind. By Saturday night, I had had enough, kissed Toni on the cheek, and drove back to Baltimore for some peace and quiet.

***

I must have been sleeping rather soundly because I certainly didn't hear Toni come home. But it was one-thirty in the morning when I opened my eyes and felt Toni's hand on my side. She was lying directly behind me, so close I could hear her breathing and feel her warm, bare skin. She moved her hand up to play in my hair, but I moved my head to get her to stop. She didn't.

From previous experience, she knew I enjoyed the affection and continued to exploit my softening exterior. Her hand was now moving down my torso, to my thigh and calf, then back up. This was one reason I had not been able to walk away from Toni. She could be so sensual and gentle in my most vulnerable moments. But her touch at this moment seemed foreign. Toni continued to touch me, and my thoughts flashed to T. *God, what is wrong with me?*

I wondered what T was doing and imagined it was her here right now trying to seduce me. Our time together had been nice. I could be myself, act silly, laugh, have fun. But we also talked about a myriad of things. She was such a refreshing presence.

"Baby, baby?"

"Huh?" I responded, extracted from my thoughts.

"Turnover."

Even though my mind was screaming "No!" I turned onto my back. Toni laid on top of me and pressed her weight in the right places. I was a sucker for her warm, naked body and Toni knew that. She moved my arms above my head and held them there, ensuring I couldn't push her off of me. Her pelvic motion became more forceful.

"Baby, you know I love you." Kiss on the neck. "I promise I'll do better, I'll cut back on hanging out." Kiss on the lips. "I just have a little too much sometimes." Kiss on the chin. "And then it's not safe to drive." Kiss in between my breasts. "You don't want me driving under the influence do you?" Kiss on my left breast. "Then that'll cause more problems." Kiss on my right breast.

Her tongue continued where her lips left off and she licked my nipples 'til they were good and firm. I wanted to be mad, but she wasn't letting me do that. Whatever nipple she didn't have in her mouth, she was squeezing between her thumb and index finger. When I stopped enjoying her mouth on me for a minute and started to speak, she put her fingers to my lips and then boldly put one in my mouth, which I started sucking without hesitation.

Toni knew she had me and instead of hearing my wrath, she decided to touch the buttons she discovered years ago. Since my breasts had been sweetly suckled, her southern travel recommenced. Skipping the preliminary licking around the edges, Toni plunged right in, simultaneously putting her finger inside of what had become an extreme wetness and wrapping her lips around my attentive clit. I couldn't do anything except enjoy the attention and make a mental note to fuss later. The building passion I felt was a combination of desire, anger, confusion, and frustration. I wanted to scream that I was sick of her shit but then she found a sweet spot and "Yes, Baby!" came out of my mouth. *Damn it!* I hated when she manipulated me like this.

"Toni, no. Toni. Oh baby, yes." I tried to push her away, hoping she was getting tired of my indecisiveness, but she wasn't. Instead, the intensity increased. She reached underneath me and cupped my ass, pressing her nails into my flesh to apply extra stimulation. I grabbed her head and tried to pull her closer, but she was already as close as humanly possible.

It felt like Toni wasn't holding anything back. Her tongue circled, flicked, licked, teased. Toni sucked and nibbled. Up until this point, I had thoroughly enjoyed oral pleasure from her and only her. Toni stayed out all times of the night but then loved me feverishly when she made it home, and I convinced myself that everything was all good and that that was enough.

I knew she was high now—which was probably fueling her overly active libido and aggressiveness—and despite being extremely irritated by that very fact, I couldn't ignore that Toni's tongue matched the pace of my thrusts. I faintly heard Toni's muffled voice, "Uhmm, hmm. Cum for me baby. Work that ass. That's right." She squeezed, sucked, pressed, flicked, thrust, squeezed, sucked, pressed, flicked…

"GODDAMN TONI, THAT'S IT!" I screamed releasing months of pent-up emotions, gripping the bed while cursing myself for giving in to Toni again, and praying for the dawning of a new day.

***

I woke up before the clock went off. I set it to make it to seven forty-five service but woke up at six a little disoriented. I glanced over and saw Toni sleeping peacefully. *Damn you*—I needed to go pray about this! I quietly got out of bed; showered and dressed quickly. I was trying to put on my shoes before Toni stirred but I failed.

"What do you want for dinner? I plan to have dinner ready early. I'm thinking about going back to D.C. to hang out at Stacey's," Toni said, now fully awake it seemed.

I picked up my Bible case off the nightstand and turned around. "Tell me you jokin'? Is that what last night was about? You know what?" I said, throwing up my hand as if that would stop the screaming in my head, "It's really beginning not to matter, go watch the game with your friends."

Toni groaned, "Look don't start, I only said I was thinkin' 'bout it. What do you mean it's beginning not to matter?" Toni asked. "I didn't say I was going. What do you want for dinner?"

"Dinner doesn't matter, and it's really okay if you go." I tried to say in a calm voice. "I'm going to church. I'll see you later." I picked up my Coach bag.

Toni's antenna, it seemed, was on full alert now. "Where are you going after church?"

"I may go to brunch or something. I'll see who's at church."

"Come back and get me. I'll go to brunch with you."

"You won't have time to make dinner then before you leave."

"I didn't say I was going, only that I was thinking about it. You trying to get rid of me?" Toni joked.

"Toni, you are going to get rid of you," I said without a trace of smile. "I'll be back after church. I'm leaving 'cause I need to get some Word in me. I'm letting Coco out, don't forget she's out there if you go back to sleep," I said and left the room.

***

I had to breathe deeply all the way to church. What do you do when you know you have to do something but don't know what to do? I entered the foyer and heard the choir singing the last phrases of "God Is in Control." I know You are. You have to be, I can't do this by myself.

By the time I stepped into the sanctuary and found a seat, the choir had transitioned to "Order My Steps," how apropos. I'm glad I got out of bed and came to church, staying at home would have only led to another fight with Toni. And I'm tired of fighting, it was draining the life out of me. We used to say fighting helped us relieve stress and share what was on our minds. How we tried to justify such toxic behavior is baffling. And it had been a long time since Toni and I had a meaningful conversation without one of us left feeling disgusted.

The choir's rendition of the song that was based on Psalm 119, verse 133, "Order my steps in thy word," was stirring something in me. How could it not? What was happening in my life right now was too much for me to handle on my own. It didn't take me long to start singing along with the choir. The soloist's raspy, alto voice belted out the verse affirming that whatever I decided to do needed to be on purpose, I needed to walk worthy and do God's will. I found myself standing on my feet with a majority of the congregation with my arms outstretched and my eyes closed, letting the intense energy wash over me. Indeed, my circumstances were changing but the one constant for me was my reliance on my faith.

"SING CHOIR!" I shouted.

The choir was reaching the song's crescendo and got to the heart of the matter. I needed a new direction—I needed a new song to sing. Tears streamed down my face. I was flooded with so many emotions, anger, sadness, regret. I was pretty sure the choir was peering into my soul in the span of their eight-minute song.

"Here sweetheart," the kind lady next to me handed me her handkerchief.

"Thank you," I mouthed, I must have looked a hot mess for her to share her beautifully embroidered and ironed hankie. I composed myself enough to enjoy the rest of the service until…

***

"There may be times when you feel like you're losing your mind!" Reverend Sampson exclaimed.

"Amen!" I and others in the congregation responded.

"There may be times when things aren't making sense to you!"

"Uh huh!"

"There may be times when you're questioning the bumps and bruises, the roadblocks and hurdles."

"Well," the hankie lady interjected.

"But I'm here to tell you, there's a plan. God has a plan, like the choir sang so beautifully. Your steps are ordered. Precisely orchestrated in divine sequence. Not left to happenstance. God leaves nothing to chance. He has already crafted every detail of your life."

"PREACH, PREACHER!" A deacon shouted.

"But you have to have faith. Jesus says if you have faith the size of a mustard seed, you can move mountains. In Hebrews eleven and one, the writer says that faith…"

"Yes!" Another deacon said.

"Somebody say faith," Reverend Sampson demanded.

"FAITH," the congregation shouted.

"Is the substance of things hoped for, the evidence, of things unseen. Hah! That means that just because you can't see it, doesn't mean, you can't achieve it. Hah! And just because you can't see beyond your current circumstance… Hah! It doesn't mean you're not in store for an extraordinary, supernatural, beyond human understanding blessing in the not so distant future." He whooped and hollered, and the congregation upheld their end of the 'call and response' relationship.

"I know that's right!" A woman exclaimed.

"As a matter of fact, Hah! God is getting you prepared. That issue you thought was a hurdle, a stumbling block, an inconvenience Hah!.. an indiscretion, a setback…"

"Yeah!?!"

"Well, it may have proved to be a rough spot, but guess what?" The preacher was in his groove now.

"What?" we all asked.

"I said, guess what?"

"WHAT?" the congregation shouted louder.

"That challenge was making you stronger. It didn't kill you. Uhhhmmm. I said, the challenge was making you stronger. Hah, Hah!! How does the saying go 'that which does not kill me?' My, my, my…"

Twenty minutes ago, I felt like the choir sang my own personal soundtrack, now Reverend Sampson was preaching on the track too, in high definition stereo. He stomped and paced and tried to keep up with wiping the sweat off of his face. "It was preparing you for what's to come. Hah! Somma ya'll didn't get that. I said, that challenge, that valley, that pitfall, that detour was merely preparing you for your supersize—hello McDonald's—blessing that's on the way. It's right around the corner. Can you see it?"

"Yeah!" The congregation said.

"Can you feel it?" he asked.

"Yeah!"

"Can you taste it?"

"Yeah!"

"My, my, my, my...church, some of you in here don't believe. You thinkin' that nothin' good is ever gonna happen to you. You thinkin' that your life is one big black hole that continues ad infinitum. Hah, hah! I'm here to tell you, that trouble don't last always! I saaiiiddd, trouble don't last always. You know what you got to have?"

"Faith!"

"Huh? Some of ya'll ain't believin' yet. What you gotta have?"

"FAITH!!!"

"Yeah, yeah, yeah, yeah...you got to have faith. Faith, the size of a mustard seed. Have you ever seen a mustard seed? My Lord! If you've seen a mustard seed, then you know, I said, you know that you just have to have a little bit of faith. Well, well, well...I'm a livin' witness that if you believe in the healing power and goodness of God, you cannot, you will not fail...on your job."

"Yeah!"

"At home..."

"Yeah!"

"In your current relationship," the pastor continued, and I heard a record scratch in the space between my two ears. What in the world? Was he talking to me?

"Yeah!" Hankie lady was on her feet again.

"In the special relationship you're about to enter." Surely, I was being punked. My chest was tightening, and my throat felt constricted by the lump that had formed there. I felt like I was

81

forcing myself to breathe. I said I was going to pray about my relationship. I asked God for guidance.

"Yeah!"

Reverend Sampson was still at it, "...the one God has planned for you. Hah! The one where it's so good you just have to shake your head and smile when you think about the person." Surely, he could not be talking about me and T, right?! Did God send T to me?

"Yeah!" The congregation was still involved too but I was focused on the internal battle in my head. Then Reverence Sampson went for all the marbles.

"The relationship where you just got off the phone, but it seems like you still have so much to talk about..."

At that moment, I didn't hear anything else the pastor had to say. He had put it out there. It was as if he had been following me around and was talking directly to me. Could this be a sign of what was to come? One thing was clear, I had been praying for quite some time that Toni would revert back to that wonderful person I fell in love with, thoughtful and caring. And just when I had given up on love, it seemed like God had another plan. "Amen, Amen, and Amen."

After the benediction, the saints slowly strolled out into the vestibule once outside. I reached into my purse to turn my cell phone back on to dial Stephanie's number for brunch but changed my mind. I flipped the phone open again to call home but changed my mind again. I didn't feel like talking. Driving with no destination in mind, I realized that I was on Light Street before I knew it so I made a left onto Key Highway and figured I would go sit on my favorite bench for a little while.

***

Sunday summer afternoons usually found Federal Hill Park slightly crowded; but it was still relatively early and only a handful of dogs and their owners were out walking around. I sat quietly and allowed my mind to wander. The leaves would begin to turn, and a chill would be in the air in a month or two. But right now, the sun glistened off the blueish-gray water in the Inner Harbor which reflected shimmering images of buildings and boats. It was warm but it wasn't blazing hot yet.

From up here, I saw tiny people moving around the marina. I assumed they were preparing their boats for a day out on the water. Several beach volleyball games were already in progress on Rash Field. The USS Constellation occupied its berth next to Harbor Place. The parking lot across from the American Visionary Museum was beginning to fill. Ballers, male and female, were playing a pickup game on the basketball court below.

Although the world around me seemed to be carrying on just fine, tears began to well in the corners of my eyes, again. Someone was going to think I was suicidal sitting on this bench crying in broad daylight. I pulled out the handkerchief from church and rubbed my fingers along the fine embroidery which I hadn't read before. It said, "We know that all things work together for good for those who love God... Romans 8:28." Lord, was that another sign?

I wiped my eyes and looked around to see if anyone saw me, not sure why I cared if they did. I sighed deeply and began to pray, "Lord, I thank you for your goodness and your protection. I thank you for my right mind. I thank you for grace and mercy. Lord, I pray for strength and ask for discernment. Order my steps in the direction that you would have me take. You said if I called on You, You would be here in my time of trouble. I truly don't know what I'm doing, but I pray for peace and your guidance. In your holy name I pray. Amen." I opened my eyes, breathed in deeply, unfolded my arms and felt my body relax.

An elderly couple walking a dog passed me. I overheard the man say, "You can't get rid of me now, it's only been fifty years, we're just getting to know each other," as he reached for the woman's hand. Fifty years. Fifty years with the same person. Could I spend fifty years with Toni? *Only if they're serving snow cones in hell!* I laughed out loud at the thought. I don't know if I'll spend fifty more days with Toni. Where will I be in fifty years? Who will I be with in fifty years? And with that, I acknowledged in my heart that my relationship with Toni had changed, and not for the better. She was getting one last chance, what she decided to do with it was her decision.

I stood to head home and saw her car first—the chick magnet—parked along Key Highway. Then I saw the chick magnet's owner stretching and bouncing on one leg across the street in Rash Field. The tightness in my chest from earlier was replaced by a warm and gooey sensation and a ridiculous, unexpected smile spread across my face. But I also felt light-headed, perhaps because I was standing extraordinarily still and holding my breath, not wanting to make a sound or bring attention to myself. This, I realized was an irrational reaction considering there was no way she could see or hear me breathing way up here, some seven hundred feet above her.

God! Even though I had just decided to give my current relationship a chance, I had an overwhelming desire to talk to her... to be next to her with no particular agenda. I wanted to stare into her beautiful eyes. I wanted to hear her laugh and see her smile.

None of that was rational and all of it was the polar opposite of staying with Toni. It was just as well, T finished her warmup routine and jogged towards the food pavilion, away from me.

***

I walked in the house and heard the television in the kitchen. I patted Coco who was lying in her favorite chair napping and peeked in the kitchen, but Toni wasn't there. I went upstairs to Toni's room. Although, we slept primarily in one room, the one considered "my" room, Toni maintained her own room. It was her place to relax, meaning she could smoke weed without my disapproving eyes. Toni was stretched out across the futon reading the Sports section of the *Baltimore Sun.*

"I thought we were going to brunch?"

"I changed my mind." I responded.

"So, where you been?" Toni questioned.

"Thinking."

"About?"

"Us," I began, "we've been together for a long time, and for the record, I think I would like us to remain together; but not like this. We don't talk, we don't spend time together, we're living separate lives."

Toni sat up. I could tell she was already agitated. "That's because we're separate people," she said throwing the paper on the floor.

"Separate people?" I repeated. "Then we need to separate," I said, looking Toni dead in her eyes.

Toni sucked her teeth, "Where's this shit comin' from?"

I sadly smiled and shook my head. "Have you been happy for the past year? How about for the past few years? Never mind," I said, holding my hand up, "you don't have to answer that. Let me tell you, I haven't been happy. I'm not satisfied with our life together. It's not about us anymore," I said, gesturing back and forth, "but you and I individually. Which would be fine if we were still growing together. But we're not! You say you're just partying with your friends, but I'm left wondering what else or who else you're doing."

"Gimme a break! Are you gonna start on that again? And," she gave the word three syllables, "you would want to be careful about the stones you start throwin'," she said crossing her arms.

"Let me finish," I said, but wondered what Toni was talking about. "In the last year, you have done nothing but complain about your finances and your job. But you aren't doing anything differently. We don't do anything together cause you always complaining about money. But that hasn't stopped you from hanging out and having a good time with your friends. Where's the substance? Where's the consistency?"

"Why you always gotta talk about me partying?" Toni asked with her lips twisted.

"Cause that's all you do! What else are you doing with your life Toni? You're forty-one years old. Cause Toni, for real, I'm just about done. I've had enough, and I'm letting you know. You are going to make me leave you! I'm done arguing."

"Well, since you finally took a breath...let me tell you a little something. You don't live in a picture-perfect glasshouse, Ms. Charles."

"What are you talking about?" I turned around at the door.

"Apparently, you been taking pictures, I saw 'em. Or should I say, somebody been takin' pictures of you. They hangin' in the mall Jasmine. And, from the look on your face right now, you didn't know. She must have forgot to tell you!" I was stunned. Toni was just getting warmed up though and I was only picking up every third word. "Owings Mills...nice...flowers...big smile...trees...her?" I walked out and stumbled back down to my room and closed the door. I fell on the bed and tried to rack my brain, suddenly remembering the day. I knew that day would come back to haunt me. But I was so caught up in the moment. *Oh my God!* Why the hell are the pictures in the mall? Why is the room spinning? T what the hell have you done? *Damn!*

Before I could gather my thoughts, Toni came into the room ready to finish what she had started. "See Jasmine, your shit ain't all that tight eitha'. You been out and about yourself. Only difference between what I do and your dirt, is my shit ain't all exposed so e'rybody in Baltimore can see it. So what, I smoke a lil' weed every now and then, that's how I reduce my stress. You go to church? I go to parties and smoke weed." Toni said that like it was almost noble, and she believed the two activities were comparable for stress relief.

"Toni, you make it seem like smoking weed is legal," I said.

"It should be! But we ain't talkin' 'bout weed right now, we talkin' 'bout why there are pictures of you on display at Owings Mills huh?" *Damn! How could T do this without my permission? Without telling me? She said I would see them. Shit!* I didn't have a response for Toni. Instead, I just prayed the moment would pass.

"Jasmine, don't act like you don't hear me." Toni threw her cool, relaxed high out the window and came across the room so fast I instinctively stood to my feet ready for whateva'. Only a quarter of an inch separated us nose to nose. Toni sneered, "Yeah Jazz, you think you all high and mighty. Who you been seein'? Who the hell is Teresa Butler?"

Oh God, Toni knew T's name. I couldn't catch my breath. My hands were sweating, and my head started pounding. I backed up to put some distance between us. "I haven't been seeing anyone," I said trying to convince myself otherwise.

"You lyin', I saw you, I saw desire in your eyes in them pictures... I saw it in your smile. Is that who took pictures of you? Teresa Butler?"

"And how did you see all of that? You probably haven't seen me smile in three years."

"You act like I don't know what makes you tick. I know," Toni squinted her eyes. "I remember when you used to look at me like that. Uh huh, tryin' to put all our problems on me, you been doin' dirt Jazz, don't think I don't know." She closed the distance between the two of us and was in my face again. Toni grabbed my hands and pinned them behind my back, she pressed all of her weight against me and tried to kiss me. I struggled and tried to push her off, "Toni stop, you're drunk and high!"

"Don't tell me what to do," she said. "You better tell that bitch, whoeva' she is, that you my woman and you will always be my woman."

"Toni stop, I'm not seeing anyone! Get off me!"

"That's right baby, you know I like it when you play hard to get."

"Toni," Toni was getting more and more physical.

"Remember that Jazz, you my wo- ahhh shit!" Toni looked down, her leg was bleeding. "GODDAMN DOG!" Thank goodness Coco was awakened from her nap with all the commotion and came to my rescue. She bit Toni on her calf. I welcomed the brief relief, pushed Toni out of the room, and locked the door.

I flopped on the bed, tears in my eyes wondering what the hell just happened? How could I have been so careless? How could a relationship that I valued so much come to this? I just knew Toni was going to try to hurt me. Coco nudged my arm. "Not now Coco, Mommy's gotta think." The dog didn't listen, she nudged me again. "Oh, all right, I'll rub you. That's the least I can do huh since you saved me from the madness." Coco and I sighed together.

***

I must have dozed off. My ringing cell phone woke me up, but I silenced it without seeing who it was. I unlocked the door, the house was quiet. I peeked out the front window, Toni's car was gone. *She was gone.* I went upstairs to see what Toni's room looked like to get an idea of her mindset when she left. Nothing looked out of place. *Damn neat freak!*

What if Toni left for good? Coco did bite her, was she hurt? Served her right. She pushed me. I don't play that! Right, wrong, or indifferent, her hands only belonged on me for pleasure. I called Toni's cell phone, it went to voice mail. It only went straight to voice mail when Toni had it off, and she never had it off. She purposely didn't want to hear from me. Alright, we would play it her way.

{NINETEEN}

T

"Hey Ms. Girl."

After my morning run, John and I agreed to have Sunday brunch at Donna's on Charles Street since we hadn't seen each other since the gallery opening. I had been busy with painting, the exhibit, and thinking about Jasmine. John was busy doing his thing, and that changed from hour to hour.

"Hey Mr. Man, how are you?" I said, greeting him with a hug. We decided to sit outside to enjoy the sunshine.

"I'm wonderful!" John beamed.

"What have you been up to, or should I say who's been up against you, that's making you smile like that?"

"Guuuurrrllll, I've been keeping company with THE most wonderful man."

"Oh really!" I was curious about who could make my friend come alive like this. "And where did you meet him?"

"At your gallery opening."

"At my gallery opening? When did you have time to meet someone in between selling paintings and running interference?"

"Are you doubting my skills?" he asked rolling his neck. "You know your baby boy got skills."

"I know you got skills. I'm just saying, we were busy."

"Well, it didn't stop you from catching a few looks, not to mention Ms. Thing you left with."

"Boy please."

"Boy please nothin', so what's up? Ya'll hook up?" John asked.

"We've hung out a few times." I said, trying not to sound too excited.

"I didn't ask if ya'll hung out, I asked you if you hooked up?" he inquired, with a crooked smile.

"No, ain't that type of party," I responded kind of nonchalantly.

"T, please. Who you think you talkin' to? It's *always* that type of party with you."

"She's different," I told John, not able to conceal my smile.

"Different?" John asked skeptically.

"Yeah, different," I blushed.

"Different how?"

"Different like she's making me rethink priorities, life."

"And you haven't slept with her yet?"

"Nope."

"You losing your skills?" John said, folding his arms and rolling his neck with the corner of his mouth turned up.

"No, don't get me wrong, it's not that I haven't thought about it. But that's not the prevalent mood when we're together."

"So what is the 'prevalent mood'?" John questioned while making goofy air quotation gestures with his hands.

"We talk, I mean talk, it's a two-way dialog. And I'm not afraid of opening up nor do I feel like I'm playing some game. It's just her and me talking about life, enjoying each other's company, sunsets, birds singing. You know, things you know are there but don't acknowledge very often. She makes me notice things. She makes colors brighter, and she brings calm…peace, you know."

"Damn! Maybe I should date her or nominate her for sainthood or some shit."

"John," I said, hitting him in the arm, "I'm being serious, like I said, she's different."

"I guess so. Anybody that makes Ms. T rethink life has got to be some kinda special."

"She is. You know after Imani broke up with me when we were in undergrad, I sort of swore off of long-term relationships."

"Sort of? T, you did a one eighty. Girl was wrong on so many levels for how she chose to disappear and then had the audacity with a capital 'A' to emerge two weeks later on someone else's arm. All while you were trying to finish your final project and graduate."

"Yeah." This unintended trip down memory lane cast a solemn shadow over me.

"To this day if I see that bit-…"

"Hey!" I interrupted my friend. "She was wrong, but calling her out her name isn't necessary." Why I felt the need to defend a person who sullied my relationship expectations, I didn't know. John ignored me.

"To this day if Ms. Imani crosses my path, I might catch a case. You may not remember how pitiful and sad you were when she left—" Of course I did, how could I forget feeling like my heart and lungs were failing me and making it impossible to breathe? John's hands flailed about as he continued. "You invested a lot of time and energy trying to make that thing work for three years. In between your art projects and research papers, you worked part time to afford food to weave all of your low-country love into home-cooked meals. You courted and loved her—hard—and what did she extend to you in return?"

"I know, I know, you are not a fan."

"I most certainly am not. Your friends—me included—had to take care of you for weeks cause you couldn't get it together. It took you a long time to recover and I'm not sure you have completely. Hell, you had to stay in school an extra semester." John sucked his teeth, in case I hadn't realized he was thoroughly irritated. I changed the subject back to him and his recent pursuit.

***

On my way home, I decided to call Jasmine, which was becoming a pleasant part of my routine and I needed some positive energy. "Hey Ms. Lady Ma'am," I said, happy that she had answered the phone.

"Hey yourself," she sounded like she just woke up.

"How are you on a fine Sunday? Up for a drive?"

"I wish I could, but today's not a good day."

My ears perked up, "What's wrong?"

Jasmine started crying. *God bless! This has been a day!* "Why didn't you tell me about the pictures? Why would you display pictures of me without asking my permission or at least telling me?" The next few questions were unintelligible due to her crying and sniffling.

"Jasmine what happened?"

"She's angry with me...we started fighting...the dog bit her!

"Whoa Jasmine, what in the hell is going on? Some woman hit you?"

"Not exactly, I'm okay, but I can't talk right now," Jasmine said sadly, "I gotta go," and hung up.

Damn! What in the hell was going on? I realized I didn't even know where Jasmine lived, not that I would go charging over there if I did. I also now knew for sure that there was a "her." But I refused to believe Jasmine was with someone who would hurt her. Could this be my fault? I wanted to take Jasmine to the mall and surprise her with the exhibit. Apparently, somebody else saw it first. Damn! This was not good. Not good at all. I was feeling helpless and awful. I tried calling Jasmine's number again but got her voice mail.

"Jasmine, please call me. I'm worried about you. I'm sorry if I caused confusion; that was not my intention. I was planning to surprise you today and take you to the mall. Let me know if there's something I can do to make this right. I, I, um. I'll talk to you later." What was the hesitation with the last line? Ugh! I was at a loss for words. This was not how I had intended to spend the day.

***

"You should have told me." Jasmine started after agreeing to meet me at Federal Hill to talk face-to-face later that day.

"I know, I wanted it to be a surprise—it all happened so fast. My principal told me about available display space at Owings Mills, I pulled together some photos fairly quickly one night and submitted the application. I thought it would be fun. In hindsight, not so much. I screwed up."

"Surprise, surprise!" Jasmine said sarcastically. "You still should have told me—my life feels like it is upside down right now."

"I'm sorry, I didn't know you had a girlfriend," I said defensively.

"That's irrelevant, don't you think I have a right to know when my image is being used, particularly in such a public place?" Jasmine asked, still very much upset and seemingly confused.

"Yes. Yes, you do, and I'm so so sorry but I think the fact that you have a girlfriend is absolutely relevant, I certainly wouldn't have used those pictures. Why haven't you talked about her?" I asked. "Jasmine, I asked a couple of times about your situation," I reminded her.

"Don't change the subject. This is not about Toni—this is about you."

"So, she has a name, and how long have you and Toni been together?"

"Teresa, I told you, this isn't about her."

"Jasmine, I'm not some irresponsible, insensitive person that sets out to hurt people. I wouldn't have used them in the exhibit if I knew about your girlfriend. That's why *Toni* is relevant. The fact that you've managed to not answer questions up until this point directly acknowledging a significant other existed is, in my mind, quite telling," I said getting slightly annoyed that Jasmine wasn't owning her part of this situation.

"She hasn't been significant for quite some time," Jasmine said under her breath.

"But she's still your girlfriend, yes?"

"Yes," Jasmine said with a sigh. "Yes she is, which makes *this* all the more complicated."

"Makes *what* all the more complicated?" I too was starting to get confused, not sure if Jasmine was talking about Toni or the exhibit situation.

"THIS! Us, Teresa," Jasmine exclaimed quite prophetically.

"Us?" I said, the corner of my mouth turned up a bit at the revelation that I wasn't losing my mind thinking there was something developing between us.

"Yes, us," Jasmine said biting her bottom lip and smiling back, slightly, but smiling nonetheless.

{TWENTY}

Jasmine

Toni spent the night out for two days and didn't call. I was worried because Toni's cell phone was still off. So, I called her job Tuesday afternoon.

"Healthcare Services, this is Keisha, how may I direct your call?"

"Hey Keisha, it's Jasmine, may I speak to Toni please?"

"Hey girl, don't know if you want to, Toni's ass been on her shoulders for two days. Walkin' round here slammin' doors and shit, mumbling' under her breath, talkin' bout loyalty and faithfulness and honesty."

Most days I got very annoyed with Toni's assistant, particularly when she was meddling and putting her nose where it didn't belong. Half the time I wasn't sure if Keisha was trying to be helpful or if she was smirking on the other end of the line. Today, her tone annoyed the shit out of me a little too much.

"Keisha, thanks for the warning and unsolicited commentary, but may I speak to Toni please?"

"Well, ex-scuzzz me!" She then converted to her nasal secretariat voice. "Please hold Ms. Charles."

I was thankful that I wasn't standing in front of Ms. Thing because I probably would have made a scene. In some respects, I sensed that Keisha was pleased that things between me and Toni weren't going well. But maybe I was just imagining things—maybe not. I heard talking; one voice undeniably Toni's, then I heard Toni sucking her teeth and a dial tone.

"What the?" I looked at the phone and started dialing again, then slammed it in the cradle. "How in the hell can she treat me like this?" I didn't like the way I felt, vindictive, hurt, out of control. I wanted to do something, I wanted to curse Toni out because I didn't foresee any of this. And even though I sensed the worse between us was yet to come, I was relieved we would be forced to deal with this mess. Perhaps Toni would recognize I was trying to make an effort.

My fury increased when Toni spent another night out, so I called her job again the next morning. After getting cleared by the Secretary of Defense, I finally talked to her.

"Toni, where have you been and when are you coming home? And how is it that you can go to work for three days without coming home to pick up clothes?"

"You ain't the only one that keep a extra set of clothes in the car Jazz," Toni snapped.

"What? Extra set of clothes? I beg your pardon."

"Jazz, I ain't even trippin,' look I got a meetin' to prepare for."

"Fine Toni, stay wherever the hell you been stayin'."

***

Toni took me up on my suggestion and stayed away from home for three weeks. Conversations, the brief times we talked, pretty much continued like they had when our argument initially started. Some days I came home, mail was sitting on the entrance table, and it seemed like more clothes were missing from Toni's closet every day. Several times the phone rang late at night, but the person kept hanging up when I answered. It was most likely Toni trying to keep tabs on me.

It was hard to stay focused. I felt like my world was falling apart and the best that I could do was just exist. Toni wasn't home and T had consistently called a few times a week expressing concern about me and my well-being. She invited me to a movie with John and his new beau on Friday. Going would involve socializing and I just didn't have that kind of strength at the moment. When I called T on Wednesday, I suspected that she wasn't going to like me declining her invitation.

"Hey Beautiful," T said answering on the second ring. "I was going to call you shortly."

"Can you chat now?" I asked.

"What's up?" T asked cautiously.

"I'm sorry to disappoint you, but I can't go Friday night," I said.

"How come?" T questioned.

"I'm not in the right frame of mind," I answered.

"For a movie? Come on, it'll be fun. Hanging out with John is always good comic relief," T tried to sound convincing.

"There's too much going on. I wouldn't be good company," I said with a sigh.

"Ahhhh, I was really hoping we could get together," T pressed.

"Me too, but I'm feeling kinda awkward meeting new people, and I don't really know what's going on here."

"Going to a movie doesn't have to be that complicated you know?" T retorted. "We say 'hello,' buy tickets, go into a dark theater, and essentially remain quiet. Tell me what this is really about."

I knew my voice sounded weary and my heart was heavy. That was what I knew for sure. What I had absolutely no clue about was how to make sense of my life right now. Toni wasn't here and T was trying to get me to open up more. But I didn't know if I was ready to expose more of my vulnerabilities or give up on Toni and me. "Yes, this is about more than a movie. I have too many loose ends to tie up. I can't make it," I said, hoping she wouldn't press further.

"Is this about Toni?" T asked me. I could hear growing frustration in her voice.

"Yes, it's about Toni. But it's also about you."

"What about me?" she rightfully wanted to know.

"I want to spend time with you and get to know you more, I do. But I also don't know what Toni and I are doing." *Ugh,* I probably said too much. I held my breath and sat completely still waiting for T to respond, yet her silence was deafening. "T, are you still there?" I asked, barely above a whisper.

"Yeah, I'm still here." She cleared her throat. "Jasmine, I'm not sure what to say." She let out a loud sigh. "I guess we'll talk later?" T sounded irritated.

"Okay," I responded. She said "bye" and hung up. Which was quite startling since she had been nothing but kind and sweet. I wasn't sure if T completely understood my perspective or not. And I didn't have the right words or energy to change that right now. I could live with a fair amount of uncertainty, but not this. *Ugh!* I need to fix this.

{TWENTY-ONE}

T

Sheila had left countless messages on my answering machine since the debacle at the café. I never returned her phone calls and hoped she would just disappear or move on. She didn't. Her messages ranged from short "Call me" demands to long rambling missives about my indifference to our relationship. I wanted to let the situation play itself out without confrontation. That plan wasn't working.

So, I agreed to meet Sheila at the Mount Vernon Stable on Charles Street and prepped myself for drama. "The Stable," as it was known locally, was legendary for happy hour and tasty ribs. Located in the heart of the gayborhood, patrons met there to enjoy the ambiance, eat, and have a few cocktails before heading out to dance at surrounding clubs until the wee hours of the morning.

My conversation with Jasmine this evening didn't go well, which meant that I was in a funky mood. But I needed to end this madness with Sheila. I looked around on the upper level but didn't see her. Consequently, I headed downstairs towards the bar. Before reaching the last step, I could hear Whitney Houston's "Queen of the Night" blasting from the 'three plays for a dollar' jukebox. The song gave me a boost. It was busy for a Wednesday evening. I assumed folks were celebrating hump day based on the volume of their laughter and frequency of glasses clinking together. Once my eyes adjusted to the dimly lit space, I saw Sheila sitting in a booth on the other side of the bar.

I intentionally took a little extra time to make her wait for me although I was already twenty minutes late. I devilishly wanted to make her wonder if I would show up at all. Perhaps she would see what other women see when I entered a room. Perhaps not.

I happened to see a couple of clients from my last show, so I went over to say "hello." One was Nia, the girl Jasmine got so upset about. I approached her and gently touched her shoulder, "Hey Nia, good to you." Nia beamed when she turned around and saw me. She stood up and gave me a hug. "Good to see you as well. How've you been?"

"I'm well, thank you and yourself?" I asked.

"I'm okay."

"I just wanted to say a quick hello, didn't mean to interrupt your dinner, have fun."

"You too," Nia said.

I glanced over at Sheila who was watching my every move. She looked restless, but I still stopped at another table to greet one of my student's parents just to make a point. Finally reaching the table, Sheila also stood up for an embrace, but I squeezed her shoulders instead.

"Hello Sheila," I said before sitting down. "Hi," Sheila replied, obviously annoyed with my cool greeting.

"How have you been?"

"Great, but I'm definitely not as *popular* as you are," she commented sarcastically.

"Popularity is a state of mind. Have you ordered yet?" I asked, trying to stay calm.

"I've already ordered a trio of appetizers. I've been waiting for you… a while, might I add."

"That works for me," I responded and ignored her comment about my lack of punctuality.

"Who the hell is the anorexic Barbie doll?"

Jesus! I had only been with Sheila for thirty seconds and she was already wound up.

"Sheila," I said looking directly at her, "not tonight. Let's not make another scene." The waiter came to take my drink order.

"May I have a Tequila Sunrise without the tequila please?"

"Yes ma'am," the waiter replied.

"Thank you," I said, handing the menu back to him and turning towards Sheila.

"Ugh! Why do you even bother? You should save the money and just have water," Sheila said, providing her unsolicited opinion.

"Just because I don't drink alcohol doesn't mean I can't enjoy a cocktail. Now, why have you been wearing out my number? What do you need to…"

Sheila started before I could finish. "You've been avoiding me, not returning my calls, you won't answer your door when I know you're home. Why are you treating me like we haven't been seeing each other for the past two years?"

"Sheila, why is it that every time you screw up, you have to remind me how long we've been dating? And if you're so concerned about longevity, you sure have a funky way of showing it. It's difficult, to say the least, to be with someone who's more obsessed with material possessions, appearances, and self-fulfillment than with anything or anyone else."

Nia walked by the table and deliberately slowed on her way to the restroom with a slight smirk on her face. Not long after, and certainly not long enough to put on lipstick let alone actually use the facilities, she stopped at our table and said to me, "I'm still waiting for you to come hang that piece for me."

I smiled and responded, "I'll give you a call soon."

"I ain't been around but a hot second and you're already disrespecting me!" Sheila fumed. The increasing volume of her voice gave me flashbacks. I really didn't hear what she said throughout her fifteen-minute monologue, but my ears perked up when I heard, "T, I've been thinking, I want us to just be friends. I mean, we are very different and we aren't in the same place, so, it's probably best that we go our separate ways."

I covered my mouth, barely containing my smile, but managed a somber, "Ok. Sheila, if you think that's best." Hallelujah! This was going to be easier than I thought. Perhaps she was a bit more mature than I gave her credit for. But Sheila being Sheila, continued talking and basically ignored my concession.

When she transitioned to pointing out all the ways that we were incompatible, I touched her arm to get her attention and shorten her award-winning speech. "I'm okay with your decision." Reality must have finally set in because she was speechless for once. Even though Sheila was trying to put on a brave performance, I saw tears forming in her eyes. She rose to leave—I did too—and gave me a dramatically long embrace. On her way out, she slowed by Nia's table. There was no doubt in my mind that Sheila gave Nia a glance that harbored both suspicion and contempt.

The waiter arrived with my drink and the appetizers. He jutted his chin towards the open seat where my now ex-girlfriend had been. "Just box them up," I said pointing at the food. "And when you get a moment, please bring the check." I loathed having to pay for another uneaten meal fooling around with Sheila again. However, I savored the moment, and my drink, because it was the last bill that I would ever have to pay for Ms. von Doran.

{TWENTY-TWO}

Jasmine

I was greeted by the delicious smell of frying pork chops when I unlocked and opened the door after coming home from church. I walked in and glared at Toni in the kitchen, who must have read my mind since I was staring at her wondering what she was doing here.

"I decided we needed to talk," Toni said, wiping her hands on the dishcloth she had draped over her shoulder. *She's about to mess up the sermon I just absorbed this morning.* The devil is still busy.

"You decided? Toni, we don't have anything to talk about. You've been gone for three damn weeks. I was beginning to enjoy the peace and quiet," I said calmly.

"See Jazz, I came back home to make peace."

"Peace? Puh-leeze. And we're doing that because you decided it's time? I've been callin' you, worried about you, and you don't even have the decency to pick up the phone, open your mouth and say 'Jasmine, I'm fine, I need some time, I won't be comin' home, don't stay up waitin', kiss my ass, nothin'!'"

"What did you expect me to say? Obviously, you been occupied, I'm supposed to just ignore that?"

"Where the hell you been for more than three weeks?"

"That ain't important, I needed some space," Toni said, turning back to the frying pan trying to act like she was deeply engaged in cooking.

I felt my neck whirling around like the Exorcist. "Have you lost your mutha' fuckin' mind?" Yep, teachings from my good gospel sermon were gone and it was on. At which point Coco came into the kitchen sensing tension between us. Toni was taken aback—she knew I only used language like that when I was really upset.

"Are you serious? You've been gone damn near a month, and we're supposed to have a good Sunday dinner?" I said walking towards her.

"I'm not doing this again Jazz," Toni said when she pushed past me after taking the pork chops out of the grease. I was glad she did, the kitchen wasn't a good place to fight, we had too many heavy pans and sharp objects.

***

"Tension." That was the title of this family drama starring me and Toni. It was an uneasy truce as we existed under the same roof. Since she decided to come back and claimed she wanted to make us work, neither of us got too close or raised our voice for fear of adding fuel to a growing fire and a deteriorating relationship. But as my gut told me, Toni couldn't miss too many weekend activities before she showed her ass again.

I had a Saturday seminar on "Teaching Adult Living Skills" and came home during the lunch break since the community college was close to the house. I didn't really feel like networking; I didn't have the energy to pretend to care.

I ran into Toni on the front porch preparing to leave the house with a packed bag. I looked long at the bag and then at Toni.

"What's up?" I asked.

"I'm going to watch the Mystics game," Toni responded matter-of-factly.

"And?" I gestured to her bag.

"I'm hangin' out afterwards, so I'm taking a few things just in case." Toni side-stepped me.

I turned around. "Toni," I called out, "let me make sure I understand...it's two in the afternoon, you're going to watch a Mystics game that comes on at four at some mystery location, and you're taking a bag 'cause you aren't sure if you'll drink too much or smoke too much and won't be able to make it home?"

Toni said, "Yep, that's about right."

{TWENTY-THREE}

T

I really liked Jasmine. During our brief conversations the past few weeks though, she sounded preoccupied. I tried not to pry but I really wasn't clear about what was really going on with her and Toni. I didn't know if they were working on their relationship or what. Much to my disappointment, Jasmine wasn't exactly forthcoming either. I thought our energy was really nice before the whole picture debacle, so I was still kicking myself for that. However, I could dwell on things I had no control over, or I could use a little distraction.

Nia and I had briefly talked a few times since meeting at my show. Our conversations were nothing serious beyond innocent flirting. After seeing her at The Stable the night of my 'official breakup' with Sheila though, I invited her to meet me at the Top of the World Observation Deck. The views of Baltimore up there were breathtaking, which meant you didn't have to chat a whole lot on a date if you didn't want to. Nia was nice enough… fine as hell, cultured, a senior vice president at a communications company downtown, and apparently deeply engaged in one of the Divine Nine sororities.

"Do you bring all of your dates up here?" she asked as we peered south over the harbor.

"Sometimes," I answered honestly.

"And I thought I was special," she said, boldly nudging me with her hip. I gently smiled at her. There was absolutely no need to commit to anything right now. "I can be if that's what you want," she continued while getting into my personal space a bit more.

I cleared my throat and returned her flirtatious energy, "That sounds enticing."

"Yeah?"

"Yeah," I responded. But I tried to be patient and get Nia to appreciate our current vantage point. "Have you been here before?"

"I have not, even though I work just three blocks away."

"So, what do you think? Beautiful, clear day huh?"

"Yeah, it's nice," Nia replied half-heartedly, seemingly uninterested in the view and focused on her own agenda. "Do you want to come over to my place for drinks?"

"Sure, that sounds nice. Heads up though, I don't drink alcohol," I informed her.

"At all?" she looked at me like I had landed from another planet.

"At all," I responded confidently.

We left Top of the World, and I followed her back to her place with the thought of exploring Nia's tight body which was nicely adorned in a fitted navy-blue St. John's two-piece suit. We didn't drive far, she lived in the Evergreen neighborhood north of downtown. The bungalow had a large porch stretching across its front façade with two wicker chairs on one side of the front door and a swing on the other. Inside, her décor was a bit garish for me, the colors were the wrong mix of cool and warm colors. But I was happy to see my work prominently displayed above the living room mantel. When she disappeared down the hallway to get us drinks, I checked out her pictures before taking a seat on the couch.

"Who are the dudes?" I asked Nia pointing to the pictures sitting on her built-in bookshelves as she handed me a glass of club soda.

"Friends," she responded cavalierly with a sly grin.

"Friends? Ya'll look a bit chummy to be friends."

"Well since you asked, my definition of friends is a bit...expansive."

"Uh huh." The hair on the back of my neck stood up.

"I have had both intimate and casual acquaintances on occasion with men and women."

"So, you're bi?"

"I don't like labels," Nia shared nonchalantly as she took my drink, put it on the coffee table, and crawled onto my lap. "My sexuality is fluid."

"Is it now?" I asked, intrigued by her boldness, disappointed in her disclosure. She kept talking.

"I've never felt compelled to succumb to the family's insistence to choose a side, one gender or the other."

I appreciated Nia's honesty and frankness, I really did. Fluidity and freedom were great for her, but not me, not anymore. Unfortunately, my experience in relationships—or even trysts, especially trysts—with bisexual women was more complicated than just the run of the mill same-gender loving ones. And since I declared my life a drama-free zone after Sheila skedaddled, I made up a lame excuse and got the hell out of there. Besides, I had bigger fish to fry.

***

A week after bombing out with Nia, I invited Jasmine to the First Thursday Gallery Stroll. Thankfully, she agreed. It was my way of seeing her, saying hello to the Charles Street gallery owners, and feeling Jasmine out about traveling with me to a mid-August Philadelphia arts festival.

After our third gallery we decided to take a break from the crowds. We bought gelato from a street vendor and headed to a park bench at the base of Baltimore's Washington Monument. "I have to make arrangements for an upcoming show and I'm going to a festival in Philly this weekend. I want you to go with me."

"What do you mean, go with you?" Jasmine puckered from her tart lemon gelato.

"Just what I said, go with me."

"I'm sorry, I can't do that," Jasmine said apologetically.

"Why not?"

"I have a girlfriend remember?"

"Do you?" I asked.

"What's that supposed to mean?" Jasmine wanted to know.

I slid closer. "It means that if you *really* had a girlfriend, you wouldn't be here having gelato with me."

"I can visit art galleries with a friend with no other pretenses in mind," Jasmine tried to sound convincing.

"Can you now?" I slowly licked my gelato off my spoon.

"Yes," she responded in a higher pitched voice.

"Is that why you're here? Because you have no other pretenses in mind?"

"Absolutely," she exclaimed.

I wasn't convinced. "And what could those other pretenses possibly be?" I questioned. Jasmine tried to backtrack and return to the original question.

"Look, I can't go away with you. Despite our current issues, I do have a girlfriend, whom I've been with for ten years. It's just not right."

"Ten years huh? That's a long time. When did she take her eye off you?" I started getting more forward.

"What do you mean?" Jasmine asked.

"I mean, at what point did she get comfortable enough to not pay attention to such a beautiful creature as yourself?"

"Stop it, you're making me blush. Besides, who said she stopped paying attention?"

"Jasmine, you didn't have to say it. It's in your eyes, it's in your actions. Women who are committed don't leave the door open for other possibilities. They don't visit galleries and chill in the park with friends," I said using air quotes. "And I don't hear their smile when I call."

"But…" Jasmine tried to interrupt my truth telling and continued to blush.

"Let me finish. I'm not trying to disrespect you or your relationship. If you tell me that us spending time together has been and will be strictly platonic, I'll respect that. I'll carry on about my business, try to not have Jasmine on the brain and think about you forty-five minutes of every hour." I looked at Jasmine very intently, trying to find an indication as to what she was thinking. She looked away and took a deep breath. I gently turned her face back towards me.

"Jasmine, all I'm saying is, your girlfriend doesn't seem too concerned about your relationship, she leaves you unattended quite a bit."

"Unattended? I'm a grown woman, I don't need an attendant," Jasmine said defensively.

"I know, I know. I don't mean you need an attendant like you're a Medieval maiden locked in a castle tower. I'm saying that if you're not paying attention to your hive, another bee may steal your honey." Jasmine smiled at that analogy.

"Speaking of which, we've not talked about your honeys," she emphasized 'honeys.'

"Geesh, where did that come from? And 'honeys' plural?"

"That's what it seems like to me. Going with your analogy, ladies seem to swarm around you."

"Hah! That's good. BUT there is no swarming and truth be told, I did have a girlfriend up until a few weeks ago. She dumped me," I confessed.

"What? Get outta here. You certainly haven't acted like you've been dumped," Jasmine rightfully observed.

"I'm not lying and you're right. Those two things, in this case, are not mutually exclusive."

"Oh?" Jasmine replied, her eyebrows raised.

"Nope, they are not. Sheila was neither good for me, my wallet, nor my sanity. And that fact became glaringly obvious the more I spent time with you."

"With me? Really?!"

"Yes, really." I placed my hand on Jasmine's. "Look, I just want to spend a little time with you away from the city. If I've overstepped the line, I apologize. If you'd like to join me, you're more than welcome."

It was getting late and I didn't want to make the situation anymore uncomfortable that it already was so I suggested we call it a night. I held her hand as we walked to her car. Jasmine unlocked the door, I opened it, and she sat in the driver's seat. I leaned inside, placed my business card in Jasmine's hand, moved further into her personal space, and whispered in her ear. "I'll leave home at one o'clock on Friday afternoon and will be back no later than three or four on Sunday, maybe earlier. Again, the invitation is out there, my address is scribbled on the back." I kissed Jasmine on the cheek with a sensuality that ensured blood still flowed below her waistline and stepped back so she could get to wherever she was going.

{TWENTY-FOUR}

Jasmine

I didn't want T to disappear. Whatever it was that was developing between us had been good. I didn't know however, if it was good because it was a distraction from my and Toni's mess or if it was good because it was good for no other reason than for the sake of being good. I did know that I wasn't ready to let T walk away, but I was also fearful of the unknown. It seemed as if this woman just appeared in my life and somehow had casually become a prominent presence in my consciousness.

Toni and I had made a life together. At the moment though, Toni didn't seem to care about our life together or how I felt about her drinking and smoking and staying out late. She just packed her bag like it was normal to want to spend the night away from your girlfriend. When *did* Toni stop paying attention?

***

I purposely hadn't called T since our gallery date. I wanted some time to think about her offer last Thursday to go to Philly. By Tuesday, the tension at home and unexpected changes at work made the walls feel like they were closing in on me. I felt restless. So, I left work a little early, picked up Coco and went for a needed walk at the Harbor. We went around Rash Field three times; Coco felt the need to bark at the maintenance crew and they laughed each time we passed them. My thoughts still unsettled; we headed around towards the pavilion where partygoers were boarding the gangway for what appeared to be an evening cruise. We turned around and walked back towards the Rusty Scupper and watched a few mariners fill their boats with fuel.

I sighed and looked at my watch. "Coco, let's go home." To be honest, I was hoping to run into T. As a matter of fact, when I caught a glimpse of a female runner rounding a corner, my heart raced until I determined that it wasn't her. Although I was beginning to miss T's sexy quirkiness, I resisted the urge to call. Why was that? I was still unsure what I was going to do on Friday. I kept looking for a sign; divine intervention would be nice.

I returned home to find a note from Toni reminding me not to forget my ticket and that she would see me at the basketball game. Yikes! I forgot that we were supposed to go to D.C. tonight. It completely slipped my mind. The season was winding down and the Mystics weren't winning much. I called Toni on her cell and asked why she couldn't have waited for me? Toni said some of the boyz were getting together for pre-game drinks so she would see me at our seats. I looked in the closet for something to wear but I really didn't feel like driving to D.C. I remembered it was airing on *Lifetime,* so I decided to stay home. At halftime the phone rang, it was Toni yelling, "Why are you still home?"

"I changed my mind."

"You've wasted my money!"

"Excuse me? I work every day," I reminded her.

"You could have given me the ticket so one of my boyz could have sat here."

That upset me, "I'll see you when you get home," I said and hung up the phone.

The Mystics lost, no surprise there. Although they had been in the league for four seasons, they had yet to put together a team that consistently won games. Everyone thought that would change when Chamique Holdsclaw was our number one draft pick in 1999, but the win-loss column didn't lie, basketball was a team sport. I went to bed after the late-night news and rolled over at twelve-thirty as Toni walked through the bedroom door. I looked at the clock, looked at Toni and smelled smoke. "Where you been Toni?"

"I got one of them flyers after the game, went to check out this little spot for a minute," Toni said as she slid underneath the covers. *Ugh!*

"Why'd you wait until halftime to call me?" I asked.

"That's when I got to our seats?"

"You and the *boyz* were together until halftime? So, I could have been on the side of the road, and you wouldn't have known until halftime."

"Yeah, but you weren't…you were here waiting for me," Toni nonchalantly said, as she caressed my hip.

I moved further to the edge of my side of the bed. "Toni, go to hell."

***

I was sitting at my desk at work enjoying a cup of coffee and reviewing patient charts when the phone rang at one minute after nine. It was Toni telling me a telemarketer woke her up.

"Why you let me oversleep?" Toni grumbled half awake.

I smiled, twirled my pencil, tried to remain calm and responded, "How old are you?"

Before she could answer, I reminded her, "You are way over twenty-one, and where does your mother live? It ain't here, she lives in Virginia. Suffice to say, you should be able to get your grown ass up and go to work. You know one of the questions on the standardized alcohol test is, 'does alcohol affect your ability to work?' Since you're already late, you may want to get up and get dressed and we'll chat about this later." I hung up the phone before Toni could respond.

***

When Toni walked in the house that evening, I was in the living room nursing a glass of wine. I saw her tense up—she knew that my drinking and waiting were not good for her.

"You wanted to talk?" I patted the sofa for Toni to sit down. Toni flexed but stood. I continued, "I understand you hung out last night after the game. That's why you said you left early, to hang out. But I won't go there right now because you want to argue about how come I didn't wake you up after you left me to go to the game to drink with your boyz, went to some hoochie party, and then stayed out half the damn night? Toni puh-leeze! Now tell me again, what do YOU want to argue 'bout?"

Toni chumped down, "Jazz, I ain't got time for this shit," she said and walked away. I drained my drink, took a deep breath and smiled, pleased that I was able to get a few things off of my chest. Jasmine one, Toni zero.

***

Thursday morning, and I still hadn't decided what I was going to do tomorrow. I looked at my horoscope, as well as Toni's and T's for a little celestial guidance... no clues. I still hadn't talked to T because I didn't want to be influenced. Toni and I were just existing under the same roof. For the last few nights, she slept upstairs. The only thing that was certain was that tomorrow was Friday and I had no idea what I was going to do about Philly. The day was basically a blur, morning staff meetings and patient group therapy sessions.

When I came back from lunch, there was a single message on my voice mail. Luther was singing "If Only for One Night." I played the message three times before deleting the song. I dialed T's cell phone but hung up before the call went through. I took out T's card to look at the address for the umpteenth time—I didn't have an answer.

That evening before I went in the house, I said out loud, "I'm not going." There. I made a decision. With that out of the way, I started dinner. I didn't cook often but decided that any change in my life had to begin with me. I thought dinner was okay however, Toni picked at her very healthy turkey meatloaf. Afterwards, instead of going upstairs to be in her own space, Toni came to the bedroom and sat on the edge of the bed.

"Jazz, we need to talk," Toni said

"Okay, talk," I responded.

"I want to be happy and I'm not. You aren't happy either. So rather than be miserable, I'm going to be leaving. We can work out details later when you aren't so upset, and we can talk about things calmly."

My heart sank and my chest tightened. I couldn't believe what I was hearing. Were we breaking up? I would be single? I wanted to be upset and kept reaching for anger. Instead, I couldn't get enough air into my lungs, my throat was constricted. Taking shallow breaths, I just sat there, numb. What the hell was happening?

Toni went back upstairs after sitting for what seemed like hours. She and I had just stared at each other. Perhaps I was in shock which felt like I had been hit with a brick...hard. Yes, we had problems, especially those three weeks apart since she never said where she was. Perhaps that took us to a place we wouldn't recover from. In spite of being in and out of sync over the years, it never dawned on me that we would ever go our separate ways and it would end like this.

I didn't know what to say or think. I laid in bed going over scene after scene of our relationship. It had been so long since we were truly happy, but those thoughts came flooding back too. Tears began to form; I could hear Toni upstairs moving about. The thought of her leaving made me extremely sad. The realization of her putting other things and people ahead of our relationship made me mad most days but we typically recovered. The dichotomy consumed me.

If she was leaving, I had to get the locks changed. I would have to adjust my household expenses to replace Toni's income. Was I ready to be alone after all this time? It wasn't supposed to be this way. Why now? What made her want to leave now? I walked upstairs; Toni was putting things in boxes. When did she acquire boxes? Obviously, she had planned this.

That made me even madder. But I didn't say anything. I just walked back downstairs, negotiating my way to my room through tear-filled eyes. I entered the room and instead of sitting on the bed, I knelt at the edge and prayed.

"Lord, it's been a long time since I've actually been on my knees. But I need to hear from You. My life as I've known it is apparently coming to an end. I know things happen for a reason, but I'm confused. I'm hurt. I'm sad. I'm mad. For the longest time, I've felt like I was in this relationship by myself. But I kept thinking things would get better. Lord, I'm here asking for strength and understanding. I'm asking for peace of mind. Finally, please watch over Toni, wherever she goes. I hope she finds peace and happiness." I crawled under the covers, the weight of emotions too much to carry right now. At some point I finally cried myself to sleep.

The alarm clock woke me up at six the next morning, the house was still. I wondered if Toni was still here. Coco came in and interrupted my thoughts, nudging my hand to let me know she wanted to go out. "Oh shit! I didn't let you out last night. Hopefully Toni did," I said to the dog. After I let Coco out, I walked upstairs. Toni wasn't there and quite a bit of her belongings were already gone. The thought that Toni already had a place to go infuriated me, but I didn't want to start the day off grumpy. I resolved that I had prayed about it and wasn't going to dwell on the negative energy.

While I waited for Coco to stop chasing squirrels—how could the dog have so much energy in the morning—I started switching purses to compliment the outfit I was going to wear today. I figured my clothes didn't have to match my mood. I dumped the contents from one purse into another; T's card fell on the floor.

"I'm not going," I said aloud, for the second time in twenty-four hours. I didn't need to convince anyone because I was alone, but just in case, I repeated the words, "I'm not going." Reading my horoscope in the *Baltimore Sun*, confirmed my intended plan. It simply read, "Move cautiously through the next moon's cycle."

I called T before leaving for lunch, secretly hoping that I could take the cowardly route and leave a message. However, she answered. *Damn!* I closed my eyes and inhaled all the air I could. "Hello Teresa."

"Awwhh this isn't good, you're using my real name. I was hoping you were calling to ask for the weekend forecast in Philly," T teased. "You aren't going, are you?"

I shook my head as if T could see me. "I'm not. I don't have the energy to travel," I said, moving papers on my desk to fulfill a need to do something with my hands.

"Wait, what's wrong? Are you okay? What happened?"

"I'm okay. I really am okay." I paused to hold back tears. "I'm single. I'm processing that. And it's not a good time," I said, trying hard to vary my voice and not sound as dull as I felt.

"Single? Really? Hmmm, I'm not sure what to say. Uhhh, what can I do to help?" T sounded concerned.

"Not much. Go to your festival, we can get together when you get back."

"So, what's all this mean now?"

"Honestly, I have no idea. I've been single less than forty-eight hours." I shuffled the papers to the other side of the desk for no apparent reason.

"How does that make you feel?" she asked.

"I've experienced so many emotions. Initially, I was in disbelief. Then I got mad, and sad, and mad again. Our conversation seeped into my thoughts," I confessed.

"What conversation was that?"

"The one when you asked me when Toni had stopped paying attention," I paused to gather myself. "T, I feel like I should fill in a lot of gaps in my story." I continued, "and I'm willing to do that but it can wait until you get back." T was silent. "Are you still there?" I asked.

"Yeah, I'm here. Just listening and trying to imagine being in your shoes."

"Thanks for that but I'll be okay, really."

"Are you sure?" T asked.

"No. But don't worry about me. Drive safely and be careful up there." I tried to muster strength.

"I don't know if that's possible—the not worrying about you part—but I'll be safe," T reassured me.

{TWENTY-FIVE}

T

Jasmine sounded flat. I had never heard her speak in such a monotoned voice, so I listened intently. I was disappointed that I would be unaccompanied in the city of "Sisterly Love," but I understood her concern. Of course, she needed time to process major changes in her life, who wouldn't? I would be lying though if I said that I didn't feel a tiny bit of joy when it was apparent there was a possibility for me and Jasmine to be together more often. But I didn't want her to be hurt for that to happen. Hell, I wasn't sure what I wanted. That wasn't true. I wasn't sure I could have what I wanted, more specifically, who I wanted. Like Jasmine, I wasn't ready to share every thought that crossed my mind or emotion I was feeling. I was, however, interested in seeing where our connection would take us. I called her back.

"You missed me already?" she asked without saying 'hello.' I could hear her smiling so that was a good sign.

"Yeah, something like that," I humored her.

"Listen, I know you don't know a lot about me but one thing that is incredibly important to me is honesty. You can thank my high school Geometry teacher."

"Okay, that's noble," Jasmine said smiling again.

"Hey, I'm being serious," I whined.

"I'm sorry, I'm sorry. Go on."

"Thank you! As I was saying," I said trying not to laugh, "honesty is important. And I want to be honest, I like you. I mean, I really like you. I like spending time with you. I like the way you laugh. I love your smile. I like being with you."

"Wow! That's, that's a lot," she said, somewhat speechless.

"I know," I continued. "And my telling you is not to scare you away or anything. I now know you have plenty going on in your life and I'll respect the time you need."

"T, I appreciate you saying those things. I agree, we need to get to know one another more," Jasmine said. "How about this... check your email after three-ish. I'm going to send you a few questions that you can think about over the weekend. We can talk about them when you get back?"

"So can I see you on Sunday when I get back in town?" I asked.

"No, I'm having dinner with some friends. What about Thursday?"

"Seriously? I have to wait almost a week to see you?" I wasn't happy.

"Yes, we just went through this T, I need time for me."

"Boooooo," I protested.

"What?"

"I'm joking, you're right," I conceded reluctantly. This girl sure did know how to keep a sistah waiting. This was definitely new for me.

"What about John Stevens in Fells Point after work?" Jasmine asked.

"John Stevens it is, I'm looking forward to seeing you," I said.

"Yeah, me too," she replied.

"Okay, bye... again," I said, pleased that we were looking ahead. She was single, I was single. What now?

{TWENTY-SIX}

Jasmine

It wasn't exactly a lie. I knew I would be having dinner with friends on Sunday. Although it wasn't confirmed yet, I knew I would see my girls because I was calling a "Red Alert," a sistah was in trouble.

Leslie and Stephanie arrived at the same time. They saw the spread, with all the Sunday fixins that I had already laid out on the table, including wine, so they knew they would be there a while. After saying grace, Leslie finally asked, "Who are we roasting?"

I replied, "My relationship."

Leslie—seated to my left—cackled, "Awh hell, I thought something was going on for real."

Stephanie—sitting to my right—went into serious interrogator mode, "What happened?"

"We broke up," I stated almost matter-of-factly.

They both almost choked.

"What?" Leslie leaned on the table with her head cocked to the side and brow furrowed.

"When?" Stephanie asked immediately after Leslie.

"No!" Leslie leaned back in her seat and crossed her arms, mouth twisted, looking suspicious.

"Stop!" I held my hands up, "I feel like I'm at a tennis match."

"Ya'll beefing or ya'll broke up?" Leslie started again.

"We're done. Over. The fat lady sang... sung her last song, her and the band have gone home," I flatly stated.

"Are you serious?" Stephanie finally asked with a hint of concern.

"When's the last time I called a 'Red Alert?' A, no questions asked, I need help alert?" I asked.

"Wow," Leslie sat back in her chair, eyes and mouth wide open. "Damn."

"How are you feeling?" Stephanie asked, the professional that she was.

"I'm feeling, I really don't know what I'm feeling," I responded.

"Okay, I'm going to put this out there. I wouldn't say this to any of my patients, but since I haven't gotten paid for any of the good advice you ignored over the last few years anyway, I'm going to speak my mind," Stephanie said as she got up to get a bigger glass for her wine.

"Don't you usually?" Leslie mocked with a neck wag.

Stephanie came back into the dining room. "Your relationship has been over for at least four years."

"Well damn!!" Leslie interjected.

Stephanie ignored her and continued, "Toni has tried every way she knew how to leave, but you kept going back to get her or letting her back in. In the words of my esteemed famous television colleague Dr. Phil, 'You taught her how to treat you.'"

I let out the breath that I was unconsciously holding and dropped my head. Leslie's hand went in the air. She mouthed amen.

Stephanie didn't miss a beat, "You accepted less and less and got less and less. Now, there are a few practical questions you need to answer. One, are both names on the house title? Two, can you afford the payment by yourself? And three, who else knows about the breakup?"

I looked up and answered her, "Only my name. Yes, but I'll need to make some adjustments. And only you two know," I lied since they didn't know T existed.

Leslie jumped in, "Only your name? I thought you got the house together?"

"No, just my name," I replied.

"You know you lied to us," Leslie stated, stunned.

"I just didn't tell the full truth," I started fidgeting.

"Chile please…why did you lie?" Leslie asked.

"Cause I didn't want to hear it," I said, still fidgeting.

"What? That you were in this by yourself, or that you had to cover for her again?" Leslie grilled.

"Where is she now?" Stephanie inquired.

"Gone, had moving boxes and everything," I responded.

"What the fu-? Did she leave the key?" Leslie asked, on a roll now.

"No."

"Did you change the locks?" Leslie shot back.

"Not yet." They both looked at me like I had lost my last mind. Then they both asked in unison, "Why not?"

"I didn't want to be hasty," I shrugged my shoulders.

Stephanie was up pacing around the table, "Let's go over this again, you broke up, she had boxes ready to move out, and you don't want to be hasty about what exactly? See," she said to no one in particular, "this is why we tape record sessions, so people can hear how they have distorted the truth into their own reality."

Leslie said, "Do you want her to come back?"

Stephanie repeated the question shortening the words to "Do you?"

"I don't know." I sniffed. I told truths that afternoon that I had held for years. Funny thing was, my friends didn't seem surprised by the revelations that I carried me and Toni financially, Toni's weed use had gotten out of hand, and I really didn't know where she was staying when she didn't come home. Listening to myself, I began to wonder when I surrendered, because I certainly felt like I had lost many battles and now ultimately the war, otherwise known as my relationship.

I was drained after they left. I was hoping T would have called this weekend, or at least responded to my e-mail when she returned from Philadelphia. I had been mindlessly going through the motions between work and home and church—T would have provided a good distraction. Maybe I should have gone to Philly. Was that why I was thinking about T so much, because I was feeling sorry for myself?

It certainly didn't feel that way. I actually thought I missed Teresa. Ironically, I wasn't missing Toni though, not like that. I missed having someone in the house and several nights had checked all of the door locks at least twice before going to bed. Not that I hadn't spent nights alone, far from it. Toni had made a habit of staying out at least one night out of almost every weekend, often times two, for over a year. *Damn!*

The thought of that truth made me angry. Where was Toni all those nights? People in relationships come home at night. Why did I allow Toni to continue spending time away from home if I wanted better for myself and more from our relationship? Questions I wasn't ready to answer.

{TWENTY-SEVEN}

T

I wanted to call Jasmine throughout the weekend but decided against it. She really didn't need me in the mix while she was going through her troubles. I also didn't respond to her "twenty-question" e-mail although I thought some of the questions were cute and some were thought-provoking.

I convinced myself that I was going to cancel dinner tonight as well, not that Jasmine needed anyone else irritating her. But I certainly didn't want to be the rebound girl while she was waiting for someone better to come along. That ain't my style. When I called to leave a message, to my surprise, she answered the phone.

"Uhhh, hey," I said, fumbling around for appropriate words, "what's up?"

"Nothin', what's up with you?"

"I wasn't expecting you to answer, thought you would still be at work, so I was just planning to leave a message," I said.

"I am still at work. Would you like me to hang up?" I could hear Jasmine smiling, which made me smile.

"No, I was just expecting to hear your voice mail, that's all," I said, forgetting the real reason I called. "What are you smiling about?" I asked her.

"What makes you think I'm smiling?" she asked, once again avoiding my question.

"I can hear it."

"What do you mean, you can hear it?" she laughed.

"I mean I can hear it in the inflection in your voice. You still didn't answer my question though."

"What's that?"

"Why are you smiling?"

"I don't know," she said, the pitch of her voice raising several octaves like a schoolgirl.

I decided to let her off the hook. I knew she was smiling because it was me on the phone. She wouldn't admit to that, but that was okay. Hearing that she was happy to hear from me changed my intention of the phone call.

"Hey, about dinner," I started.

"Are we still on to meet at John Stevens tonight?" she asked anxiously.

"Actually, I'm not feeling going down to Fells Point."

"Oh, that's why you wanted to leave a message, to cancel huh?" she sounded disappointed, her smile obviously gone.

"No, Jasmine that's not it," I lied, honesty out the window.

"What is it then?"

"Why don't you come over for dinner?" I asked before I developed the idea fully.

"I don't know T," Jasmine expressed her reluctance.

"Why not?" I wanted to know.

"That sounds kinda… kinda…"

"Kinda what? You were going to meet me for dinner, right?"

"Yes," she said hesitantly. "But coming over to your place implies intimacy."

"It doesn't have to, besides, we're just friends right?" I said teasing her.

"Stop it."

"I'm sorry, I was just messing with you. You were going out… you're still going out, it's just here," I said trying to convince her while coming up with a quick menu in my head.

"I just don't know if I'm ready to be in someone else's space just yet."

"I get that," I said. "Well, if you change your mind, you know how to find me."

"T?"

"Yes?"

"I was looking forward to dinner. I wanted to see you tonight," Jasmine admitted.

"Then come see me," I said emphatically. As far as I was concerned, it was just that simple. I understood she didn't want to jump into anything, but it wasn't like we hadn't been seeing each other since the beginning of summer.

{TWENTY-EIGHT}

Jasmine

I could hear a scuffle outside my office door and told T that I would call her right back. When I opened the door, two patients were pushing and shoving each other. Other staff members heard the commotion at the same time and came running to help me diffuse the argument. It could be funny what patients get into it about. This time the discussion was about the correct words to the theme song from the *Jefferson's,* amazing what the human brain can become fixated on.

I returned to my office, looked at the phone, and laughed to myself thinking about what I had been fixated on... my relationship ending, my lack of focus, my preoccupation with Ms. Teresa. *Damn it.* I started trying to compare the advantages and disadvantages of seeing T at a restaurant or her house. The last few times we were alone, the energy between us was pretty intense. I wasn't sure I could trust myself to do the right thing, if there was such a thing in this case. And I wasn't sure if I was ready for all possibilities.

Who the hell was I kidding? I truly enjoyed the few times I was close enough to T to identify the type of soap she used. But I certainly didn't want to give the impression that I wanted to sleep with her, even if the possibility lingered in the back of my mind. Plus, I felt like T was putting me on the spot. If I didn't go to her house, would she cancel dinner altogether? That was kinda like an ultimatum, and I didn't like ultimatums.

Paula walked into the office joking, "I smell smoke, deep thinking, very deep thinking. Why all the concentration?"

"I was invited out, or over should I say, for dinner," I confessed.

"Hmmm, most people would find that rather cute, going out on a date with the one you love to keep the relationship alive."

I looked at her kind of strange, remembering that she didn't know. So, I gave her the Cliff's Notes version of the breakup. Paula asked incredulously, "She moved out?" But she didn't wait for a response. "Certainly doesn't sound like Toni wants to continue working on it. And you're dating already? When the hell did that happen?"

See this was why I felt guilty about seeing T and hadn't told anyone, I wasn't ready for the questions, criticism about seeing someone else, or unsolicited armchair relationship therapy. People made assumptions when they didn't have all the facts. I gave Paula the shortened version of that part too.

"And now she wants you to come to her house for dinner? So, what's the problem?"

"You're no help," I said, tossing a balled-up post-it at Paula to get her out of the office.

I picked up the phone and called T back. "Why did you give me an ultimatum?"

"Hello again to you too. Ultimatum?" T asked.

"Yeah, explain how dinner at your house even became an option. You called to cancel, didn't you?" I didn't wait for a response. "If I say I don't want to have dinner at your house, are you canceling our dinner plans?"

"I'm not saying that."

"Is that a 'yes' or a 'no'?"

"Why does it have to be like that? Look, I figure you have a lot going on. You just broke up with your girlfriend..."

"Stop!" I interrupted T, "I thought you were seeing somebody too."

"Nope, we talked about that." T steered the conversation back. "We're talking about your situation remember?"

"Teresa, are you seeing anyone?"

"Wait a minute, what's with the irrelevant interrogation? But, 'no' for the record your honor, I told you before going to Philly that I wasn't seeing anyone anymore."

"Well then, is it a good idea for me to be at your place so soon?"

"My situation is not an issue. Are you coming to dinner Ms. Christie Love?"

"Mizz Smarty Pants, I don't even know where you live," I informed her.

"Bullshit!" T exclaimed.

"Excuse me? Why you gotta use that language and tone of voice with me?" I asked, surprised by her response.

"I'm sorry, you're right. I didn't mean to offend you. Look, I told you, I like you. I'm just tryin' to ask a nice woman over for dinner for a nice evening and nice conversation. Is that too much to ask?" T tempered her tone and lowered the volume.

"Okay, okay, fine, where do you live and what time?" I asked again.

"It was on my card, unless you threw it away. Is seven okay?"

"No, I didn't throw it away," I said rolling my eyes and smirking. "Seven is fine and what about the questions?"

"We can talk about them over dinner, deal?"

"Deal!" I agreed.

{TWENTY-NINE}

T

Jasmine arrived promptly at seven dressed unseasonably warm. She had on a black mock turtleneck, cream cardigan, and black pants. No cleavage or legs showing, hair pulled back, and no suggestion that anything except dinner would be happening tonight.

"Did you come straight from work?" I asked, dressed in impeccable linen with sharp creases.

"Why do you ask?"

"You're either dressed for a funeral or an early cold spell," I joked gesturing to the mirror by the door so she could see what I saw.

"I just wanted to dress appropriately." She looked and laughed sheepishly.

"Yeah okay, at any rate, please come in. May I take your sweater before you burst into flames?"

"Smart ass," Jasmine murmured.

"Scuse me?"

Jasmine whispered, kind of cutesy-like, "I didn't say anything. Thank you for taking my sweater."

"Uh huh. Would you like something to drink?"

"Yes, what do you have?"

"Juice, wine, water..."

"Wine please. I thought you didn't drink?"

"I don't, but like you, it's here for visitors," I answered her.

"And do you have many visitors?" Jasmine wanted to know.

"You know you never gave me a proper greeting," I said not answering Jasmine's question. I opened my arms and said, "Good evening Ms. Charles, it's a pleasure to see you."

"Good evening, Ms. T," Jasmine said, falling into my embrace.

We stood there for a minute, not talking, just enjoying the moment. Jasmine had said that she was looking forward to seeing me but getting reacquainted so quickly was an unexpected surprise. I was certainly looking forward to seeing her and experiencing moments like this. Jasmine pulled back from me, of course she couldn't seem too comfortable or give me the impression that she wanted to be here.

"Is that your van out front?" she asked nodding towards the street.

"Yeah," I smiled. "It's usually parked in the back, I needed to run a few errands today. But that's how I make the magic happen."

"Ewww."

"What do you mean ewww? Get your mind out of the gutter. I mean, that's how I carry the magic… my work?"

"Yeah, okay," she replied with a skeptical look on her face.

"Trust me, the thing is outfitted with storage racks and not much else. I won't be impressing anyone with that thing anytime soon," I said. "Excuse me Dr. Ruth, I was on my way to get your wine." She poked her tongue out at me, which made me inadvertently lick my lips." Good Lord, focus T, focus. "Please make yourself at home. The living room is right here." Before disappearing into the kitchen, I pointed across the hallway towards a cranberry-colored wall with a mural painted on it similar to the artwork from the gallery opening at the beginning of summer. Jasmine stopped in front of it. The art was showered in soft yellow light.

"Bring back memories?" I whispered as I came up behind her handing her a glass of wine.

Jasmine accepted the glass. She took a quick sniff and sipped it. "Nice." She smiled. "Yes, it was a full evening, a gallery opening, a wonderful dinner, an averted catfight."

"See, why you have to go there?" I teased her.

"What? There are a lot of memories from that night," she said with her beautiful smile.

"Fair enough." I drank from my own goblet.

"Wait a minute now," Jasmine said inquisitively.

"What? You wanted wine, right?" I asked.

"Yeah, but what's in your glass?"

"Would you like to taste it?" I smiled and handed Jasmine my glass.

"I don't know where your lips have been."

"Maybe not but I know where I want them to be." I stepped closer.

Jasmine sighed and turned away, but I could see her smile. She took a little swallow from my drink. "Hmm...is that apple juice?"

"It's not just apple juice. Mott's is just apple juice."

"Uh huh, so what kind of apple juice is that?"

"You don't know nothin' about this," I said.

"So, tell me."

"It's Martinelli's!"

"I thought they made sparkling apple cider?" Jasmine asked.

"They do. But they made apple juice first," I said like I was a seasoned apple juice connoisseur. "When I come to your house for dinner, this is my favorite."

She ignored my comment. "This is your home and your studio?"

"Yes."

"Do you have showings here?"

"Not often, but I have folks over occasionally to see what I'm working on," I answered.

"So, you stick to galleries?"

"Mainly, I can reach more people that way plus, you don't want too many people knowing where you live. That's an occupational hazard."

"Yeah, guess you have to be careful, there are no referees here."

"Here you go. Why does it have to be like that? I like my privacy." *Women always sabotaging shit.*

Jasmine smacked her lips, "Okay. Have you lived here long? Bolton Hill is such a diverse area."

"I've been here almost ten years, bought it not long after moving to Baltimore."

"About that, you aren't from Bawl-more are you?" Jasmine asked using local vernacular.

"How could you tell?" I laughed.

"There are a few local dialects, and you speak neither of them," she said laughing too. "Anyhoo, you must do very well with your paintings."

"I do alright, the day job helps. Truth is, I bought the place when the market was down and it needed a lot of work, but had loads of historic character and details you know?"

"I can see that. I like the modern décor, did you do a complete renovation?"

"At this point, I guess you could call it complete. I gradually completed small projects over time, it was a lot. I'm sure you're familiar with Bawlmore rowhouses," I said, mimicking her. "Obviously I removed a few interior walls and floors but kept much of the original perimeter brick and wood molding, replaced badly damaged windows, restored others, and kept the doors. I also refinished the floors, removed three layers of Antebellum Era wallpaper, and added my own touches here and there like the cable railing along the mezzanine and the industrial light fixtures."

"Nice, I love the stained glass and high ceilings," Jasmine said, "you seem to have an eye for design."

I smiled. "Yeah, that's what happens when you take one little Intro to Architecture course in undergrad and then hang out with architecture students. That's where I met John," I said, "he would stand out anywhere, but he *really* stood out in that program. Not many Black people to speak of and certainly not many Black people wearing brightly colored bowties and matching eyeglasses." I chuckled, thinking about John giving his professors hell during project critiques. The boy had always been a mess, in a good way.

"Lord have mercy, I can only imagine. Where did you all go to school?"

"Savannah College of Art and Design, better known as SCAD."

"Hmmm, so living around the corner from Maryland's premiere art school is right up your alley huh?" Jasmine asked.

"Yeah, I guess you could say that," I responded, "birds of a feather."

"So, who did you hire to do the work here?"

"John actually helped me with the design. On the contractor front, I started off working with *your* people. Then when they missed the third deadline and still hadn't removed the first plumbing fixture or light bulb, I hired a Jewish contractor that employed a handful of Latinos who understood that time was money."

"See, why you got to go there? That's so wrong on so many levels," she said.

"What?" I asked immediately.

"We need to do business with our people."

"Hey, I started off trying to do my part, but everybody ain't ready," I said.

"I still think we can hire *our* people and get our money's worth."

"Yeah well, I like getting paid just like everybody else. When I take someone's money up front and tell them their painting will be done in a month, it probably should be. If it ain't done in a month, they probably won't be pleased with me and may not patronize my business again and oh, by the way, will tell all of their sistah friends how lousy I am. But if I finish a week early, and it looks better than they expected, I probably have a customer for life."

"That's a great business philosophy," Jasmine said, then asked, "can I get a tour?"

"Not yet. If you don't mind, let's eat first, dinner is getting cold."

"Where can I wash my hands?" she asked rolling her eyes.

"There's a bathroom under the stairs," I said pointing in the direction of the front door.

When Jasmine came to the dining table, it was set, the lights were low, candles lit, and I was standing there waiting to pull her chair out. "Are you ready for the first course?" I asked.

"Sure, what are we having?" Jasmine asked as she sat down, and I placed a linen napkin in her lap.

"Tonight, madam we'll start with avocado slices and grape tomatoes on a bed of greens with balsamic vinegar with fresh herbs," I said in my best proper voice. "Then? We'll have seared salmon steaks with wild rice and steamed vegetables also with fresh herbs. For dessert, I have coffee or a selection of herbal teas and your choice of chocolate-swirled cheesecake or chocolate chip cookies."

"Who cooked or better yet, where did you order this from? Because four hours ago, you were calling to cancel dinner," Jasmine said suspiciously.

"I cooked, except the cookies and cheesecake. I'm from the south, we know how to cook."

"T, you made all that food?"

"What do you mean ALL? It's just veggies and fish? I can't prepare a nice dinner for a beautiful woman?" I asked, picking up the remote and filling the room with the sweet sounds of Brian Culbertson.

"Whatever…I'll have my salad now, thank you." She folded her hands in her lap like she was waiting for service at a restaurant. I went to the kitchen again.

I came back in the dining room and was met by Jasmine's giggles. "What's funny?" I asked carrying the salads and warm bread.

"Nothing, just had a stupid moment," Jasmine laughed, still smiling.

I smiled. I forgot how giggly women could be. Sheila was anything but. I joined Jasmine at the table and reached for her hand to say grace.

"Would you like more wine?"

"Half a glass please, I need to drive home," Jasmine responded.

"Not necessarily," I said slyly. Jasmine just stared at me through the candlelight. "Hey, I want to keep you safe."

"Umm hmm," Jasmine said, looking skeptical. "Hmmm, this salad is tasty."

"Glad you like it," I said, smiling.

"No, I mean like really tasty," she insisted.

"You know why?" I asked, still smiling.

"Why?"

"Herbs."

"Herbs?" she asked. "What? I mean, I know what herbs are, but my herbs don't make salads taste like this."

At this point, I was laughing out loud. "They're fresh herbs. I grow them."

"You have a garden? I'd love to see it."

"Okay, but I wouldn't call a bunch of pots a garden. However, I grow my own oregano, thyme, basil, sage, and tarragon," I announced proudly. Jasmine just stared at me with her eyebrows raised. "And I dry it and store it," I continued.

"Really? Are you serious?"

"Of course I'm serious. I love the way they make everything taste."

"Wow! That's fascinating. Creativity wasn't the only thing we have in common... we both garden."

"Yeah, I guess so."

"But I've never met anyone who made their own seasonings. You know we swear by McCormick's products here in Baltimore," Jasmine laughed.

"Well, we've already established 'dat me naw from 'roun 'dese parts," I said harking back to my Geechee heritage. I took the opportunity to shift the conversation. "So how was your day?" I asked, settling into my chair.

"It was fine, typical for a full moon," Jasmine responded.

"Full moon?"

"Sorry, psych humor. And yours?"

"Alright, getting ready for school to start. Summer seems to have flown by," I replied, somewhat melancholy thinking about going back to work.

"How was Philly?"

"It was okay, productive. Made a few contacts at the festival. I met with several clients for upcoming shows and a few commissions."

"What's the name of the piece with the women's bodies?" Jasmine asked.

"I don't know. I haven't named it, give me a name," I responded.

Jasmine shrugged her shoulders. "Can you sell untitled art?"

"Absolutely! I can name it one thing and a buyer could think it should be named something else. I don't always name them, they just are, you know?"

"No, I don't really, but okay," Jasmine admitted.

"I'm just saying, my effort is in creating the piece, someone else can come up with what it's called. My brain and creativity only have so much capacity. Like the one you like. Now, I would call that *Jasmine* because you like it," I said smiling. That made her smile.

I served Jasmine, displaying my best table manners, serving from the right, picking up from the left, catering to her every whim. Jasmine said she liked the effort and was impressed by my culinary skills. We laughed like old friends, had good conversation, and bantered back and forth.

I returned from taking the dishes into the kitchen. "Coffee is brewing that we may partake with dessert," I announced and noticed Jasmine eyeing the studio on the mezzanine. I reached for her hand, "Would you like your tour now?"

She didn't have to answer. When she put her hand in mine, our fingers interlocked, and I guided her up the stairs to the studio on the second level. Jasmine slowly took in unfinished paintings in various stages, stacks and stacks of prints, large art-related books, photographs, paint, lots of paint. I turned on the track lights in the rear of the room and one photograph caught Jasmine's eye. Her own image, about two by three feet, was staring back at her with intense eyes and a knowing smile. Her hair was slightly wind-blown. I thought it captured her sexiness perfectly.

"What are you doing with that?"

"Nice photo, huh?"

"Maybe," Jasmine said, shrugging her shoulders, voice obviously five octaves higher than normal.

"You like?" I wanted to know.

"I've never seen a picture of me that large. What are you going to do with it?"

"That's one of the photos that was in Owings Mills."

"Hmmm…yeah, I'm still salty about that. With all the fallout, I didn't have a chance to see them," Jasmine said, her eyes getting very wide. "Can I have it?"

"Why?"

"I've never had a picture of me that big."

"Yeah, you just said that. And what are you going to do with it?"

"Maybe you'll come help me hang it," she said, laughing at her own sarcasm.

I just smiled. "Oh, you know that was funny," Jasmine said playfully hitting me.

"Don't you think it would be kind of odd having such a large photo of yourself in your own house?"

"No, people have enlarged pictures of themselves hanging up all the time. Remember Michelle and Thomas' house? I was just going to put it on a wall, it's not like it was going over a mantel piece."

"I'll consider it, if you're nice to me."

"What's your definition of nice?"

I pulled Jasmine closer to me and held her by the small of her back. "I know what it will cost you."

Jasmine swallowed hard. "What?"

I leaned in to kiss her, tasting the wine lingering on her lips. *Good lord, they were so soft.* Our energy was palpable. "Eh hem, eh hem." Jasmine pulled away and pointed, "What's up those stairs?"

"Are you sure you want to go up there?" I asked.

"I don't know, what's up there?" she inquired.

"My personal space."

"Hmmm, think the coffee's finished?"

"Probably not, it's a slow brew," I answered, not letting Jasmine off the hook.

We reached the top of the landing. My entire third floor was one big open space, except for the bathroom. On one side was the bedroom, where the bed sat on a stepped platform elevated above the hardwood floor. I thought the contemporary rosewood furniture gave the room an earthy feel.

Some of the walls were brick, some were painted cranberry. The lighting was soft and warm. The other side of the third level was a sitting area with a relatively large flat screen TV mounted on its own credenza with surround sound Bose speakers and enough CDs to open a decent music store. The furniture could also be considered contemporary, but it wasn't stuffy. A sexier illumination showered this area from the moon shining through the skylight. Jasmine let out a low whistle. "My, my. Who you got to know to get up here?"

Sensing an opening, I pulled Jasmine close and looked deep into her eyes, "Me."

"Oh really?"

"Yes," I answered her.

"Who else has been granted super-secret, confidential access?"

"Jasmine Charles, I am a single woman spending time with a single woman who just happens to be standing in my personal sanctuary. You have access."

"Okay. Yes ma'am." Out of the blue, Jasmine asked, "Number four of the twenty questions e-mail asked dogs or cats? Since I didn't get a response to my e-mail, dogs or cats?"

"I didn't respond because you said we would talk about it over dinner, thank you very much. Ummm, cats? Hell, I don't know."

"Uhhh, zero for one." We both laughed.

"Cats don't tackle me like your dog does. Who got the dog in the divorce?"

"Coco is my dog!" Jasmine informed me then boldly asked, "Is there space for Coco over there in the sitting area?"

"Perhaps," I said smiling.

"Are there any yes or no answers with you?"

I put my index finger to my lips. "Hmmm."

"It's time for coffee." Jasmine said as she smacked her lips, turned, and headed for the stairs.

I grabbed her around the waist and pulled her back. "I know that's not the only question you wanted to ask."

"You didn't answer the one I asked."

"Yes. Yes, is the answer to your Coco question," I complied.

"Okay then. Since you're holding me against my will. Beach or mountains?"

"Beach."

"Why?"

"I like the water, the rhythm, the calmness. I think we talked about this during one of our first conversations. Next."

"Favorite color?"

"Black."

"That's not a color," Jasmine protested.

"Please, it's all colors in the spectrum combined." She rolled her eyes.

"What kind of animal would you be?" she continued.

"An eagle."

"Why an eagle? I thought maybe something a bit more aggressive."

"Ahhh, you never know do you? Eagles soar, they're graceful and beautiful. They have keen vision."

"Do you have keen vision?"

"With my glasses," I laughed.

"You're such a smart ass," Jasmine said. She came closer and whispered another question that I must have missed in the email. "Top or bottom?"

"Both."

"Oral or penetration?"

"Why does it have to be either or?" I whispered in Jasmine's ear and nibbled on it just enough to make her giggle. "You'd like to find out, wouldn't you?"

"T, stop," Jasmine quietly pleaded. I didn't. Instead, I put my hands behind Jasmine's head and tilted it up so a little bit of her neck was exposed. I smelled her aromatic fragrance, a bold, heady musk that drew me in. It was a lingering, "when can I see you again" scent that always stayed in my mind long after Jasmine and I parted. I was thankful that I was getting a chance to experience it more closely. Jasmine seemed too weak to stop me and was enjoying the closeness too much to protest. I got the sense that she didn't want to.

I turned the table, "Fast or slow?"

"They're my questions, you haven't finished answering them," Jasmine whined.

"Seemed like you were done, and I believe you're adlibbing."

"What was the question?" she conceded.

"I said, fast or slow?" I rubbed her back, tangibly emphasizing the slow part.

"Both."

"Lights on or off?"

"Off. Friday nights or Sunday mornings?" Jasmine turned the line of questioning around again.

"Both and, not either or, thank you very much."

"I hear you. Trumpet or sax?"

"Sax."

"Why?" Jasmine asked.

"Sexier sound," I replied. "Although I do enjoy Chris Botti."

We were still standing at the top of the stairs when I backed her against the wall. I held Jasmine's hands above her head, pressed against her body and kissed her neck over and over again. I traced her ear with my tongue then whispered, "Any more questions?" Jasmine didn't speak; she merely shook her head from side to side. Receiving confirmation that she didn't object to where the mood was going, I softly kissed her on the lips and parted her legs with my own thigh. I wedged myself there and continued to put pressure on Jasmine's lower body. Jasmine met my pelvis with her own. It was as if we were slow dancing, our bodies in rhythmic harmony.

I let Jasmine's hands go so I could feel her curves. My hands traveled down her torso. I placed my hand behind her neck and firmly pulled her lips closer to mine. I inhaled Jasmine's scent again, gently kissed her nose, one eye, then the other, her forehead, back to her nose again, then proceeded to kiss Jasmine in a way I hoped she wouldn't soon forget. Our tongues danced together, hearing the same melody our bodies heard. We kissed and kissed again and kissed some more. We liked the exploration; we felt the unspoken energy.

I leaned back to look at this woman who had occupied my thoughts this summer. Usually, I would have been on top of conquests by now, them calling my name and exclaiming what I knew to be true. That I was a great lover and knew how to push women's buttons. But Jasmine was different. I didn't want to spoil what we had established; I didn't want to go there just yet. I wanted to stare into her eyes. I wanted to know more about her. I wanted to be in Jasmine's mind, not just inside her essence. She was making me realize there was more to relationships than drama and empty sex.

Jasmine pushed away. "T, I should go. It's getting late."

"Now?"

"I have to work tomorrow remember?"

"I know," I said kissing her forehead.

"You're not making it easy."

"Easy to do what?" I asked.

"Leave."

"Do you want to leave?"

"No."

"Then stay," I simply said.

"It's not that easy," Jasmine reasoned.

"What's so complex?"

"How would that look?"

"To who?"

"To, to," she stumbled.

"Yes?"

"To?"

"You're single remember?" I reminded her.

"I know, but I haven't been for so long, I forgot what it feels like."

"Jasmine?" I pulled her close again.

"Yes?"

"If you want to stay, stay. For once, do something because you want to, not because someone else wants you to."

"Why do you make it sound so easy? In my mind, it's not that easy. Besides, I didn't bring anything with me to stay," Jasmine rationalized.

"What do you need? I have clean pajamas, t-shirts, a toothbrush."

"A toothbrush? Why do you have an extra toothbrush?"

"Jasmine please. I happen to have bought a new one for myself today when I was at the grocery store. You're more than welcome to have it. What else do you need?"

"Ummm,"

"I didn't think so." I started kissing Jasmine again, this time backing her up to the platform where the bed was perched. We stopped shy of the first step.

"Teresa?" Jasmine interrupted whatever was about to happen.

"Yes?"

"May I use your restroom?"

I exhaled. "Of course, it's right there," I said pointing to the only door on the third level.

"Thanks, I'll be back, the wine is catching up with me," Jasmine said twisting her hands.

"Take your time, I need to turn the coffee off, do you still want some? Cheesecake? Cookies? Anything?"

"No, not right now, I'm still stuffed from dinner."

"Okay, I'll be back," I said and headed downstairs.

{THIRTY}

Jasmine

Oh God, I was here in this woman's house, in her bathroom, her personal space. I took a few deep cleansing breaths and tried to compose myself. I was conflicted. I wanted to be here, but was it too soon after Toni? Why did I even care? As Stephanie reminded me, Toni and I hadn't been on the same page in years. I guess that was the good girl in me, placating, always trying to do right, or taking the high road. My thoughts were erratic.

T served an impressive dinner, no fried chicken and now I was lusting her and this great color palate in the bathroom. The colors reminded me of a sunset—it was gorgeous and spacious—and three people could probably fit in that soaker tub. I felt one of the towels on the towel bar. Nice fluffy, expensive spa-like towels. Hmmm… you don't put these out for everyone. I smiled.

I didn't want to give T the wrong impression. What was the wrong impression? That was funny, her impression was I came to dinner dressed for a funeral. I was foolishly overdressed, giving off a Morticia Addams vibe. It wasn't like we just met, and this was a first date. Was this a date? It felt like a date, I mean, I prepped and danced around like it was a date. What was wrong with me? She had obviously gone out her way to make me feel special. Oh God, please give me a sign. Should I run? Should I stay? ARGH!!!!

After Toni moved out, I exchanged house keys with a neighbor for emergencies. I called and asked her to let Coco out. I certainly hadn't planned on being here this long.

T was right too. I had not looked out for me—only me—for a long time. And why shouldn't I enjoy a night out, even if it was Thursday. Who said dates only had to be on the weekend? I made a mental note for future date nights, T enjoyed Dave Coz, Gerald Albright, Najee, Walter Beasley, Candy Dulfer, and Kim Waters, nice! She spared me on the country music front.

I needed to live a little and stop being so predictable and cautious. But caution wasn't such a bad thing, was it? I mean, it was one reason Toni could leave and my finances weren't drastically impacted. As a matter of fact, I might save a little money on utilities. I definitely would save on gas without running up and down the road to D.C. to whatever party Toni wanted to go to, and whatever the hell else.

And here I was with this woman who was sexy as hell, who obviously invested time to maintain her incredible body, and who apparently wanted to spend time with me.

I finished in the bathroom and after washing my hands moisturized them with the lotion on the counter. Even the damn almond scented lotion smelled good! I could get used to this.

{THIRTY-ONE}

T

I came back upstairs, lit more candles, and picked up the entertainment system's remote to summons Luther's soothing vocals. Jasmine came out of the bathroom and stopped to let her eyes get adjusted to the dim lighting. "Are you okay?" I asked.

"Yes, just trying to see."

"Come here," I said.

Jasmine seemed to like my confidence. "Yes?" She approached me. I reached down for her hand.

"Be careful," I said guiding Jasmine up two steps. I sat on the bed, and she stood in between my legs. I held her waist gently and rested my head on her stomach and let out a sigh. Jasmine took the band from around my locs and let them fall. It was the first time she had seen them down and ran her fingers through them. From her reaction, I surmised she liked them.

I lay back on the bed, pulled Jasmine on top of me, and gripped her firm rear. We kissed again and our tongues continued exploring the other's just where we left off. I rolled Jasmine over, stood up, and looked at her.

"What?" Jasmine asked seemingly becoming self-conscious.

"Just looking."

"Why?"

"Because you're beautiful."

"Stop, you probably say that to all your girls."

"I'll ignore the *all* part but no, I don't. I recognize beauty when I see it." I reached for Jasmine's left foot.

"What are you doing?"

"I'm taking your shoes off. Is that alright?"

"Yeah, I guess," Jasmine said shyly.

"Relax."

I took Jasmine's pump and knee-high off. I reached over to the nightstand for a little lotion and began massaging Jasmine's foot, first the top, following the bones to her toes, then kneading my thumbs into the soft flesh on the bottom of her foot. I rotated Jasmine's foot in a circular motion. The massage wasn't confined to the foot, but also Jasmine's lower leg, knee, and calf. I stroked and kneaded and massaged. As my hands worked their magic, Jasmine closed her eyes, sank into the bed, and for once did what I suggested, she relaxed. I repeated the same on Jasmine's other foot and leg.

"Hmmm."

"You like?" I asked.

"Yes."

"Good."

I joined Jasmine in the bed and lay on my side beside her and propped my head on my hand. I ran my hand along her arm and thought to myself how much I was at peace. Being with Jasmine was calming, soothing. We lay there in silence enjoying the music and each other's breathing. The other being afraid to interrupt the amazing energy in the room.

***

"Jasmine," I whispered. It seemed like we laid there for a long time, but the clock indicated only forty-six minutes had passed.

"Jasmine," I shook her gently, standing next to the bed with a set of pajamas.

"Huh?" Jasmine said.

"Put these on."

"Huh?"

"Here, change your clothes," I said.

"What time is it?"

"It's after midnight."

"Why did you let me sleep so long?" Jasmine asked.

"Because you were tired."

"I need to go."

"Why? Just stay baby, I promise you'll make it to work on time."

"Did you just call me baby?"

"Did I?"

"Yes."

"Hmmm. Anyhoo, you're here, you're comfortable. Change your clothes and go back to sleep," I said trying to convince her to stay.

She reluctantly went into the bathroom to brush her teeth and change. I could see her hesitate. I guess you'd have to be a cruel person, which Jasmine was not, to move seamlessly from one relationship to the next without blinking. When she came out of the bathroom wearing my pajamas looking sexy as hell, I was already in bed. "Did you find everything you needed?" I asked her.

"Yes."

"Good, come back to bed," I patted the spot where Jasmine had fallen asleep.

She sat on the edge of the bed with her back to me, "T?"

"Yes."

"It's been so long since I shared a bed with someone other than Toni and spent the night at someone's house other than my friend Stephanie's."

"Okay."

"I'm nervous," she admitted.

"Understood."

"I, I... there are so many thoughts running through my head right now. Tonight was nice. The foot massage was nice. What do you know about reflexology?" she asked, turning to look at me.

"I know a little sumthin' sumthin'. You relaxed, didn't you?"

"Yeah, probably too much."

"Why do you say that?"

"I shouldn't be falling asleep in someone else's bed," Jasmine said.

"I'm not just anyone."

"I know, but anyway."

I moved over and sat behind Jasmine and let her fall into my embrace. "Jasmine, I'm sorry about your relationship, I really am. I don't like to see bad things happen to good people. But you must know that things happen for a reason."

"I know, it's just hard. So much of my life is changing, my daily routine, how I see things, the places I go."

"And that's a bad thing?"

"No, when you put it like that, I guess not."

"I didn't think so, let's get some sleep."

I helped Jasmine get underneath the comforter and joined her. I spooned her body and put my arm around her. "Jasmine?"

"Yes?"

"You teach people how to treat you," I said borrowing a line from Dr. Phil.

"I know Teresa, I know."

{THIRTY-TWO}

Jasmine

I was tired. It wasn't like I needed to rush home to anyone or anything in particular once Coco was taken care of, so I stayed at T's insistence. Although I still didn't want to lead her down a path I wasn't ready for, I freshened up a bit just in case. In case of what? I wasn't sure, but I could never be too prepared since I would be in someone else's bed. As always though, T was incredibly gentle and understanding.

I woke up disoriented and glanced around to see T sleeping peacefully and smiled. I couldn't believe that I had spent the night at this woman's house, and she didn't make a move other than to massage my feet. "Oh shit! Coco needs to get let out!"

T opened her eyes, looked at me, and smiled. "Good morning, how'd you sleep?"

"Surprisingly, I slept very well," I replied.

"Would you like some breakfast? Coffee? Tea?" T asked.

"No thanks, I need to get home and get ready for work, feed the dog, let her out." I laughed and said, "I'm just going to brush my teeth, wash my face, and get home." After I got dressed and came downstairs, T walked me to the door, and we embraced for quite some time. This felt so right. She kissed me on the lips and near my ear and whispered, "Next time bring Coco so you won't have to rush home." *Have mercy!*

On my ride home, I felt my phone vibrating, six missed calls. I checked voice mail and found that I had four messages. Three were from Stephanie; all of them contained some combination of, "Are you okay and do I need to call 911?" As I walked in, the house phone rang. Breathlessly, I answered, "Hello?"

"I've been calling you all night, where have you been? Are you okay?" It was Stephanie.

I giggled, "Girl, I'm fine. I'll explain later, but I need to get ready for work, I'll call you later."

During a lull in my morning routine, I called Stephanie back. After exchanging pleasantries with her assistant, I was transferred.

"I got an appointment in ten minutes, heifer talk fast."

I giggled again, "I was on a date. I didn't know you called until this morning."

"What! Let me tell Rachel to hold my calls for a minute. Where the hell were you?"

I said coyly, "I was with Teresa."

"Who the hell is Teresa and why are you spending the night with her already?"

"Why don't you and Leslie come over tonight so I only have to tell the story once."

"No, you got six minutes. Tell me NOW. Who is Teresa?" Stephanie said emphatically.

"Long story short, I met her at the Harbor. She's a teacher and an artist, and I spent the night at her house."

"So let me get this straight, and I may charge you for this session. You met some woman at the Harbor and you're already sleeping with her?"

"I didn't say I slept with her," I defended myself.

"You said you spent the night."

"That doesn't mean I slept with her, but you're not letting me tell the story."

"You got two minutes."

"She gave me a foot massage."

"Ahhh hell, what time should I come over?"

"Around seven."

"That's good. My last appointment is at five-thirty."

"Okay, I'll call Leslie," I said.

I left a message on Leslie's work phone, "I met a new honey, I spent the night, details at my house at seven o'clock." I laughed as I hung up the phone. When I returned from an afternoon meeting, there was a message from Leslie, "Alright Jezebel, I'll see you at seven."

***

I ordered two pizzas, one with meat for Stephanie, a veggie only for Leslie, and opened a bottle of wine. Leslie arrived first and tried to get me to share details before Stephanie got there. "I'm only telling this story once, hold tight," I told her. Both were at my house before seven.

The mood as we sat around the table was much different than the last time we had all gathered. We joked, laughed, and teased each other. I shared the juicy details of my and T's meeting from the first evening at the Harbor to the open invitation to return to her place again. Then the rapid succession of questions started.

"You like her?" Stephanie asked.

"Yeah," I said coyly.

"What about the foot massage, who the hell does that?" Leslie chimed in, "That's some *Jason's Lyric* type of shit right there!"

"Guuurrrrlll, I'm tellin' you what," I let out a low whistle.

"What?" Stephanie and Leslie said in unison.

"She's gentle, considerate, sexy, and *cooks!*"

"Cooks? You datin' a femme?" Leslie asked with a skeptical frown on her face.

"No, stupid… Toni cooked, remember?"

"You mean she ordered food and put it on nice dishes?"

"No, I mean she cooked. Salmon and wild rice, steamed vegetables, simple, yet charming. And oh by the way, it was delicious!" I couldn't contain my smile.

"What?" they said in unison.

"Yeah, apparently she grows her own herbs and…"

"Herbs? She grows weed?" Leslie interrupted me.

"Nooooo!" I protested. "Herbs like spices, oregano, basil."

"Was everything neatly arranged on the plates? Did you have to take your shoes off? Did she keep washing her hands?" Stephanie asked going down her list of personality disorder symptoms.

153

"Nooooo," I said trying in vain to defend myself. "She's different."

"Different? Good different or I need to call my shady cousins different?" Leslie questioned with her mouth twisted to the side.

"What? Different like somebody you dream about," I plead my case.

"Ah hell, she dun went Cinderella on us," Leslie said throwing up her hands.

"No, there's no white horse. She does drive a beat-up white van though—she carries her art in it. And get this, she likes country music."

"What the fu--? She's white?" Stephanie exclaimed.

I let out a sigh, trying to not let my friends exhaust me. "And what's wrong with that if she were?"

"You dun lost your damn mind. All the fine black women in Bawlmore and you had to find a white woman?" Leslie asked.

"No girl, not just a white woman, but a white woman with a beat-up ass van who's growing weed in her basement," Stephanie said while high fiving Leslie.

"Ya'll have added a lot of sauce to this story," I said, shaking my head at my friends' narrow minds.

"Girl, you better bring us some more wine," Stephanie said raising her empty glass, "to get this story down."

I giggled—something that I was doing more of these days—and went to the kitchen to fetch the bottle. After I filled their glasses, I sat down and proceeded to stick up for myself. "One, I'm sure as my good friends, you all would support me if I fell in love with a woman of ANY color. Two, I believe love is love. And three, T is a fine, caramel-colored Adonis whose skin has been kissed by the sun."

"Thank you, Jesus!" Leslie shouted. "Thought you had bumped your head. But don't think we missed that fell in love statement."

"I didn't say I fell in love," I said.

"You said you were sure we'd support you if you were in love with a white woman," Stephanie reminded me.

"Right, I didn't say I was in love, I said if."

"Uhh huh," Leslie said questioning my response.

"I haven't been out of love long enough to be falling in love," I pleaded my case.

Stephanie leaned back and said, "Oh no honey, you've been out of love for a minute."

"Heifer," I hissed peering at her.

Stephanie countered, "I only do truth."

"Look, all I'm saying is, yes, Toni and I had been on the outs for a long time. And truth be told, T has been a good—dare I say necessary—diversion. I met an intelligent, thought-provoking, easy on the eyes friend and it's been fun these past few months getting to know one another." I didn't tell them T said she liked me. That would have been too much fuel for the fire.

Stephanie whirled around, "Wait a fuckin' minute! I thought you just met Ms. Gentle, Considerate, Sexy, Intelligent, Thought-Provoking..."

Leslie cut Stephanie off, "What the hell is her name?"

"Teresa," Stephanie said.

"Teresa who?" Leslie asked.

"Teresa Butler." I also didn't tell them about T's vagueness or how I initially got her name from a handcard rather than directly.

"Is she looking for money? A girlfriend?" Stephanie asked.

"What? No! I don't know?!" I said throwing up my hands.

"That's okay! We have enough to do a background check. Where's she from?" Leslie asked.

"I don't need either of you to do a background check. Anyway," I said, ignoring Leslie, "It's only been a few months and it's early in the getting to know you stage."

"It ain't that damn early, you dun spent the night with a woman and you don't seem to know much about her."

"Ooh Jezebel," Leslie said shaking her head back and forth.

"You two, I'm telling you when you meet her..." I chimed in.

Stephanie interrupted, "The first thing I'm going to ask is what are her intentions."

I responded, "Well, you do that. Up until this point it hasn't come up. But as I was saying, she's nice, different than a lot of women I've met here in Baltimore."

"Oh, she ain't from round here?" Leslie asked.

"No, she's from Savannah, Georgia."

"Now how she know that and she don't know what her intentions are or where THIS is going?" Leslie asked Stephanie doing finger swirls in the air.

"I don't know, she must have been too busy enjoying foot rubs and whatnot," Stephanie answered.

"'Scuse me, ya'll act like I'm not sitting here," I said.

"Rubbin' her feet, she'll be rubbin' your hair and next thing you know Ms. Country Bama is puttin' a root on you," Leslie said as usual putting more than her two cents in the plate.

"Both of you, go home, I fed you, we shared libations, and this is how you treat me?" I said laughing.

"Girl, we just watchin' your back," Leslie said.

"Is that what you call this?" I asked. "Go home, it's time to go home. Now!"

I was lying in bed reflecting on the conversation with my two crazy, but concerned, friends. I was certain they would love T too. Would they love her? Did I love her?

***

Unlike Mondays with new hospital admissions, Tuesdays weren't generally difficult days. But driving home Tuesday evening, I was exhausted, it had been a long day. It couldn't be a full moon already...the patients, staff, everyone was crazy today. Even Paula and I openly disagreed at the morning meeting. I felt off. Maybe I'm PMSing. The phone rang as I turned into the driveway, "Hello?"

"Hey Jazz."

Uhhh, more negative energy. "Hi Toni, how are you?" Not that I really cared but 'nothing beat good manners' I heard my grandmother saying.

"I'm good. I uh, hadn't heard from you and wanted to make sure you were okay."

"I'm good too, everything's cool," I replied.

Toni paused, "I umm, uh, was wondering if you wanted to get together for dinner or something."

It was my turn to pause, I hadn't heard from Toni in a month. I tried not to be suspicious, but it wasn't easy. Toni's unpredictability was cause for apprehension. "I'm kind of busy for the next week or so," I carefully responded.

"Come on Jazz, I know you can make time for a, a, a friend. How 'bout I bring dinner over on Friday?"

"Friday? You want to spend Friday night having dinner with me?" Bells went off. "I haven't seen you on a Friday night in a year and you want to spend Friday with me? What's up Toni?" I asked slightly annoyed.

"Baby ain't nothin' goin' on, just wanted to spend some time with you," she replied.

"Well, this Friday isn't good, I have plans. What about Friday after that?"

"I was hoping to see you before then, you don't have any time for me?"

I felt slightly torn, God only knew why because I knew Toni was up to something. "I'm free Tuesday," I groaned inwardly.

"Okay, next Tuesday it is. I'll see you then." Toni hung up before I changed my mind.

***

A week later, things had settled down at work. Paula and I were on speaking terms again and decided we were better allies than adversaries. I couldn't put my finger on it, but I could feel something in my spirit was different. I felt like burdens were lifted and vaguely remembered a sermon about change and had started to employ a few tenets.

Toni called while Paula and I were at lunch. She left a message saying she would be at my house by six with General Tso's Chicken, my favorite. I've heard an ex is an ex for a reason and Toni was going to test the veracity of the saying. What was she up to? Toni also closed her voice message by saying she was really looking forward to spending some time at home. I replayed the last part to make sure I had heard the word 'home.'

Toni arrived a few minutes before six. When I opened the door, she had a funny look on her face. "Hey there," I said.

"You changed the locks!" Toni said, more a statement than a question.

"Uh yeah? Are you coming in?"

She came in with two bags of food and a bouquet of flowers. I almost laughed; Toni hadn't bought me flowers in a long time.

"These are for you."

"Thanks, they're nice. I'll get a vase."

Toni followed me into the kitchen, Coco was on her heels trying to get some attention. She silently took plates out of the cabinet and brought the food out while I arranged the flowers and sat them on the table. I almost lit a candle but decided against it. Toni's tone and her mood had shifted from the voice message earlier, she seemed a little more tense. I attempted humor, "What army did you think you were feeding? This is a lot of food," I chuckled.

Toni looked at me and asked, "Why did you change the locks? How am I supposed to get my mail?"

Here we go. "Toni, I assumed you had already changed your address. You haven't had much mail over the last few weeks." I got up from the table and got Toni's mail from the office.

"I just mean, I thought you would have told me instead of me putting my key in the door," she yelled loud enough for me to hear.

"You don't live here anymore, why would you put your key in the door?" I asked returning to the dining room table.

"I don't know…"

"Like you were at *home*? What's goin' on? You seem bothered by the fact that you couldn't just walk in here at your convenience and had to ring the bell."

"Like I'm a visitor," she had the nerve to say.

"You are. You moved out remember?" I virtually shouted.

"Well, that's what I was hoping we could talk about."

I sat down; I wasn't feeling steady anymore. Toni got up and sat on the floor with Coco. "I was thinkin', nobody breaks up for good. We hit a rough spell and I'm willing to forgive you."

I could feel my brow furrowing, I honestly hadn't anticipated this conversation even though I suspected Toni was up to something. I took a deep breath and responded, "It's mighty kind of you to forgive me, but I'm neither asking for forgiveness nor do I think I've done anything that I need to be forgiven for. As a matter of fact, I thought you would initiate apologies. But let me just cut to it. I don't want a roommate, or at this particular moment, a girlfriend. I'm enjoying the peace and my new routine."

"Does that routine include seeing that girl? The photographer?"

"I think it's a fair assumption that we're both dating Toni."

"So, it's like that?"

"Yeah, it's like that," I said confidently.

Toni got up off the floor, brushed her clothes off, and headed for the door.

"Guess I don't need these." Toni took her old keys off the ring and threw them in the bowl on the console near the door.

"Absolutely not. What about dinner?" I wanted to know. Not because I wanted her to hang around, I just didn't understand the point of all the effort she made.

"Not feeling dinner anymore."

Keep your head. And with as much grace as I could muster said, "Well, it's been a quick visit and it was good to see you." I walked to the door and held it open for Toni. She was tense, brushed passed me and paused, "Yeah, I'll see you, I hope you're happy."

I stared at the door after locking it. "Peace," I said into the air, tempted to return to my old school Pentecostal roots and anoint the door frame with oil. I uttered a "Sweet Jesus" for good measure though. I squared my shoulders and had a *Color Purple* moment like when Celie said, "My house, this is my house." I didn't know why I suddenly felt better or was smiling, but it—whatever *it* was—was going to be okay.

***

Sam, the Director of Nursing at the hospital, invited me to an end of summer, pre-Labor Day party that he was having the Saturday after Toni's little stunt. He told me he hadn't invited a lot of people—just a small intimate group—which I didn't believe.

159

I invited T to go with me, something a little different from our one-on-one close encounters. We agreed to meet at T's house since Sam lived less than ten minutes away. Walking may have been more practical if it wasn't damn near ninety degrees at five o'clock in the afternoon. Especially since Bolton Hill residents had figured out how to limit outsiders from their insular neighborhood, having successfully lobbied for permit-only parking. Any parking beyond two hours was subject to zealous towing. So, T drove. She would have better luck finding a space with her smaller car. We parked down the street from Sam's house.

"Is that music coming from his house?" T asked, "this is a small gathering?" We could hear "It's Time for the Percolator" pumping from the house as I opened the wrought iron fence in the front yard.

"That's what he said, but you know the boys never do anything small," I replied.

"I know that's right," T laughed. "You've met my cousins."

We made our way to the back and were both surprised to find just nine people in the lush terrace—the yard meticulously landscaped with wrought iron garden decorations. Neatly trimmed boxwood hedges defined the property edge, red geraniums were spilling over their containers, and fragrant climbing coral roses twisted and wound their way up wood trellises. I was surprised I could smell them in addition to the smokey aroma from the grill that made my stomach growl.

After introductions and getting a bite to eat, T and I settled into a lounge chair—me leaning back into her, comfortable as the day was long—next to a male couple on one side and Paula and her cute lesbian cousin, Jael, on the other. Turned out, Sam and Jael were friends from way back in the day. Which wasn't surprising, the town was sometimes called Smalltimore for a reason. The conversation among everyone was free flowing.

Unfortunately, Jael expected her reserve unit to be activated in the next few months considering all the rumblings about supposed weapons of mass destruction in Iraq. "I have several friends in the Navy and Marine Corps that always talk about walking a fine line not to be outed. How do you handle being in the closet and in the military?" T asked.

"It can be tough sometimes. I was deployed for about three months during the first Gulf War when I was on active duty," Jael said. "I'm potentially looking at twelve months now… that's a long time to be undercover," she lamented with a shrug.

"You got that right," one of the men entered the conversation.

"Yeah, but it's something I volunteered to do, you know? On the flip side, I've gotten some good benefits over the years… traveled, finished my degree with the G.I. Bill, and will have a decent retirement check in the future. At the end of the day, no matter how I feel about one particular policy, it is an honor and privilege to wear the cloth of our great nation," Jael confessed and bit into a rib.

We were all a bit stunned by her patriotic declaration. No one spoke for a few seconds until I broke the silence. "That's interesting, dare I say, principled even, that you choose to focus on the positive."

Jael responded, "What you choose to focus on or devote energy to makes a difference right?" T nudged me, I tried to ignore her. Jael didn't wait for a response but chuckled a bit. "How does the saying go? You have to laugh to keep from crying?"

"I guess," T said with an eyebrow raised.

"My cousin is being modest. She has done well… she's a commander in the Navy. Not too many people are gunning for her," Paula chimed in.

"Not yet Cuz, soon though. I'm still a Lieutenant Commander," Jael corrected her.

"I'm claiming the promotion for you," Paula declared.

"Thanks. You're right though, not many folks are paying me and my personal life any mind," she said to her cousin. "But the hardest part?" Jael said turning to the group.

"What?" several of us asked in unison.

"I'm a damn good leader and my troops and my superiors trust and respect me, at least I think so. But T hit the nail on the head. Staying so deep in the closet *and* being away from my family that the commander-in-chief says shouldn't or doesn't exist is rough."

"No doubt. You have a girlfriend?" T asked.

"Yeah, my partner and I have been together for five years and she has an eight-year-old son. They're at a birthday party."

"Good grief. I can't even begin to imagine navigating that mess. So, what does that even look like in the day to day?" T was into this story.

"I'm not so sure it's incredibly different than how we all manage our civilian lives. Like, it's 2002 sure. But I'm sure you're cautious about who knows you like girls, right?" Jael answered.

"You got that right!" I chimed in, laughed, and looked at Paula.

"But here's an example," Jael continued, "while everybody else gets to have their families milling about when we ship out or return home, I don't. Their presence may raise questions." She sighed. "So I've been a great officer, followed the rules, and served in silence."

"Damn!" T and I said under our breaths.

***

Prior to sunset, I sensed T had had her fill of meeting new people and socializing so I suggested we head out. We went inside and I went to get my scarf that Sam put in the hall closet. When I turned around, T was right behind me, smiling wickedly, and backed me into the dimly lit space.

This is crazy. I couldn't believe I was in here with T's hands already gripping my ass. But I didn't protest. Ever since she opened her door when I arrived earlier today, my imagination took me to places it hadn't been in a minute. T was hot as hell in a black tank and linen shorts. *She sure does like, a looks good in, linen?*

In an instant after our lips locked, I was no longer concerned about our current environment. Once my eyes adjusted to the darkness, I tried to look into T's penny brown eyes for confirmation of what was next. She gave me a seductive wink—or at least that was what I saw—and it was on. I was surprised that I let her feel me up as much as I did.

"What are you doing?" I whispered.

"Nothin'," T answered with her head buried in the crook of my neck.

"It doesn't feel like nothin'," I replied.

"What does it feel like?"

"It feels like you're trying to seduce me."

"Does it?" T asked, now with her tongue in my cleavage.

"Yes."

"I'm just trying to get to know you better."

"Maybe we should start with something simpler," I said. "Football or basketball?"

"Excuse me?" T asked, pulling away and looking at me.

"The email? Football or basketball?"

"You're kidding right?" T asked, puzzled by my sudden shift.

"No, I'm not," I smiled anyway. "I've spent the night at your house. You've rubbed my feet. We've been to dinner multiple times. And I want to continue getting to know you. Like, what school do you work at? I know you're from Savannah but who are your people?"

"You know I teach art and I'm an artist. You even know where I live, which is saying a lot," T interrupted.

"Yeah, but there's more to you than that," I responded.

"Is it that important?"

"Are you runnin' from the government? Or in some type of witness protection program?"

"I was just wondering where the questions came from. They are totally one-eighty out from the moment I thought we were both enjoying."

"T, like really. Are your parents still alive? Do you have siblings?"

"Wow! What if I told you I was raised by wolves?" T said laughing.

"Okay," I started getting agitated. We were in a closet, and she was dodging my questions.

"Jasmine, I'm not in the witness protection program, neither are my parents. And I'm not running from the government. The questions just took me by surprise. What? You need to do a background check?"

I was not amused. "We need to go," I said trying to get around T, but she firmly held me still.

"Baby, wait… My parents are Harold and Mary Butler of Savannah, Georgia. They've been married forty-two years. I have a forty-year-old brother who hasn't figured out what he wants to be when he grows up. And as far as my mother is concerned, the sun rises and sets on him. My social security number is…"

"Teresa stop," I interrupted, holding my hand up. "I was talking to some friends, and it occurred to me there was still so much that I want to know about you. I have no intention of doing a background check or…" Suddenly the door opened. Sam was as startled as we were.

"Oh, I see it's no different than work, you're still in the closet," Sam said laughing.

"Shut up boy, we were just having a little chat," I said and punched him in the arm.

"Umm hmmm, here? There are plenty of chairs in the backyard. I even have some in the kitchen."

"Sam, it's my fault, I couldn't keep my hands off of your co-worker," T said smiling and walking past Sam with me in tow.

"Umm Sam, thanks for inviting us, this was nice," I tried to keep from laughing. "See you next week?"

"Not me, I'm heading to Hotlanta's Black Pride for Labor Day. You know the boys are usually in a frenzy to end the summer."

"I know that's right. Well, have a good time, be safe." I kissed Sam on the cheek, T shook his hand, and we were out the door.

"Where to Ms. Charles?" T asked.

"You're driving remember Ms. Butler," I said nudging T as we walked towards the car.

"Oh, so now you want to be nice? A few minutes ago, you were getting an attitude because your friends couldn't google me and search for my prior convictions."

I punched her too. "Uh unh, google you? That's a verb now?"

"If it isn't, the important word people will make it so. That's the future of the interwebs you know," T said smiling.

"Yeah, okay."

"But don't think you're off the hook," she kidded me.

"T, don't be like that. They brought up some good points that's all."

***

The work week flew by following Labor Day; they always did after a holiday. Much to my disappointment, I hadn't heard from T all week. Not like we were a couple or anything, but I expected a phone call every now and again. I picked up my desk phone and dialed T's number and smiled while listening to the brief and throaty directions to leave a message. I hemmed and hawed my way through a message, wanting to sound a bit more intelligent and coherent, wishing I had an ability to erase and re-record.

Wouldn't you know she would call when I stepped away from my desk for a hot second. I listened to her message three times. "Hey beautiful... thanks for the call. It's been hella busy at work. Talk soon."

I didn't call back, but I toyed with the idea of riding past her house on the way home but decided against it. I could use a quiet night with Coco. I also thought about T being evasive last Saturday when I started asking her questions and I got agitated again. They were common questions that people attempting to get to know one another ask. "I don't know her!" I said aloud. She was very guarded. We should protect ourselves, but damn. Plus, she only answered half of the questions on the twenty-question list.

Dinner was done, I sauteed chicken, onions, and peppers and spread them over rice. I placed my plate on the table and believed a glass of wine would be nice. I laughed out loud. It was all downhill from here. I was eating and drinking alone. So not only did I pour myself a glass, I poured a large glass of wine. I blessed my food, picked up the fork and the phone rang. *Ugh,* it better not be a telemarketer! "Hello," I answered with slight agitation.

"Hello Ms. Charles."

"Well, hey Ms. Butler."

"That's my name."

"Yes, you are one of The Butlers from Savannah," I smartly commented.

"See, I just wanted to say hello and return your call."

"That's very kind of you, it's the first one this week."

"You know what? I'm gonna go, I've had a busy week getting me and my classroom ready for the new school year and you givin' grief is just too much right now," T said in her defense.

"Oh, that's right, I'm sorry," I said. Here I was likely being a bit selfish and throwing myself a pity party. I may have been spoiled by T being available on summer break. "When do the kids come back?"

"Next week," she answered.

"Are you ready? All your boards done?"

"Boards?" T asked.

"Yeah, your bulletin boards."

"I haven't put much effort into bulletin boards in a few years. After two weeks, the boards are pretty full of all the little Van Goghs' work. But we had to sit through hours of presentations about changes in the curriculum and quite frankly, I would not have been a good conversationalist. What are you doing this evening?"

"Nothing much, I was sitting down to dinner."

"Alone?"

"Yes, alone. Interested in joining me?"

"Are you inviting me to your home?"

"Nooo. I'm going to have the food delivered to your house. Of course!"

"I appreciate the invite, and know it wasn't extended lightly, but I'm kinda beat. I'm gonna chill for a bit. Call me when you finish eating?"

"Okay," I muttered, disappointed that T didn't accept my invitation. I heated my food up again, but my appetite had faded.

{THIRTY-THREE}

T

"Hola," I answered the phone.

"Hey, it's me. Still chillin'?"

"Yeah, kinda…vegetating really," I answered.

"Okay, we can chat later."

"No rush. We can chat now, I just needed to recharge. You know, introvert thing and all."

There was a significant pause. "What do you want to talk about?" I said breaking the silence.

"I don't know, you could answer some of my questions."

"Oh no, not tonight. Can we just talk without an interrogation session?"

"Why does it have to be interrogating? I'm just trying to get to know you. I feel like I'm sparring with you?"

"Jasmine please, that's not my intent but I'm not feeling like twenty questions tonight. I like it when we just talk, you know?"

"Okay T, maybe you should just chill then."

Ugh! "I will, later."

"Much."

Damn! That last comment Jasmine uttered was cold. I was bone tired. I had been working like a dog, and attending mind-numbing, beginning-of-the-year, everyone-has-a-bright-idea conferences. I was also trying to work on my next show that was coming together slower than I wanted. And why the rush? She made it seem like I had been intentionally evasive, I hadn't. Yes, I had been careful about revealing too much information too soon. It wasn't often that

I let anyone I was seeing get too close anymore. Women get information, assumptions are made, and then I had to deal with the fallout and their feelings. But I also knew Jasmine was special. I liked spending time with her, laughing with her, being in her presence. I liked *her* and she knew that. So, I called her back…

"Hello?" Jasmine answered on the second ring.

"Hey," I said simply.

"Hey," Jasmine replied.

"Look, I didn't mean to upset you. And I don't want it to be *much* later, as you proclaimed, before I talk to you again. I'm just tired, physically and mentally. I haven't had a chance to run lately since the days are getting shorter, so my usual boost of energy isn't there."

"Uh huh."

"Jasmine seriously, don't dismiss me so quickly. Let me try again? May I come see you?"

"Tonight? Don't you think it's getting late?"

"Yes, it's getting late, but let me just come over to talk face-to-face."

"Why should I?" Jasmine asked, being difficult.

"Because I want to see you. I wanted to see you when you offered, and I should have been forthright and said that."

"Why *didn't* you say that?"

"I'm not sure. Must we belabor the point right now? Do you want to see me or not?" I pressed.

"Yes," Jasmine virtually whispered.

"What's your address?"

"426 Lochlea Road in Mount Washington."

"Mount Washington? You movin' on up huh? Quite persnickety," I joked with her to lighten things up.

"Not really. Come up the Jones Falls, get off at the first Northern Parkway exit, make a left onto Falls Road, make another left on Kelly, and make a right onto Lochlea Road."

"Okay, that's 83 to Northern Parkway, left onto Falls Road, left onto Kelly, right onto Lochlea."

"Yep."

"I'll see you within the hour. You still have some chow for me?"

"Maybe," Jasmine said coyly.

"Don't play with me woman." I said jokingly. "Well, I haven't eaten in a minute so if I can trouble you for some warmed-over vittles, that would be much appreciated."

"Anything for you. Ummm, I'll have a plate ready for you."

I laughed, "I'm going to pretend like I didn't hear that, for now anyway." That was amusing—I think I may have gotten through Jasmine's cool exterior.

I packed a few things in an overnight bag, certainly not to be presumptuous, but one must be prepared right? I threw my toothbrush and a few other essentials in. The drive up 83 was quick; of course it was after rush hour so that helped. Nothing like watching folks fleeing the city on Fridays—or any weekday afternoon for that matter—like they might turn into pumpkins when the streetlights came on.

My goodness, old girl must have done quite well living in the high rent district. Mount Washington was geographically in Baltimore City, but it didn't look like my part of the city. It was dotted with walking trails, cute little shops, and restaurants. I pulled into the driveway of a beautifully preserved Craftsman house and got out of the car, still surveying my surroundings. It was kind of dark out here. I rang the bell and anxiously waited for Jasmine to come to the door. Coco's loud, energetic bark only added to my anxiety because she sounded like she was ready to jump me. Jasmine was gorgeous when she opened the door. I mean, she's usually beautiful, but she was especially radiant tonight or maybe I was just happy to see her, happy that she reconsidered her invitation.

{THIRTY-FOUR}

Jasmine

Coco jumped off the sofa and started barking before T rang the bell. Her timing was perfect; I took crescent rolls out of the oven before heading to the door and transferred the food to real plates as opposed to the paper plate I was eating off of. I did a slow three-sixty turn to survey the results of my flurry of activity. I had dusted, swept, cleaned the bathrooms, changed the sheets and plumped the pillows before she got here. I was almost too damn tired for company. I came up the old-fashioned way, that amount of cleaning generally took half a Saturday morning with 95.9 playing on the radio in the background. I couldn't believe "Anything for you" came out of my mouth. *Shit, did I say that out loud?* Take a deep breath...

I opened the door and there she was, smirking and waiting for me to invite her in.

"Hey," I said with my coy, I'm-sexy-but-I'm-not-trying-very-hard-smile.

"Hey, you look nice," T said.

"You're just saying that to get in the door."

"No, I assume you wouldn't invite me out here to Hell's Half Acre and not let me in. I was merely speaking truth."

"I don't know if you have an objective bone in your body," I said, certain of my response.

"That may be true when it comes to you, but I'd prefer to debate that point inside rather than out here on the porch with these killer bugs hanging around the light." T moved closer into my comfort zone.

"Oh, I'm sorry, where are my manners?" I apologized and backed up.

"No worries. I know I get you all flummoxed," T said sarcastically. I gave her a shot in the arm.

Who the hell used the word flummoxed? She was so different. Unlike any other woman that I had met. Unlike any other woman that I would normally spend time with.

"Your house is gorgeous. You were talking about my place, you must be doing well yourself."

"Girl, this place was so sad when I bought it," I said.

"Really?" T asked.

"I know right, we put in a lot of sweat equity," I said shaking my head at the thought.

"Well, you all—whoever 'we' is—did a great job. Hey, I got something for you." T handed me a beautifully wrapped gift the size of a large pizza.

"What's this?"

"Open it," she said.

I shook it, trying to guess what this could be but that didn't provide any clues. I tore the wrapping off to reveal a hubcap. "What in the world?" I asked.

"Hey, you needed one and I was thinking about you." T was apparently pleased with herself.

"Thanks?!!"

She laughed.

"This is probably one of *the* most practical, thoughtful gifts I've ever received."

T raised one eyebrow.

"Seriously, thank you," I said.

"I know it's a bit odd and certainly not the sexiest of gifts," T stated the most obvious thing ever.

"Yes, you're right and I appreciate the effort," I replied honestly.

"Speaking of practical, thought that you would like these too." T took the hubcap and handed me a bag.

I reached in and pulled out a small jar labeled, 'OREGANO.' I looked up and smiled and pulled two other jars out, perfectly labeled like the first... 'BASIL,' and 'THYME.'"

"Ahhhh, now these I really appreciate," I said, my smile extending ear to ear, and kissed her cheek.

"Good, now what smells so good?"

We made small talk over dinner, and I shared a few war stories from work. After dinner, we moved to the living room to get comfortable so, I slipped my sandals off. T reached for one of my feet and once again started massaging it, but I stopped her.

"No thanks, tonight, I'm going to help you relax," I said.

"Oh really? What do you have in mind?" she asked.

"I'll be right back." I returned with a large black towel and a bottle of lotion and told T to take her shirt off.

"Excuse me?" T exclaimed.

I stood in front of her, smiled and said again, "Take off your shirt." T did as I asked and began to unbutton her shirt but then stopped. "What do you have in mind?"

"You obviously aren't used to taking orders." I put the bottle on the coffee table behind me, bent down on my knees between T's legs, finished unbuttoning her shirt, and took it off. If this were my own shirt, I would have just tossed it haphazardly across the armrest, but since T is a bit more fastidious, I made the effort to fold it neatly. I spread the towel on the full length of the sofa and told T to lie down. She hesitated.

"Ms. Butler, it's your turn to trust me," I said as convincingly as I could.

T gave me the side eye, but she laid on her stomach anyway. I picked up the stereo remote and turned the XM radio to the Spa channel. The room filled with the calming sound of nature. I rubbed my palms together to warm them, unhooked T's bra, and gently touched her back in strategic spots to center her and bring her into an awareness of the moment. I started kneading T's back in long, rhythmic strokes with my hands. I wasn't sure, but I thought I heard T moan a few times.

"I'm almost too relaxed to move," T said.

"Then don't," I whispered. "You're welcome to stay here or come with me."

T took too long to make a decision, so I made it for her. "Come with me." I reached for her hand and led her down the hall. I winked at T and facetiously said, "I'll make sure you get to work on time." I smiled.

"You got lots of jokes, huh?" T asked grinning.

"Do you need a toothbrush? I doubt it though. I bet you have a bag in the car huh?"

"You're on a roll," she pointed out.

"You know I'm joking." T rolled her eyes. "I suspect this isn't your first late night visit." I laughed. Toni always traveled with a bag, perhaps that was par for the course.

As we entered my bedroom, I saw T appreciating the room's colors, which reflected me totally, grey for coolness and purple 'cause every queen needs that regal look. I joked, "I'm not sure you want to relax in any of my PJs, I can offer you an oversized t-shirt."

"That's good enough for gubment work," T responded.

"Do you need a washcloth or towel or anything?" I asked.

"I'll take both, if you don't mind," T answered.

I came back with a big, fluffy towel, the kind that you would find at the Ritz Carlton next to slippers embroidered with a fancy emblem, and a flowered patterned t-shirt my grandmother would have worn.

"Oh no!" T exclaimed, "I'll be right back." She promptly left the room, and I heard the front door open. She came back a few minutes later with a bag.

"See, that is how you roll," I said.

"Hey, I didn't know how long I was going to be here. You could have kicked me out after dinner. But no, I don't usually roll like anything. You may be surprised to know that I very rarely spend the night out anywhere in Baltimore, with anybody."

"Really? Why is that?"

"Let's just say I like my own space."

"Yeah okay. You can freshen up and I'm going to do a security check."

"I locked the front door when I came back in," T said.

"Girl please, there's a process. You saw how wooded it is around here. A girl has to be careful."

"Right, right... should I come witness the process?"

"Are you assuming this won't be your last visit?"

"No, I'm not assuming anything, but I hope not. But I'll let you do your thing," T said.

I methodically went through the house checking not just the front door, but the French doors that led to the patio and the door to the basement. I turned off the radio, made sure the windows were closed and locked, and finally armed the security system. Coco came back to the room with me this time, company or not, she was ready to get comfortable on her pillow in the corner.

"Has Fort Knox been secured?" T asked as she came out of the bathroom.

"Yes, smart ass. One can never be too careful living in the city."

"Damn suburbs, this ain't livin' in the city," T countered.

"It is not the suburbs. All the houses look alike in the suburbs. This house is uniquely its own and doesn't look like any other house on the street. And my property taxes, water bill, and car insurance clearly reflect that I live in the city."

"Yes ma'am, I hear you," T said and pulled me closer.

"Whoa cowgirl, it's my turn to go in the bathroom for a minute."

{THIRTY-FIVE}

T

While Jasmine conducted her security routine, I surveyed the room a bit closer which included framed pictures of who I assumed was Toni. I wondered why they were still here but didn't internalize the passing thought very long. I didn't think that I had ever been this comfortable in a woman's house because I was usually eager to get back home. The artist in me liked her space, it felt warm and inviting. Jasmine herself likely had a lot to do with that. I noticed she had multiple gallery-style picture arrangements on the walls, but I really liked the sunset pictures going up the stairs. Jasmine had nice taste in art.

I have had my share of booty calls over the past few years... this was so not that. I got a delicious meal that wasn't take out, Jasmine went out of her way to make me comfortable, and the massage put me in a good place. Even Coco sitting at my feet during dinner seemed a bit, dare I say, family-like. Jasmine came out of the bathroom and interrupted my thoughts.

"I'm just going to wrap my hair tonight; I usually wear rollers but..."

"Go on and wear your rollers, put cold cream on your face, whatever. Don't do anything special on my account," I joked.

She laughed. "I don't wear cold cream to bed thank you very much. But *if* you come back, I may put rollers in next time."

"What's the *if* contingent on?" I asked.

"I don't know... fighting me in your sleep, sleep walking, snoring too loud, talking in your sleep...then again, if you talk in your sleep, maybe I'll get to know you."

"I am lying in your bed, what else do you need to know?"

"I don't know," Jasmine said in a higher octave than normal, "but we'll come back to this conversation."

Jasmine sat on the bed cross-legged next to me as I propped myself up on an elbow.

"This isn't a slumber party Ms. Charles. It's damn near midnight, come to bed." Jasmine got up, took her robe off, threw it across the edge of the bed, and a revealed a short, pale yellow nightshirt with ruffles around the V-neck collar.

"What kind of frock is that?" I asked, having seen sexier lingerie on Barbie.

"Hell, look what you got on. I wouldn't classify Joe Boxer shorts and a plain white t-shirt as the pinnacle of sexiness. You called me at the last minute, you don't get the Valentine's Day special," Jasmine said, slightly annoyed.

"Hey, this is as good as it gets. You better be glad I have on clothes at all. What does the Valentine's special consist of?" I asked, as Jasmine lay next to me. I pulled her closer, and held her from behind.

"Be here Valentine's night and perhaps you'll find out," Jasmine said looking over her shoulder.

"I should have known that was coming, but you know, Valentine's Day is really a plot by the man."

"What? A plot? Spoken like a playa' who travels with her essential, well-appointed overnight bag. A card and a little candy never hurt anybody to express that you were thinking about them."

"Well, I'm glad you didn't say anything about those triple-priced flowers. But the way I look at it, I don't need somebody else to tell me what day to treat my woman really special," I said and kissed the nape of Jasmine's neck.

"Yeah, yeah, yeah," she said settling further into my arms and falling into a deep sleep.

***

"What? What the hell! What's that noise?" I sat straight up in the bed and looked over to see the clock flashing "5:30."

"I'm sorry, I forgot to turn the alarm off," Jasmine said, reaching over to shut it off. "What time do you have to go?"

"I don't have to go anywhere this early on a Saturday morning."

"Well, do you want some breakfast?"

"At five-thirty on Saturday? Woman, go back to sleep," I said. I laid back down and threw my arm around Jasmine. But Jasmine's lingering orange, ginger, cinnamon scented oil from the night before awakened my senses.

"Hmmm, you still smell good," I said, burying my nose in and running my fingers through Jasmine's hair, "you sleep yet?"

"Isn't that what you told me to do?"

"You got to be one of the most difficult women," I said as I spooned Jasmine closer and cupped her left breast. Jasmine let out a low moan, "Ummmm, you feel good."

"Yeah?" she asked, barely above a whisper.

"Yeah."

I rolled Jasmine over on her back and propped myself over her in a sort of plank position that revealed my defined arms. Jasmine caressed them, which made me grateful for my workout routine as I lowered myself onto her and kissed her neck and ears. "I thought you wanted to go back to sleep?" she asked.

"Not now," I replied, "You smell too good."

"So, now what?"

"What do you want?"

"I want to brush my teeth before this goes any further," Jasmine said, rolling out from under me and out of bed.

"Of course you do."

She turned around and smiled, "Of course I do."

"I'll go with you."

{THIRTY-SIX}

Jasmine

Since we were already in the bathroom, I suggested we freshen up a bit. I put on a shower cap, turned the water on, dropped what T had deemed a "frock," and gestured for her to join me. Without hesitation or giving me a chance to change my mind, T undressed and stepped into the double shower, designed for two people to share rather comfortably.

I paused a beat and moved towards T, intently looking into her beautiful eyes, not breaking eye contact. I wasn't sure where the courage was coming from, but I moved in closer, letting our bodies touch completely naked for the very first time. T firmly gripped my butt so that I couldn't back up even if I wanted to. But I didn't want to—that was the last thing on my mind. I finally admitted to myself that what I wanted was for T to have every part of me.

My heart was pounding in my chest; I wondered if T could feel it too. I was feeling extremely vulnerable since I had been with one person for so long. But I also felt protected. I had been waiting a long time to feel this way again. To want to be with someone, not out of obligation but because of pure, unbridled passion and desire. I wanted T to have me so badly right now, but I also didn't want this feeling to end. I wanted to feel her body next to mine. I wanted to grab her head as she traveled southward to places I'd been fantasizing that she would go for months. I wanted her tongue to dance with my essence and make me scream her name.

T reached around me, picked up the bar of soap, and let the water wet it. She cupped it in one hand and started to lather my body, using her other hand to swirl the suds around. First on my shoulders, then my neck and down my back in long slow strokes; I could feel every sensation. Her hands moved to the front of my body to lather my breasts, then my belly. She stopped short of moving further down, returning to my backside to make sure my butt was soapy before her hands traveled back up my back. Making her way down my legs, T made sure my entire body was covered in suds before returning the soap to the dish. This felt so good, so relaxing, yet my body wanted more. I wanted more of her.

With my back to her, T cupped both of my breasts and pressed her body against my ass, which moved in rhythm with her and physically signaled that I wanted more. Our bodies moved and rocked to the beat of music that only we could hear while the water continued flowing out of one of the showerheads and rinsed us both off.

I moved away from T to wash my essentials like I intended to do from the beginning. My washcloth met the stickiness generated from the last fifteen minutes, which made me blush. I dared not look at T 'cause I knew I wanted her to finish what we started. T turned on the other showerhead and bathed too, so I thought that perhaps we would finally take this party back to bed. However, much to my surprise and delight, she kneeled down, raised one of my legs onto the tiled seat in the back of the shower and pulled my center to her.

It started slow at first; she was very methodical. First, T smelled me and let out a deep sigh like she was dining at a three-star Michelin restaurant. Then she gently nibbled my inner thighs, at which point I wanted to scream, the anticipation was getting the best of me, and I let out a moan. But that didn't make her go any faster. T spread my vaginal lips and licked the creases on either side of my clit. *Can I scream yet?*

I involuntarily started thrusting my pelvis toward T's mouth, the building pressure getting to be too much. I was wet and she still hadn't gotten to the most erotic zones. Just when I thought I would cum, she switched up the rhythm and put her tongue on my clit and licked it like I was an ice cream cone, like a vanilla dipped in chocolate on a scorching hot Sunday afternoon ice cream cone. *Ahhhh! Why was I thinking about food?* My mind was wandering all over the place. But T continued to lick, slowly, making her tongue as flat as it could be. Her moaning created a sort of vibration on my vagina that was also surprisingly sexy.

I was pretty sure that I was having an out of body experience when T switched it up again and started circling my clit with her tongue. She also went inside of me, finding a spot that I didn't know existed, motioning her index finger in a "come here" sort of stroke. She circled and stroked, circled and stroked. My body had never felt this good. Not even with Toni, and Toni was good but *THIS*! This was something entirely different. This was other worldly. So. Damn. Good. *THIS* had to be illegal.

Just when I thought I couldn't hold it together any longer. Just when I thought perhaps this was a mistake because I wasn't tryin' to fall all over anyone. Just when I was pretty sure my eyes rolled in the back of my head and I saw Jesus himself, my body exploded with rolls of energy and ecstasy, and I rode T's face like *this* was the first and last time I had and would ever have sex.

I was spent and felt like I wanted to cry. To cry? Why was I so emotional? I peeled my leg from behind T's back where it had been lodged for God knows how long and sat down. Tears formed and started to fall. T sat down next to me and pulled me into her arms. I lay back and opened my mouth to say something, but nothing came out.

"Shhhhh," T whispered.

"But…" I tried.

"Shhhhh," she said again and kissed the side of my face. Since we got in the shower, I realized we had never said a word.

{THIRTY-SEVEN}

T

I joined Jasmine in the kitchen. With the exception of saying she was going to prepare us something to eat, we hadn't said much to one another since getting out of the shower and then back in bed for an hour. Jasmine looked up at me when I walked in and gave a sort of half smile.

"Hi," I said to break the silence as I sat in the breakfast nook where Coco decided to come get a rub. The nook was perfectly situated so you could look out into Jasmine's backyard which was filled with brightly colored plants, mature trees, and sunshine. What a wonderful space, I shouldn't have expected anything less.

"Hi," Jasmine replied.

"Jas-"

"T," she said at the same time.

"You first," I offered.

"T, I told you. It's been a long time since I've been with anyone other than Toni."

"Yes, and..."

"And nothing," Jasmine's voice trailed off.

"Yes, there is something. What's on your mind? You haven't said much of anything in a minute."

"I don't know what to say," she responded.

"Listen, I know you probably want to take things slow. And I want that for you too. But I don't think we need to apologize or feel bad for engaging in grown folks' business. If you're enjoying me, cause I'm certainly enjoying you, we don't have to apologize to anyone, for anything. I also think that in order for us to continue enjoying each other's company; we have to do it fully and honestly.

"There you go again making *this* sound so simple," Jasmine interjected.

"Why does it have to be complicated?" I asked.

"Because life is complicated T. Life is not always rainbows and unicorns. I am barely out of a relationship and here you are spending the night, sleeping in my bed, doing things to my mind and body that I cannot explain…"

I smiled and thought I understood Jasmine's point. "Listen, I get it, I'm feeling you too."

"No, I don't think you do," Jasmine countered. "My life had been pretty measured and predictable before I met you. I am usually the adult in the room, the designated driver. The reliable, dependable friend."

"Certainly you aren't saying you no longer possess those traits?" I asked.

"Not exactly, but now? I don't feel like I'm being very responsible. That very fact is making me both crazy and excited and it scares the hell out of me."

I stood up and walked over to Jasmine with my arms outstretched. "Come here." Jasmine stopped chopping vegetables, wiped her hands on a dish towel, and did as I instructed. She stood in my space with her head slightly down.

I lifted her chin and ever so gently kissed her lips. "Nothing is going to happen that you don't want to happen. You are in control of this," I said drawing an arc in the air around us. "We take this as fast or as slow as you want. All I ask is that you one, enjoy the moment and two, be open and honest with me about what you're feeling at any particular moment."

"You think it's really that simple don't you?"

"Here's what I think," I said.

"What do you think?" Jasmine managed a slight smile.

"I think humans, particularly those of the female persuasion…"

Jasmine interrupted me. "You're of that persuasion, so be careful."

"You're proving my point. Anyhoo," I said, "I think humans are extremely skilled at overthinking situations, making them far more complex and worse in their minds than what actually manifests in the real world. I honestly believe that we, you and I," I said gesturing between us, "should not saddle ourselves with strictures of what something should or shouldn't be. What we should or shouldn't be doing. Or what someone else does or doesn't think of us and what *this* is."

"T, I just don't want to dive headfirst into what felt like just a few hours ago a relationship."

"Relationship? No one said anything about a relationship," I said.

"Oh, I'm not good enough for you to be in a relationship?" Jasmine suddenly sounded offended.

"Wait, what is happening here?" I asked. "You were just making the case that you don't want a relationship. That you and Toni had been together for so long that it's hard to get the idea of that out of your head. Or take her pictures down, I might add. I respect that, but what I don't understand is the self-sabotage. You've told me what you don't want multiple times. What, or shall I say, who is it that you do want?"

{THIRTY-EIGHT}

Jasmine

There hadn't been a morning after of hugs, smiles, and sensual caresses from a new lover in over a decade. Unfortunately, instead of relishing in the swoon of a night and early morning well spent, T's presence brought more questions. And, I didn't have any answers. I knew T was right, my psychoanalysis of every single thing, person, and situation sometimes got in the way of enjoying life and living in the moment. I can't say that I'd ever enjoy spontaneity, but it wouldn't hurt to be a bit more open to new possibilities. On the other hand, I'm thirty-eight years old and honestly, I don't know if I trust myself right now to make smart decisions, let alone trust someone else. If I was completely honest with myself, I would acknowledge that my heart was still hurting because of the death of my relationship. It was amazing how much Toni's and my life were intertwined without the benefit of state legal protection.

For a time though, I thought Toni and I had something special. We proudly told people how long we were together all of the time. Our friends would then offer praise and congratulatory flourishes as if sharing the same address and saying we were girlfriends for X number of years was somehow an accomplishment. It was all a front that was crystal clear for me to see now that I'd been mentally released from bondage and had the extraordinary benefit of hindsight. Not to mention, Teresa's presence, gentleness, intellect, and thoughtfulness had created a stark contrast that even a blind mouse could see.

My parents—whom I loved fiercely—have been married for almost half a century. But some days, they acted like they didn't even like each other. I did not want to follow that model. Quite frankly, I didn't know what model to follow. Was there a model relationship? Maybe 'Chelle and Thomas? Not because of their big house and fabulous vacations. T had a point; there was something about the way they looked at each other in those photos. But who knows if they were a good model or not. I should be the first to admit that you can't judge a book by its cover.

I walked from room to room, looking around and removing pictures that encapsulated my previous life with Toni. We were all smiles when we spontaneously hopped on Amtrak just to go to a concert in New York's Central Park and on trips we took to Rehoboth, P-town, and Jamaica. Toni certainly didn't take any pictures with her when she moved out, at least none that I could tell. I guess for her, moving wasn't a sentimental task, just one that needed to be done. I hadn't paid much attention to the fact that her pictures were still in the bedroom until T slid that in; I honestly saw past them. I packed the pictures in boxes and placed them on a shelf in the basement.

What does one do with ten years of pictures and stuff? I pushed the boxes to the back next to holiday decorations. I would know by Christmas what I was supposed to do with the stuff… perhaps. I was tempted to burn a little sage but after all the rushed cleaning last night prepping for T's arrival I wasn't interested in dusting burned ashes. I still felt restless.

I couldn't settle my mind; it was racing and all over the place. I hadn't had time to sit and think, like really think, about what I wanted in a minute. So, I decided to turn on my computer and write my thoughts in an email to T. I took two deep cleansing breaths like instructors encouraged patients to do during meditation groups. I sat for a minute with my fingers interlaced, took another deep breath, and started typing. I wrote two sentences, deleted them… sat quietly… closed my eyes, and started typing again. I highlighted words—too mushy—deleted another sentence, then worried about what T would think. What if she thought this was childish? This made me remember a note in grade school that I received from some little boy. "I like you. Do you like me? Check 'Yes' or 'No' with little boxes next to each." Hah! I got up walked to the window and looked out at my untended garden. I shook my head, rolled my neck, let out an "uughhh," thought again about the last few months, and returned to the keyboard.

Hi T,

Sometimes I find myself so overwhelmed that I write to communicate intelligible thoughts and prevent my head from exploding. After you left this morning, I wanted to pick up the phone and talk to you more as if we weren't just together. To fight the urge, I decided to write.

I had a REALLY nice time when you were here. And it wasn't just about the sex, although that was sooo nice, I enjoyed you being here. I enjoyed us being together and getting to know each other better.

It's hard to admit that, and probably shouldn't be as hard as I make it sometimes. But please understand that being vulnerable on any given day scares me. Being vulnerable with you so soon after my breakup scares the shit out of me. I don't know that I would survive being hurt again. You asked that I tell you what I want rather than what I don't. I'm going to say this at the risk of sounding silly, but I want the fairy tale. Certainly not like Cinderella cause I'm not trying to be mistreated by evil step sisters or clean up after their trifling asses. I want to be treated with kindness. I want someone who will think of me and then let me know they were thinking of me with a simple phone call or email. I want to sleep in on Saturday mornings and snuggle and spoon and just breathe. I want less drama. I want to be wanted.

I say all of that to say again, I don't want to be exposed, out on a limb by myself. I want a partnership. To show you that I can live a little, LOL. I know I declined your previous invitation, but I'd like you to go away with me for a weekend. Perhaps we can steal a little time away to just breathe, together.

Email sent, I decided to expend a little physical energy in the backyard. Coco agreed. Once I opened the door, she shot straight out to chase a squirrel who dared to scavenge in her domain. I hadn't walked my garden in forever. I laughed to myself—you have been a little busy! Next time T stayed over, I would serve a meal out here under the pergola. It was pretty festive in the evening with lights strung around the walls and trees.

Plumes of dust were sent airborne as I beat the patio furniture cushions together. I had neglected the trice weekly container watering, so I gave each flowerpot of geraniums, marigolds, and nasturtiums a drenching shower. I swept pine needles from the outdoor rugs and shifted tchotchkes back into their varied places.

The late afternoon sun was bright and beginning to lower as I continued my day long reflections. I lounged in one of the wicker easy chairs and looked around the patio space I had finished cleaning. I came back to the question, 'what did a model couple, gay or straight, look like?' Hell, gay or lesbian, it was so hard to be who you were, less known a model couple. There was so much pressure to conform to societal norms to avoid fire and brimstone, being fired, and our eyes brimming with tears. Quite a bit of energy was spent on the basic act of existing and surviving, much less thriving.

But the skeptic in me was alive and well. No rational person should read very much into their feelings for someone who seemingly appeared out of thin air. Nonetheless, I found myself longing to be with T and laughing with her and doing absolutely, positively nothing…with her. Especially after our glorious night and morning together, why wouldn't I have feelings for her?

I shouldn't be pining for some woman that I met at the Harbor by happenstance. Or was it happenstance if I call myself a believer in the divine order of the universe? Who made the rules and why did I feel obligated to follow them? I was grown.

Why couldn't I want to want T? Was that insane? To answer this—like other questions I have had in my life—it came down to precise, unbiased, scientific data. I picked up a Shasta daisy growing along the garden retaining wall and plucked petals from the stem.

I want her, I want her not, I want her…

{THIRTY-NINE}

T

I tried to be excited, but I really don't like surprises. Jasmine gave me a heads up in a beautiful email a few weeks ago that she wanted time away together, which I was down for. Then she called yesterday to say we were "going out of town for a 'fall getaway.' *Ugh!* One, it was still hot as hell even though it was supposed to be fall, the temps are still hovering around the high nineties most days and two, I don't know where we are going. Chalk it up to my innate impulse to be in control. Plus, I was feeling kind of apprehensive. Jasmine implied she wanted to be more exclusive, although she hadn't come right out and said that, and I refused to even attempt to read anyone's mind.

Truthfully though, I had not been seeing anyone else with any regularity although the opportunity had presented itself. Just last night I was out to dinner with John and Dre and a gorgeous woman with the smoothest dark chocolate skin I'd ever seen sent a drink to the table. I raised the glass and mouthed "thank you" without engaging her in conversation. Ugh, I was losing my edge.

All of this ruminated in my mind as Jasmine and I made small talk in the car on the way to God knows where. I tried to relax and put on a happy face as we headed out Interstate 70 in bumper-to-bumper traffic. But when she took an exit headed towards Virginia, I found myself instantly irritated. I'd never been a fan of the more remote areas of Virginia, hadn't even wanted to drive through them. There was not enough melanin out here for me. And there was too much talk about family values and being Christians with inconsistent evidence of either.

Once we passed I-66 and started seeing signs for Luray Caverns, Jasmine announced that that was our destination. I'd heard of Luray Caverns of course, the stalactite formations were beautiful on brochures, but they weren't necessarily on my bucket list of places to see.

"You know we've passed that same gas station three times now," I informed Jasmine.

"Yes, I know. I'm a bit turned around," she admitted.

"And when were you going to say something?" I asked, amused by her being so headstrong.

"I don't know. Ah!" She exclaimed as we turned into a motel driveway with pine trees and a bear on the modest welcome sign. Jasmine actually looked excited, and I tried to match my facial expression to her mood but was having a hard time catching up. "Wait here," she told me, "while I go check us in." A woman with the motel's logo on her shirt walked past the car, glanced, and lingered slightly longer than I thought necessary. I was not generally a suspicious person, but my intuition was already hyper-vigilant. The woman turned to enter a sliding glass door.

Jasmine came out with keys, and we drove around the short, squat building that needed a paint job twenty years ago. We gathered our bags and upon opening the door, Jasmine looked puzzled. "This can't be our room, I requested a king room," she said. The room we were standing in had two double beds. *Uh oh, here we go.* "Wait here, I need to rectify this," Jasmine instructed and went back to the registration desk. I stayed put in the dank-smelling concrete box, knowing this was going to be ugly!

Jasmine came back cussing! "This is bullshit! I paid for a king room!" She said she ended up having to speak to the manager who said there were no king rooms left, but also threw in that king rooms were for "couples." She said their argument escalated when she asked for a refund of the difference. She informed the manager she would take it up with her credit card company and would not be staying the second night. Secretly, I was relieved that we wouldn't be staying any longer than necessary in this one-star room.

The next morning didn't go that well either. Before heading to the caverns, we went into the little office to return the keys. "Ma'am, we have to charge you for leaving early."

"Excuse me?" Jasmine questioned.

"You reserved the room for two nights. We charge for early departures," the lady behind the wood-paneled, Formica-topped counter said.

"Have you lost your ever-loving mind? You will NOT disrespect us!" Jasmine responded.

I fully expected to see the local sheriff show up. I had never seen Jasmine so much as raise her voice. By the time the manager was called again, there was no doubt he was glad we were leaving because somehow the fee immediately disappeared, probably because it didn't exist in the first place.

Needless to say, by the time we finished with Bob and Becky and all of the extracurricular activity, I wasn't feeling the tour, especially since I was unprepared for the drop in temperature inside the caverns. It was dark and freezing down there! I really couldn't appreciate the rock formations—although I must admit, they were stunning—and Jasmine knew I wasn't listening to the tour guide. She offered to buy me a sweatshirt and I foolishly exacerbated the already tense situation when I responded that I didn't want anything with this place's name on it.

We rode back to Baltimore in virtual silence. I didn't want our first trip together to be our last... the traffic, getting lost—apparently Jasmine's sense of direction was a bit skewed—and having to deal with other people's perception of how they viewed love were all a bit much. In my mind, if my money was green, I should get respectable and appropriate service. What was Jasmine thinking? It may as well had been 1952 because that was what western Virginia felt like to me.

I wasn't very cordial when she dropped me off. Jasmine had tried to do something nice, something different. I should have asked her to come in, but I was grouchy and tired and just wanted to take a shower and rest. I jumped out the car, grabbed my bag from the backseat, and said, "Let's chat soon."

{FORTY}

Jasmine

I hadn't been technically free on a Saturday night in many years. Though I didn't always like the weekend adventures and rides to D.C. for parties, I knew it was part of the relationship and Toni's expectation. Tonight, I didn't have anything planned. I wasn't lonely, but alone was new for me. With the exception of brief chats, it had been radio silence from T after the disastrous Shenandoah experience. I telephoned Stephanie who begged off and asked for a raincheck after a trying week with her staff and patients. So, I reached out to Leslie, she was child free since Portia was with her father for the weekend and up for an adventure. Great!

I started pacing in the bedroom immediately after hanging up with Leslie. Now I could go out without worrying about a timeframe to return home; I was no longer tethered to anyone. Preparation for a girl's night out was much different than a date night, it was less intense. I wasn't trying to coordinate an outfit with anyone, I could wear whatever I wanted. But the broad range of choices and my indecisiveness proved to be a challenge. I finally settled on my third outfit.

I went with weekend chic, white shirt, jeans, and strappy sandals. Right before heading out the door, I ran back to the bedroom and grabbed a hip scarf. The delicate bells jingling, purple pattern, and gold fringe threads gave me a little something extra. I rarely wore the scarves anymore, throwbacks to my belly dancing days. I started belly dancing for the exercise; practicing drum solos, figure eights, and traveling steps for two plus hours worked up a sweat. And I enjoyed the sensuality of making my hips shake. Toni wasn't a fan though and one season WNBA games coincided with my evening classes, so I reluctantly stopped. I tousled my curls, posed to the left, then turned to the right and stared at the woman in the mirror for a few minutes; she looked cute. I smiled, blew her a kiss, and left the house.

The ride down 83 was easy and I lucked up and found parking on Read Street. Leslie and I decided to meet halfway between our houses and settled on Central Station downtown. At some point, the nightclub was renamed "Grand Central" but many of us still simply called it 'Central Station' or 'Central' for short. They had a decent upscale menu with small plate options. Most folks started in the restaurant, then took their party downstairs to the bar.

When we arrived, the place was beginning to get crowded, and it took a minute to wade our way through to the hostess. We were seated at a table farthest in the back where we could still feel the bass music thumping, but we didn't have to scream to talk or strain to hear. After handing us our menus and identifying the specials, our waitress asked for our drink orders. Still feeling sassy, I ordered a Cosmopolitan. Leslie gave me a look, "Why didn't you order that before we were seated. It's two dollars more up here." The waitress nodded her head in agreement and left us to chat. Leslie put her menu down. "Sooo, you really doing this? Your first outing as a single woman."

"I am, I'm glad you could come out," I said looking around the room then at my menu. "What looks good to you? I should be careful what I order right? I shouldn't eat something with a lot of garlic. In case I dance with somebody? I think I'm sad. I should be sad for a little while, right? No, I'm not sad, I'm nervous."

Leslie laughed. "Oh wow! That was a serious stream of consciousness—light or no garlic is best. No, you're not giving a sad vibe. Are you excited? I mean you're antsy, squirming in your seat. Do you need a drink?"

"Maybe," I answered. "Nervous, that's what I'm feeling. About what exactly, I don't know."

"That's completely understandable, By the way, I know I was Plan B. You called Stephanie first, didn't you?" Leslie asked out of the blue.

"What?" Leslie looked at me with her head cocked to the side.

"Yeah, I did. Why? You sound a little sensitive about that."

"Perhaps," she admitted.

"I only called her first because she doesn't have to plan around childcare. I try to be mindful that you are a mother." I shrugged and then looked directly at Leslie. "You know you do this all the time."

"Do what?" Leslie asked defensively. "What do I do?"

"Ask me who I called first. Does it matter?" I wanted to know.

"I know it shouldn't, but it does."

I stared at Leslie and tapped her with my menu. "Seriously, are we doing this on my first night out? Your friendship is just as meaningful to me as Stephanie's."

"I know, I know, it's me. I just want you to call me first sometimes. I don't always have childcare issues. Portia is getting older so I can come out and see what's happening too," Leslie laughed and wiggled her eyebrows. "That's a story for another night."

The server returned with our drinks. I sipped the drink which is usually pink; it was so strong it was fuchsia. I started swaying to an Ultra Naté song playing in the background; the drink color and my mood couldn't have been brighter. She asked if we were ready to order.

"We haven't really looked at the menu yet. What are we doing after dinner?" I asked Leslie. "That'll decide how much I'm eating. I may need food to soak up this alcohol," pointing to my drink.

"Please, not from that one drink you'll nurse all night! Decide what you're eating," she commanded. The server left again to put in our orders. Leslie offered a toast, "To you and your happiness!" She said it so loudly that folks two tables over yelled, "Cheers!"

"What are you looking forward to?" Leslie asked more quietly.

"That's easy, new adventures," I responded.

"With Teresa?"

"Possibly, I really enjoy being with her," I shared.

"Wow!"

"I haven't heard from her in a few days though, which is quite disappointing."

"Have you called her?"

"What? Why would I do that?" I asked incredulously.

"Why wouldn't you?"

"I don't know," I admitted.

"You want to?"

"Yes."

"Then, call her!" Leslie was emphatic.

"Anyhoo..." I said, "I said that I felt nervous tonight. That's true but I do think I'm sad."

"What are you sad about? Are you sad? You don't look sad?" Leslie cocked her head to the side again and raised her eyebrows.

"Sad that Toni and I couldn't make it work. Sad we couldn't get the flow restarted after a long ebb. But it's done, and I'm okay."

Leslie leaned in, "But is it really done?"

"Chile, I'm so done. I'm going to speak in language a seamstress can relate to," I said.

"Okay?!"

"After sewing the wrong sides of delicate fabric together, would you want to remove each stitch by hand?" I asked.

"Hell no! It would be easier to just start on a new pattern," she replied.

"Exactly!" I snapped my fingers for added emphasis.

"Your message is crystal clear, you're done," Leslie laughed.

Leslie and I ate, whooped loudly, laughed until tears ran down our cheeks, and caught up for the remainder of the evening. And we had to get a little dancing in as we edged towards the exit when Black Box's "Everybody Everybody" got everybody on the dance floor, which was packed with bodies gyrating, arms waving in the air, and lots of grinding hips. The DJ then mixed the hell out of Chaka Khan's "I'm Every Woman" and it took us another fifteen minutes to make it outside.

It was after one o'clock in the morning when I walked back in the house. It was peaceful. Coco was too sleepy to be bothered with my late-night antics, she stayed in her bed and didn't greet me. I came home feeling less anxious and more empowered than when I left.

Was single life going to be my reality or something else? Either way, I was going to be just fine.

{FORTY-ONE}

T

Winter was on the way. Nightly temperatures were consistently dipping into the mid- to low thirties. The chill hung in the air during the day, leading me to put on more layers to run and me running in late afternoon rather than early evening.

At the beginning of November, my mother called to see if I was coming home for Thanksgiving. I hadn't given it much thought considering all the plates I had spinning at work but thought it would be a nice break. So, I asked Mom if I could bring a guest. She quickly agreed but did not miss the opportunity to give me grief since I hadn't brought anyone home since undergrad, fifteen years ago.

I called Jasmine after hanging up with my mother. "What are you doing for Thanksgiving?" I asked her.

"I'm going to stay in my pajamas, watch the Macy's parade and some kind of televised dog show, and find a meal somewhere," she responded. "This is the first time in a long time that I won't have to do anything."

"You aren't going to your parents' house?" I asked.

"No, too much drama."

"Well, I'm going home for the holiday. Come to Savannah with me," I suggested.

"I want to be quiet and still. On a good day, traveling from Baltimore to like Richmond is a day trip because of the heavy traffic. You want to knowingly venture onto the speedway or parking lot— otherwise known as I-95—on one of the most traveled weekends of the year? No and thanks."

"Ah…" I whined.

"Besides, meeting your parents also implies something I'm not sure we want to imply."

"Why not?"

"T, you asked me to be honest. That's what, nine hours from Baltimore on a good day? Can we fly?"

"Noooo, that's no fun. Driving is part of the journey. I want to stop at Potomac Mills to say hello to a friend who owns an art gallery there. And there is this great joint in Kenly, North Carolina that has the best barbeque this side of the Mississippi. Besides, spending last minute airfare on a teacher's salary is a good example of insanity."

"I appreciate the invite," Jasmine said quietly. I didn't say anything, so she filled the silence on the phone, "Maybe next time?"

I tried my best not to be irritated with her—the mixed signals were wearing me out. After I pouted for two days, I called Jasmine when I came home from work with a different approach. "I want to see you, can you meet me for dinner?"

"I'd like that," she said.

"What are you doing tonight?"

"Seeing you, I guess," she laughed.

"Great!" I was excited.

"Are you cooking?"

"Nah, I don't feel like it. There's a little diner on the corner of Kittery and Cold Spring Lane?"

"I know the area, I'll find it."

"Is six-thirty okay?" I asked.

"Sure."

**

I was already seated when Jasmine arrived.

"Hey, I've not heard from you for a few days!" She said, sliding into the booth and squeezing my hands. "I've really missed talking to you."

"Did you now?" I asked, surprised that Jasmine was admitting that she had a vulnerability.

"And that's hard for me to say," she said, twisting her glass around a few times before taking a sip of water.

The waitress came back and placed a basket of bread with squares of foil-wrapped butter on the table. She highlighted the evening specials and took our dinner orders.

"Because?" I asked after we were alone again.

"Because…because I don't know. Because I'm questioning my judgement again. Because you've seeped into my consciousness."

"And that's a bad thing?" I asked.

"Not necessarily, but it's scary," Jasmine said.

"Fair enough. Can I share something too?" I asked, leaning in.

"Sure," she smiled

"Do you know I haven't taken anyone home to meet my parents since undergrad?"

"Really? Undergrad?"

"Yes, undergrad."

"Why not?"

"I never thought they were worthy," I answered.

"Wow! That's somewhat pompous don't you think?" Jasmine asked.

"Maybe, but you gotta understand the context," I started. "I believe I mentioned it before, but my parents have been married for forty-two years. Forty-two years! I've missed being around them and their old school romance."

"That's sweet," Jasmine said.

I continued, "They are sweet. They have an enduring relationship that I hope to have one day. I can't just bring any ole trick to their house."

"Hmmm," she said, listening intently.

"Their expectations for me and my brother are high. My brother is still figuring things out on the employment and career front, but he has somewhat gotten the relationship thing right. But me? Not so much. I was hurt pretty bad years ago and have been cautious… probably overly cautious ever since. This is the first time in a long time that I've really felt a connection with someone and can see beyond tomorrow. I've been excited. I want to take you home to meet my family."

"Whoa, why didn't you say that?" she asked.

"I didn't think I had to," I said. "I asked you to go, I didn't know I needed to qualify my request with a long, drawn-out explanation." Jasmine paused. Based on her furrowed brow, I assumed she was reconsidering my invitation. "Okay, I'll go but I can't leave until after work on Wednesday. I didn't take the day off because I hadn't planned on going anywhere. You're looking at the skeleton coverage for the department," she said pointing to herself.

"If we leave after six o'clock on Wednesday, we won't get to Savannah until three a.m. on Thanksgiving Day."

Jasmine shrugged, "Here's a compromise, I'll fly down and ride back with you."

"I was hoping to introduce you to a few friends along the way," I countered.

"What's this my debut?" Jasmine asked, laughing nervously.

"No, but I don't go home often so I wanted to maximize our time."

"Sorry, I can't this trip. I'm offering to pay for my ticket and fly one way. You can pick me up at the airport and we can get my introductions started," Jasmine proposed, shrugging her shoulders with her palms up.

"Do you know how expensive that ticket is going to be?" I grumbled.

"Yes, I have a pretty good idea with Thanksgiving being two weeks away," Jasmine nodded.

"Okay, we'll split the cost," I sighed.

"Up to you."

"It's settled then," I responded.

Our dinner arrived, I took her hand and formally announced I was saying prayer. I winked when she shot me a side eye.

***

Tuesday before Thanksgiving, I jumped in my already packed car before the last bell finished ringing and headed south. Jasmine was absolutely right about traffic on 95, it was heavy and slow until I was south of Fredericksburg. I stopped for gas, a bathroom break, and barbeque but decided to forego any other detours. All in all, I made good time.

Even though my windows were rolled up, as soon as the car wheels reached the Talmadge Bridge, I knew that I was home. The undeniable smell of oil, brackish water, heavy industry, and the weight of history—both good and bad—hovered over my hometown. It sort of crept up on you and seeped into your bones. I saw the huge letters of my alma mater—SCAD—mounted on a building as I crossed over the Savannah River, bringing back a flood of memories of late nights and early mornings in art studios, galleries, and libraries. I pulled up to my parents' home in a little more than nine hours after leaving Baltimore.

When Mom opened the door to our family home, the warm goodness of baking cinnamon and sweet potatoes hit my nostrils. I closed my eyes to savor the moment. My mother on the other hand, disrupted my olfactory experience and hit me with the dish cloth that had been draped across her shoulder. "Ow!" I exclaimed.

"You're alone?" she asked, looking disappointed to see just me standing on the front porch.

"Hi Ma', how are you?" I asked, leaning in to kiss her on the cheek.

"I thought you were travelling with someone?"

"I am, kind of… she's flying into SAV after work tomorrow. I'll pick her up then," I said, trying to squeeze past her with my bag and realizing I hadn't updated her about the change in travel arrangements.

"Oh, Teresa, we were looking forward to meeting your girlfriend," she said.

What in the world? I didn't think my eyebrows could rise any further. "Ma', we're just friends," I replied.

"That's what we're going with?" she wanted to know. *Ugh!* I hadn't cleared the foyer yet and she was already marrying me off.

"Mary, let the girl in the door for goodness' sake." Dad, likely awakened from a nap, wandered into the conversation and chided Mom, then turned and kissed me on the cheek. "Hey baby girl."

"Hey Dad," I said, smiling at him. *Yes! Pops to the rescue.*

"I heard you stopped in Kenly. I know you got some leftovers." *Well, that welcome party didn't last long.* I handed him a takeout box, translucent in areas saturated with grease stains. My mother rolled her eyes at the both of us and bumped my father with her hip as she headed towards the kitchen. He in turn gave her a pat on the butt.

Harold and Mary were fun to be around because they acted like they were still as much in love now as they'd always been. I found that kind of deep, abiding love soul-stirring and longed for it in my own life. Now that I was getting older, I'd come to appreciate their example more. My mother still sat on my father's lap like they were teenagers at the local soda fountain. I imagined it couldn't be as easy as they made it look, but I wished they could bottle their secret sauce and share it with the rest of us. I was looking forward to Jasmine meeting them.

On Wednesday night, Mom and Dad stayed up—and my brother and his family even came over—to meet and welcome Jasmine despite her late arrival. My mother personally showed her to the guest bedroom after a quick house tour and asked if she needed a snack. Jasmine declined and thanked her for the offer. After I heard my parents retire to their bedroom, I snuck into the guest room which used to be my brother's, there was no trace of him in here now.

"What are you doing in here?" Jasmine whispered.

"I've missed you," I responded.

"Really?"

"Yes, really. I just wanted to give you both a proper greeting and bid you a good night."

"What does that entail?" she asked.

"This." I leaned down, closed my eyes, and kissed Jasmine slowly and deeply, sucking on her bottom lip before I stopped. "Goodnight Jasmine."

"Goodnight," she replied, unsuccessfully trying to stifle her smile.

***

Thanksgiving at home was great. Mom invited our cousins—the measured, dignified, A.M.E. Butlers—rather than the sho-nuff country, unbutton your pants at the dinner table Butlers, or the moonshine drinking Butlers. Otherwise, I wasn't sure Jasmine would have hung around. The food, as I anticipated it would be, was ridiculously good. My mother's cooking was exactly why I started running track in middle school. I couldn't resist having too many helpings of her oyster stew, shrimp and grits, red rice, fried chicken, and homemade biscuits.

Once the extended family departed, we all changed into more comfortable clothes with forgiving waistbands for a second round of dessert and lounged in the family room. Dad lit a fire and settled into his recliner that matched Mom's. My belly was full, I was cozy and leaning on Jasmine on the sofa and had just closed my eyes.

"T what are you planning to do tomorrow? I know you aren't shopping," Mom asked, piercing the tranquility.

"Definitely not shopping, unless you want to," I said, glancing at Jasmine. "I hadn't really thought about it. Any suggestions?" I asked my mother.

"Why don't you take Jasmine on a walking tour?" Mom said.

"We are NOT going on one of those tours where they whitewash the city's history. Mom, that's so cheesy, plus you could do a better job. You grew up hearing the same stories. Why would we pay for a tour?" I responded.

"You could go on Wayne's tour," Mom said.

I turned to Jasmine and pointed at my mother, "Mr. Wayne is her high school classmate and was my high school history teacher."

Dad interjected, "He was sweet on your mama, I stopped all that." Mom swatted at Dad and laughed. Jasmine laughed too.

Mom rolled her eyes at Dad, "Wayne owns a local tour company, he gives a great African American history walking tour."

"I don't know, do you want to go?" I asked Jasmine with one eyebrow raised.

"Sure," Jasmine said casually and smiled. "I've never been to Savannah; I'd like to hear about history that was purposefully omitted from my schoolbooks."

The next day, I talked Mom into going with us to make the day more interesting. We arrived early and peeked into stores and store windows along the brick sidewalks in the historic district until it was time for the tour.

If you imagined a history professor in your mind's eye, Mr. Wayne Hamilton would fit the bill. Wearing the requisite tweed jacket with elbow patches and round, rimless eyeglasses, he waltzed towards us and the circle of tourists waiting at the designated park monument. He hugged Mom and planted a kiss on her cheek.

"Hi Wayne," Mom said, pulling away from him and blushing, "you remember my daughter Teresa?"

"Come on now Mary! I may not remember much but how could I forget Georgia's Miss Track and Field? Not to mention one of my best students." He was certainly embellishing that last part as he hugged me. Stepping back, I turned to see Jasmine staring at me.

"But ya'll look more like sisters now," Mr. Wayne was pouring it on. Wait! Was he saying that I looked old or that my mom looked young? My mother went with the young option without hesitation.

"Oh Wayne, you're too kind. And this is Teresa's friend, Jasmine." Jasmine extended her hand, "Pleased to meet you Mr. Wayne." He tipped his hat, which tickled her. "The pleasure is all mine. Now, let me get on with this here tour."

Mr. Wayne proceeded with practiced flair to highlight interesting tidbits about life as a Colored, Negro, Black and African American person during the Civil War, the great migration, and up to present day. Mom leaned over often and whispered additional information about the southern chef who passed black employee recipes off as her own and how First African Baptist Church participated in the Underground Railroad to Jasmine during the tour. Ending promptly ninety minutes after starting, he thanked us for our time and reminded us that gratuities weren't included with payment.

When we got back to the car, Mom directed me to drive through historic Cuyler/Brownsville for her bonus version of the history tour. My parents grew up in this neighborhood and the four of us lived here until it started changing. She explained that she and many other Black children were loved, supported, and protected by neighbors who looked out for each other. She pointed out buildings important to their segregated lives, Florence Street School, Charity Hospital, and several churches.

I weaved through the one-way streets, saddened by the changes I saw. The neighborhood—once a thriving working-class community—had clearly seen better days. A combination of a downturned economy, the eighties crack epidemic and the erosion of good paying industrial jobs led to increased poverty and crime, which in turn meant people needed to protect their property and families. Which begat the prevalence of bars over windows, extra security doors, abandoned corner stores, and boarded up and dilapidated homes.

"Watch," I said, "In twenty or thirty years, these Craftsman homes will be prime real estate and fuel opportunities for gentrification." Both Mom and Jasmine agreed.

***

Dinner Friday night was Thanksgiving leftovers. I was helping clear the table when Mom said slyly, "I like Jasmine. And since I can't remember the last girlfriend we've met of yours, seems like you like her too." Mom chuckled. "Wait...," she snapped her fingers. "I do remember. Sheila! We met Sheila a little over a year ago up there in Baltimore."

"Ugh! Sheila is old news," I said rolling my eyes at the thought of that human nightmare.

"Good, I didn't much care for her."

"Thanks for the confirmation Ma'...but hold on a minute. Yes, Jasmine is nice. Yes, I like her. But truth be told, she has been clear about wanting to take things slow." I continued, "Like, I had to work hard to get her to come down here with me. But it's just as well, I like keeping my options open."

"What?!" My mother looked at me like I had two heads. "Options? You need to settle yourself down. You need to exercise the option to focus on one person..." She held up her index finger for emphasis. "One person that you can create a future with. What are you afraid of T?"

"I don't know," I said honestly.

"I think while you're keeping your options open, Jasmine is going to move on, and you're going to realize what you could have had too late."

"That's coming from someone who's been with the same person for forty-plus years," I mumbled.

"Exactly!" She hit me with another dish towel. "It's good advice from an excellent source," Mom shot back, smiling.

"Yeah, I'll keep it in mind," I sighed.

"Do that, I'll let your father talk to you about what he almost missed out on trying to see who else might come along," Mom responded, just short of twisting her neck.

I walked back towards the family room—in the direction of a lot of whooping—and trash talking to find Jasmine, my father, and brother playing Spades. Jasmine was dancing in her chair, waving her hands in the air, and laughing and my father was congratulating her on a win.

"Your brother here reneged a book and she," he said, pointing at Jasmine, "cut my ace."

"I wanna play," I jumped in.

"Mr. Harold, you want to be my partner?" Jasmine asked Dad.

"Not me?" I asked, pointing to myself.

"Nope, I want to be on a winning team, and you don't want a partner," she responded which sent my father and brother into howls of laughter.

"Oww, that hurt." I was serious, that kind of hurt. Nonetheless, Jasmine and Dad beat me and my brother mercilessly. On the last hand which set us back again, we folded. They high fived like they were best buddies and Jasmine announced she was heading to bed. She had the nerve to add, "My work here is done." I stuck my tongue out at her. My brother said goodnight and headed out too. That left me and my father.

"That girl can play," Dad said.

"She's alright," I smirked.

"Yeah, okay says the sore loser," he chuckled. "I liked her game, the lady counts cards."

"What? Who?"

"Your friend Jasmine. She counts cards," Dad repeated.

"How do you know?" I asked.

"Cause I know. This wasn't my first game, you don't know nothing about that though," he laughed. "I like her."

"You and Ma' are obviously in cahoots. Why do you like her, 'cause she counts cards?" I laughed.

"No, she's good people. I would say good southern people, I suspect. But we were playing cards and kicking your butts, her credentials were none of my business. Where's she from?"

"Baltimore… not our kind of southern, but southern enough," I replied.

"Well, Maryland is in the south according to Mr. Mason and his comrade Dixon, she's good," he said, smiling.

Very interesting. That was a huge compliment coming from my father. He didn't bestow the 'good people' honor on very many people. I put the card table up, kissed Dad on the cheek, said "goodnight," and headed down the hall to my room. But I knocked on the guest room door first.

"Come in," I heard Jasmine say. I stepped into the room and leaned on the doorframe.

"Hey," I said.

"Hey yourself," she replied in that familiar way I'd come to enjoy.

"Just checking on you, everything good?" I asked her.

"Yeah, I'm really enjoying your family. I'm glad I came," she admitted.

"Me too."

"You have your father's eyes," she observed.

"That I do. Mom always said that made us closer."

"How so?"

"I don't know, maybe 'cause you can clearly see that we favor. Who knows?" I shrugged.

"Miss Track and Field?"

I smiled and huffed a little. "Yeah, that was a long time ago."

"How come you hadn't mentioned that?"

"What was I supposed to say? 'Hello, my name is Teresa Butler, I was Georgia's 1985 Miss Track and Field?'"

Jasmine laughed, "That would have been a bit odd huh?"

"Uh, yeah!" I agreed. "Plus, you know I run so that's not a surprise."

"You said you run 'cause you liked the way it made you look and feel."

"And that's true," I confirmed.

"I don't know T, it just seems like the more I get to know you, the less I know. Like, running for exercise is one thing, being the best in an entire state is something totally different."

"Fair enough," I conceded.

"SCAD is an art school, right?"

"Yeah," I said, amused that Jasmine was getting a glimpse of my background.

"I'm surprised you didn't run in college."

"I had a scholarship to a state school and ran for one indoor and outdoor season. I loved the challenge. But I loved art more, so I came back home. I don't have to tell you it took Mom and Dad a minute to get over that," I confessed.

"Wow! You followed your passion."

"Yeah, I guess you could say that. You want to know something else?"

"What?" Jasmine sounded intrigued.

"I want you right now," I whispered as I moved towards her.

"T," she whispered back, trying to shove me away but I didn't budge.

Instead, I smiled and raised her chin up as I bent down to kiss her, "Yes?"

"We can't," she protested, blushed, and leaned away from me.

"Awwhhh," I whined. Jasmine gently pushed me away.

"Ooo-kay, I'll settle for kissing you goodnight." I kissed her on the forehead and made my way to my room feeling warm and fully alive.

Saturday morning, I walked into the kitchen to find my mother and Jasmine having coffee and talking like old friends. They stopped when I came in and had the nerve to laugh.

"Well good morning, Sunshine," my mother said with a smile.

"Good mornin', Ma'," I said rubbing her shoulders. I had never kissed a woman in front of my mother, and I wasn't about to start now. So, in a slightly awkward moment, I lightly pinched Jasmine's arm. Although she was hiding her face behind her coffee mug, I could tell that she was smiling by the crinkles in the corner of her eyes. This made me smile too.

"T, you wanna ride into town with me?" My father asked as he walked into the kitchen fully dressed.

"What on earth are you going into town for on a holiday weekend?"

"Don't question my motives woman, only your mother can do that," he jokingly said to me. "Where are my manners? Good morning, Jasmine. How'd you sleep?"

"I slept very well, thank you for asking," she replied. And then she squealed. "Are those Gabriel Trumpets?" My mother stood up and went to the door next to Jasmine who was looking out over the backyard.

"You know about those?" Mom answered looking surprised.

I had never seen Jasmine so excited. "Yes. I've never seen purple ones."

My mother beamed. "You garden?"

"Yes ma'am. I've only seen white ones, but I don't have any because they're poisonous and I have a dog. They are beautiful! Do you mind if I take a look?"

"Absolutely not! Admiration is both allowed and encouraged," Mom said, happy that someone wanted to venture into the yard with her. Jasmine stepped out onto the patio. My mother was right behind her. "I'll show you my garden. It's nice that the plants are still blooming, we've had a warm fall season." Jasmine was laser focused and never turned around to say goodbye. My father looked at me, "You might want to ride with me, you won't see them anytime soon."

***

As we packed up the car on Monday morning, my mother gave Jasmine a few cuttings from her garden. "I thought you might like these." And Mom invited her back to Savannah with the promise to do a Garden and Historic House tour the next time she came.

Jasmine gladly accepted. "Thank you, that's really sweet of you."

"Are you coming back for Christmas?" Mom asked.

"We hadn't talked about it, I needed to see how well your daughter and I traveled together," Jasmine said while laughing.

"She's like her daddy, I understand," Mom laughed too placing her arm around Jasmine's shoulder.

"Please continue to talk about me like I'm not here," I exclaimed.

My mother gave Jasmine a warm embrace and told her how much she enjoyed her visit and hoped to see her again, real soon. My mother whispered to me "I like her. Be nice to her."

My father and I made small talk about which route we were taking and wanted us to call periodically. He reminded me that I was in the south and still needed to be careful driving while Black. He hugged Jasmine and told her that it was a real pleasure meeting her and to call him if she needed any help because his daughter could be a handful. They both laughed; I rolled my eyes.

The ride back to Baltimore was uneventful; we recapped the last five days and laughed at my family's antics and unsolicited commentary. When I dropped Jasmine off, she kissed me on the cheek and thanked me for the invite.

"It was nice to meet your family. I had more fun than I thought I would," she beamed.

"I'm glad you enjoyed yourself. I enjoyed being there with you. They liked you too. As evidenced by them explicitly saying so."

"No, they did not!" she chuckled.

"Yeah, both of them on separate occasions. And they extended a Christmas invitation. I don't usually go back for Christmas, but we'll see. Let's keep our holiday options open."

Jasmine laughed and shook her head. "That's right, let's keep our options open."

{FORTY-TWO}

Jasmine

Stephanie had been hosting a holiday dinner for her co-workers for the last five years and always invited a few additional friends, so everyone didn't talk shop all night. She rotated the invitations but there were always standing offers extended to me, Leslie, and Rachel—Stephanie's assistant was also a superb events planner who could throw a fabulous party like nobody's business. It was a chance for us to put on something sparkly, eat well, and dance like no one was watching.

I originally invited Paula from work. She was single and I figured she could use a little festiveness. As the holidays got closer, she had become more somber and irritable when staff and patients talked about their upcoming celebrations. Holidays were not the same for Paula since both of her parents passed away. And this year her brother was with his wife's family. She initially said she would think about going but Paula eventually declined my invite, said she just didn't feel like mingling.

T was my backup plan, but I didn't tell my friends she was coming so they wouldn't have time to prepare for oral arguments and cross examination. We parked around the corner and walked to The Pointe, an upscale, black-owned restaurant in Fells Point. It was two nicely converted Baltimore rowhomes—with lots of cherry wood paneling and a grand fireplace—that was now a destination for Baltimore's classy elite. I felt good and was looking forward to being out. Although not as sexy, I was glad I wore block heels, the uneven cobblestone streets wreaked havoc on stilettos, my shoe of choice when I was trying to make a statement.

"The Pointe huh? I heard about this place," T said before we went in.

"I have too but not only do I not hang out on this side of town often; I believe the last time I was over this way was when we went to T.K.'s down the street on Thames Street. By the way," Jasmine said hesitantly.

"Uh oh, what is it?"

"I didn't tell my friends I was bringing a date."

"Really? So, this is *my* debutante debut?"

"Or maybe our couple's debut," I said.

"Are we a couple?" T asked.

"Well, what are we?" I said with an inflection in my voice, unsure if I appreciated T's question.

"I don't know, you tell me. A month ago, you didn't want to meet my parents because you said it implied something that you weren't ready to imply. Now, you're getting upset because I asked a simple, but very appropriate question? Jasmine, the vacillating back and forth is making my head hurt."

"You know what? I don't feel like fussing with you tonight. We're not a couple, just two people keeping our options open," I reminded her. "Let's just have a good time. By the way-" I paused and put my arm through the crook of T's. "You may want to answer my friends' questions."

"Questions? I don't understand, why would I answer questions that you have to warn me about?" T asked. "This sounds like a setup."

"Well, why are you here?"

"Because you invited me. Why do you have to answer a question with a question? I'm going to spend time with you and meet your friends. I don't, however, expect to spend the entire night on the witness stand; interrogated and judged about who I know, what I do, what organizations I belong to, and what church I go to."

"They're not going to ask you about church. Those heifers do brunch." I tried to lighten the mood. "They gave up years ago giving money to mostly men who damned them to hell just because of who they loved."

"Well, amen to that. That's something we agree on," T said.

{FORTY-THREE}

T

Jasmine and I had established a nice little routine since returning from Georgia. We chatted in the evenings after work and then again right before bedtime. And while our conversations were nice, I hadn't seen her in a few weeks, and I missed her. An invitation to a Christmas soiree was a welcomed surprise, until Jasmine dropped a bomb walking into the restaurant. She told me it was a professional holiday party hosted by her friend Stephanie and she expected most of their closest friends there. I hadn't met any of them, which meant tonight's unexpected introduction was swiftly taking "us" to another level.

Relationships took on new meaning when you started introducing friends and expanding the nucleus of the relationship. Relationship? I still wasn't sure that's what was going on here. Life as I'd known it didn't routinely include my lover's friends. I certainly limited my contact with many of Sheila's friends, I interacted with that stuffy crowd only when absolutely necessary. And other friends with benefits typically meant just the two of us. So, once again, all of this was new, uncharted territory.

I took deep breaths to reduce my irritation with Jasmine on the way back from dropping our coats off. The cutie on coat check duty gave me an extra big smile, that helped. It was the holiday season, we were out, may as well have some fun.

I met and exchanged pleasantries with a few people I recognized from summer gallery openings. One of them gave me a heads up about a new opening near Cross Street Market that may be looking for 'diverse talent,' code for 'Black art.' He was chatty. Nice enough though in that he identified and provided a little intel about the party's host. I suspected Jasmine's other friends were the ladies huddled around Stephanie. They were watching me, and I was watching them. It was quite comical in the way we were all sizing each other up from a distance. Looking around the space, I finally saw Jasmine through the crowd and watched her laughing so hard with a guy that they were holding on to each other's arms. I chuckled. Jasmine—still laughing and wiping her eyes—seemed to be having a nice time.

I took a position near the bar after getting a glass of orange juice when Stephanie caught my eye. She smiled and walked towards me. Since Jasmine said Stephanie was one of her closest confidants, there was no doubt in my mind that she was coming for me with nothing but fire. I tried to smile as she approached but started putting my guard up. Jasmine claimed there would be questions. By the reaction of the wait staff and others in the room, I surmised Stephanie was accustomed to being deferred to. I didn't know if that was true, but in the fifteen seconds it took her to walk across the room, I probably made a lot of assumptions.

"Teresa, we haven't had a chance to meet. I'm glad you were able to come tonight," Stephanie said offering her hand. I shook it.

"Thanks. Jasmine told me yesterday that we had an event to come to." *Ugh!* Did that sound like I didn't want to be here? I just needed to survive the night without drama.

"Oh, so she didn't give you any warning either?" Stephanie laughed and nodded in Jasmine's direction.

"Warning? Warning for what?"

"Warning that her friends are her fiercest allies. We pride ourselves on watching out for one another."

I didn't know why Stephanie's response annoyed me. My chest was tight, my pulse was increasing, and my palms started to sweat. "That's cool. But look, you're hosting a swanky party here. I think your interrogation can be tabled for another time. Hmmm… that's probably not the right term. Jasmine mentioned your psychology background, so I don't know if it's interrogated, evaluated, or studied." I smiled, trying my best to play nice.

Stephanie smirked and responded, "I had no intention of doing any of those things. Why are you being so defensive?"

"Steph-"

She put her palm up as if to say, 'Stop talking.' *Ugh!* This wasn't going to end well. I rarely felt the need to explain myself beyond any opening salvo, but I wanted Stephanie to know I wasn't some pushover. I continued, "I get it, you and Jasmine are friends. But the Jasmine I've come to know is an adult and really doesn't need anyone to make decisions about her life. She's fully capable of deciding who and what is important to her. I'll say this, Jasmine and I mutually enjoy each other's company."

Stephanie leaned in and lowered her voice, "I didn't realize you would have a tough time having a simple conversation."

"What?!" I exclaimed. This woman had some nerve.

"I came over to merely say 'hello' and that I looked forward to getting to know you. But since you think you know what Jasmine is capable of, I need you to know an important fact about my friend."

"And what's that?" I asked.

"Jasmine loves being connected. She loves romance and being courted. As much as I always want to protect her from herself, my friend loves love. I hope you enjoy being connected, with and to Jasmine. If that's not your thing... if you feel the need to 'keep it light'—Stephanie used air quotes—or aren't interested in committing, you are wasting her time and yours."

"Thank you very much for the advice," I said sarcastically and took a sip of my drink just so I could do something other than standing here being pissed off.

Anyone looking at us may have presumed it was a delightful conversation replete with smiles and air quotes. Little would they realize the verbal sparring that was taking place. I wasn't sure if I was irritated for thinking she was mocking me or that I may have been wound pretty tight. Maybe both.

She nailed it though—I was being defensive. I felt the need to protect myself from a perceived threat. As far as I was concerned, I was a better catch than Jasmine's ex. But leave it to lesbians to have the U-Haul packed before the end of the first date. Jasmine and I were still figuring out what this was. Were we in an exclusive relationship? I didn't think I was quite there. Nor did I think Jasmine was either. I had no idea what she had told her friends but she herself was far from committed. What was different now though was that I was open to new possibilities. The thought of settling down no longer made me feel like running across the country like Forest Gump.

Stephanie was still staring with a half-smile, half challenging expression. I tried to smooth the conversation out. "Stephanie, I think it's fair to say that we are both concerned about and care for Jasmine. I hope you'll see that as time goes on."

"You won't have long to figure things out," she countered.

"Really? Her ex had a long time."

"That's why Toni's an ex. You don't have the history with Jasmine for her to continue a relationship that doesn't demonstrate commitment. I'm not sure when or if you've ever had an all-in relationship. If that's not your mindset with *my* friend, you two won't be together long and I won't remember your name next Christmas."

I was pretty sure I had ground a layer of enamel off of my teeth as I tried not to lash out. Stephanie filled in the silence. "It was so good to meet you. I hope you'll keep our conversation in mind as you and Jasmine grow closer, or not." Stephanie squeezed my forearm and walked away.

Ouch, that hurt! Not the squeeze, but her frosty words. I turned my back to the crowd and leaned on the bar. *What the hell was that?* Jasmine walked up and put her arm around my waist. "Hey, I've been looking for you."

"Have you now?" I asked, trying to smile. It probably looked more like a grimace.

"Of course, are you having a good time?" she asked.

"I was, until I was castigated by your friend."

"Uh oh, should I apologize now?"

I shook my head. "No apology necessary. Stephanie was very clear that she cares very deeply about you."

We prepared to leave the party with the majority of the crowd. As we said goodnight, Jasmine hugged Stephanie before Stephanie extended her hand to me with a firm handshake. "You take good care," she said. I wasn't sure if she was sincere or what but that didn't mean I couldn't be cordial. "Likewise," I replied.

Compared to the party's festive atmosphere, the ride up 83 was quiet. I didn't have a lot to say. I pulled into Jasmine's driveway and neither turned off the car nor did I give any indication that I was getting out.

Jasmine reached over and grabbed my hand, "Is everything okay?"

"Yeah, why do you ask?" I replied, staring out of the windshield at the darkness.

"I thought maybe you were staying," she informed me.

"We hadn't talked about me staying so I'm going to head home."

"T, look at me," Jasmine said, sounding concerned.

I took a deep breath, swallowed, and turned to face Jasmine.

"I'm not sure what's going on, you don't need an invitation to stay." She stroked my hand. "At what point can we just assume we're spending the night at each other's house?" she asked.

"I didn't know that's where we were. Why would I assume anything? I never make assumptions about staying at a woman's house," I replied.

"Really? A woman's house? I'm not just some woman Teresa." She snatched her hand away from mine. Jasmine didn't bother saying goodnight and slammed my car door.

***

Jasmine fluctuated between "I want consistent conversation and visits" to unexplained disappearances. Which spurred me to ask if Toni had returned, but Jasmine assured me that she hadn't. Jasmine did accompany me to TK's private family and friends pre-New Year's dinner. The boys closed the restaurant for one night between Christmas and the new year to celebrate with those they were closest to. Jasmine and I were all smiles, giggles, and good loving that night.

However, Maryland's unpredictable winter weather wasn't helping us maintain whatever we were doing. Nights that we planned to get together in January were overcome by harsh weather conditions. On the other hand, the last "big" snowstorm that was predicted for MLK weekend resulted in a dusting. And here we were again, another holiday weekend potentially being impacted as WBAL's meteorologist was calling for five to six inches of snow.

Warnings started Tuesday evening, but I wasn't falling for it this time. By Wednesday afternoon Baltimore was in full tilt for an increasingly common President's Day weekend snowstorm. News anchors were reporting that grocery stores had run out of toilet paper, milk, and snacks. Plus, hardware stores had virtually sold out of shovels and salt for sidewalks. I always watched and listened in amazement at the dire predictions and people's responses. So, when Jasmine asked what my plans were, I suggested she come over for a few days, thinking we'd have a nice time for one, maybe two nights. Sheila was the only woman that had stayed here overnight, and no one had ever been invited during a snowstorm. I was taking a risk.

"You know I have to bring Coco right?" Jasmine reminded me. *Oh shit, that's right.* "Of course," I finally said.

"I'm a package deal remember?"

I laughed. "Yes ma'am, I would be happy to host the full package," I conceded. Heretofore, we hadn't had many overnights together and typically I was at her place for this very reason. My house was neither child nor animal proof and that was about to be put to the test.

Maryland state personnel services had already announced personal leave for non-essential employees and Baltimore City, in atypical fashion, declared school closures for Friday. Jasmine and I could relax and do whatever suited our fancies. I was really hoping to stay horizontal with her as much as possible.

Jasmine arrived Thursday evening after work with lots of bags, mostly dog stuff. She brought Coco's bed, medications—I didn't know dogs had allergies—food, and more toys than some children had. I had her place all the stuff on the other side of my room away from the bed. Coco was busy sniffing around but didn't look pleased when she saw her bed tucked in a corner.

As predicted, snow started falling slowly around nine o'clock, making everything outside white and bright. I put music on, lit candles, and made dinner. Jasmine was going to be dessert. We ate, laughed, and watched television reporters try to outdo each other's stories about the "catastrophic" storm. I'd never understood why people of generally sound judgment had to report *in* inclement weather... slipping on sidewalks, wearing hip waders in flood waters just to tell us to stay inside because it was bad outside. Here in Baltimore, it was snowstorms, at home, it was hurricanes. In either case, it didn't make sense to put yourself in danger.

Around midnight, Jasmine let Coco out for the last time, I was grateful the back yard was fenced. It took Coco a long time to decide to get things moving, strange environs, I guess. She kept looking at us watching her. "Where's your shovel?" Jasmine asked. "If the snow keeps up at this pace, I'll need to make a path for Coco in the morning."

"Shit! I broke the handle during the last storm. I forgot to buy a new one," I suddenly remembered.

"What? Are you serious? They're now calling for eight to ten inches! What were you thinking?"

"The weather people just said four to five inches," I replied.

"T, it's four inches now. In the morning it'll be eight to ten if not more."

I went to the shed to see what we could use. The only shovel I had was a garden shovel, more suited for digging small holes than moving snow. Nonetheless it was perfect to dig a dog path and it had to suffice. Jasmine shook her head and slanted the shovel up against the back wall. When I stood the shovel upright, she moved it again, continued shaking her head, and said, "Do you want trouble Smarty? You might as well put up a neon sign 'Break Glass Here.'"

"You're right, but we also don't want it buried in the snow. Let's compromise," I said. "I'll put it inside the back door."

"Fine." Jasmine stuck her tongue out at me.

It was almost one o'clock in the morning by the time we finished showering and brushing our teeth. So why did the damn dog start whimpering as soon as we got in bed? *What the hell?* Coco was standing there looking pitiful. Jasmine got up, tried to console her, and brought the dog bed to her side of the bed. Ultimately Jasmine ended up giving her a Benadryl to calm down. When Jasmine got back in bed, I didn't say anything, I just looked at her.

"She's a little anxious but she'll be okay," Jasmine said.

"Dogs down south would be outside this time of night," I responded.

"Don't be like that Twan," Jasmine said trying to lighten the mood.

A tree branch crashed and knocked over flowerpots at three in the morning. At least I hoped the breaking noise was just pots. I peeked outside and saw everything glistening. Oh hell, never had the meteorologists mentioned ice. Snow was one thing; ice was a totally different ballgame. Everything stopped for ice. I started taking a mental inventory of what food I had in the cabinets and how many rolls of toilet paper I had. I was starting to think maybe I miscalculated this little adventure.

Coco woke up promptly at five-thirty like she had a damn job to go to. I put the pillow over my head to dampen her barking. Jasmine got up to let her out. Much to my annoyance, I eventually had to get up after Jasmine hadn't come back to bed after like fifteen minutes. Expecting her to be standing at the back door, this crazy woman was outside shivering in a nightgown. "What in the world are you doing out here?" I asked her after grabbing a coat to put around her shoulders.

"I didn't know about the ice. I was trying to get in the shed to look for salt."

"No need," I said. "I'm out of salt."

"Did you not hear the forecast?" she fussed again.

I shot back, "They didn't say anything about ice."

We both looked as Coco whimpered; she was walking gingerly and sliding on the thick ice. "No shovel, no salt. T, do you have food and toilet paper?" Jasmine asked. "Did you not think about us. You made great meals, it was fun for a time, but this isn't how you keep the family safe."

"What family?"

"Exactly! You are singularly focused, and not very well may I add. I know the invitation was last minute, but they have been calling for bad weather all week. At what point in *this*, whatever *this* is will you make room for anyone other than yourself?"

Damn! A woman with a dog doesn't automatically constitute a family. Jasmine had a point, but I wasn't conceding that easily, hence the awkwardness for the remainder of the morning. By two in the afternoon, the ice melted a bit and the city crew had treated the road making it possible for Jasmine to beat feet and make her way home. I knew it was my imagination, but it seemed like she packed everything up in ten minutes. Coco didn't look back and neither did Jasmine. I closed the door and sighed. That was a train wreck.

{FORTY-FOUR}

Jasmine

I couldn't get home fast enough but I had to be careful driving. The roads were still hazardous, and people were speeding as if it was July, dry and sunny. I didn't like the Jones Falls Expressway on a good day. I liked it even less when the roads were icy. I pulled up to the curb in front of my house. The driveway was still completely covered in snow and what was likely an inch or two of ice underneath. It needed to be broken up before I could even think about navigating the incline. I parked, grabbed my purse, and gingerly carried Coco in the house. I picked up the phone to call Stephanie 'to process' as she liked to say but she made it clear after the holiday party that she was not a T fan. Which wasn't surprising; Stephanie was fiercely protective and wasn't a Toni fan either. I put the phone back on the hook, I didn't need to be scolded. Instead, I changed into my snow boots with the good traction, they were not cute. Cute was for the club; you needed functional gear in dicey weather.

I grabbed the shovel from the side porch, the one hidden from view so that someone wouldn't think it useful to break a window and burglarize the house. *Ugh, T!* I shook my head at the thought. Taking tiny steps down the driveway, I wanted to avoid the same fate as my former neighbor, Mrs. Weinberg, who fell last year and laid outside for about an hour before anyone knew she was out here. Her kids banded together, moved her to a swanky Roland Park retirement community, and sold her house before she knew what happened.

Surveying the enormous task ahead, I got to work using my new ergonomic shovel, supposedly the curved design would make lifting easier on my back. I wasn't crazy about shoveling, but I bought it in December after realizing that I was now the Charles Family snow removal crew. Toni used to do it however, since she didn't live here anymore, it was me, myself, and I.

Whew! One side was finished. Breathing heavily, I paused at the end of the driveway and laughed to myself. Therapy wasn't this hard. Thankfully, it warmed up a little; breaking up ice *and* shoveling was the worst! I walked back to the top of the driveway to work my way downhill this time.

What was T thinking? Her single lifestyle was apparent in how unprepared she was for me and Coco during the storm. It wasn't attractive. She invited me over for a weekend and was no more ready for guests than the man in the moon. Who didn't have a snow shovel in Baltimore for goodness' sake? T raised my hopes and dashed my expectations all within forty-eight hours. I secretly thought her invitation was going to usher in a solid start for us. We had been starting and stalling for months.

I couldn't put all the onus on T though, some of this was my fault. The possibility of being in a new relationship, especially so soon after Toni, made me feel unsteady and somewhat mentally paralyzed. Every time I thought that I should see who else may be out there, T and I would go out or have a wonderful conversation and I started believing in a possible fairy tale again. I loved being with her and her family for Thanksgiving. Her mother even sent me the most delicious cookies for Christmas along with Savannah Sun Marigold seeds, which I can't wait to see bloom in the spring. I liked T's attentiveness when we were together. I had forgotten how good it felt to be the focus of someone's attention.

But then? This weekend it became obvious that she was prepared for dinner and sex, yet not much beyond that. I was nobody's booty call. I thought I was okay with our nightly calls and occasional dinners and dates. Last night though, it became abundantly clear to me that I wanted and needed more. And if I was being honest with myself—on this point I was the ill-prepared one—I wanted more with T. Somehow, we had managed to avoid discussing whether or not we would be exclusive. *Ugh!* Was I being too harsh and judgmental?

I stopped halfway back down the driveway to catch my breath. The sun had made the temperature tolerable in my down winter coat and fuzzy-lined gloves. Now that dusk had crept in, I was starting to get cold, and my fingers were numbing. The neighborhood was quiet. It didn't look like many cars had been moved from other driveways or spots along the curb. Few people had driven on the street even, the pavement was still covered in a slushy tan mess, a mix of frozen water and sand.

Exhausted seemed to be an inadequate descriptor that came from tiring physical activity and my mental gymnastics. I dragged myself up the porch steps, plopped down, and sighed. I hadn't dated anyone else since T and I started spending time together. I wasn't certain if I could say the same for her. I noticed how other women noticed her, after all, she was easy on the eyes. Did T follow up on that energy? I didn't know. What I did know was that I was not interested in being among a cadre of women. I just shoveled all this snow, there was no question that I was a strong, independent Black woman. That thought made me laugh out loud. Screw that… next time I was going to hire someone to shovel. On a positive note, I guess I didn't need Stephanie for this session, I had worked my irritation out on my own.

***

"Hey," T said when I answered the phone that night.

"Hey yourself," I replied.

"What are you up to?"

"Nothing really, I just got out of the tub. I needed to soak a bit; my muscles were soar from shoveling."

"Hmmm, the thought of you naked is delightful."

"Uh huh…" I tried to be annoyed but a tingling between my legs got in the way.

"Sorry, I digress. I would have helped you if you had asked," she said.

"With what T? You don't have a proper shovel," I said rather abruptly.

"You're right Jasmine, I made a mistake. I don't have a snow shovel right now. I told you, I broke it last month. And I didn't think about it again until it was too late. There wasn't a shovel or salt to be found anywhere. But obviously you have a shovel, I could have shoveled with your shovel," she said. I could hear the smile in her voice.

This made me smile, but I didn't let her know that. Through all my frustration with T, she was still making me smile.

{FORTY-FIVE}

T

A month after the disastrous sleepover, I was still down in the dumps. I reached out to John. It was his birthday month, and he was due a meal anyway. We had hardly spent time together lately and I missed my best friend. We met at our favorite Indian restaurant. Since Johns Hopkins was buying up all the property surrounding its campus and expanding, café after café, restaurant after restaurant opened along St. Paul Street to capitalize on the pool of hungry students and staff. The plain aluminum-framed storefront the restaurant occupied was in its second incarnation having once been a classic American diner.

There was nothing special about this place's ambiance. The faux leather booths gave you serious skin burn if you sat in one place too long and then tried to shift. However, the food was excellent and tasted like it came directly from Mumbai. Sitting in our usual booth in the rear of the restaurant, I filled John in on the twists and turns of my life since Ms. Charles became a constant presence in it.

"So, she just packed all her shit and left?" he asked.

"Yep, she bolted like the damn house was on fire or something," I told him.

"Have you talked to her?"

"We see each other here and there, talk just about every day, and enjoy the occasional night out. You know it's hard for anyone, Ms. Jasmine in all of her coolness included, to stay away from all of this good lovin'," I said teasing.

"Uh huh," John said with one eyebrow raised.

"But she really hasn't had much in-depth conversation for me, and her mixed signals are tiring. Quite frankly, I've been incredibly busy producing new stuff for the spring and summer festivals as well as putting in extra time in the after-school program."

"How do you feel about that?"

"Jasmine or putting in extra time with the kids?" I asked.

"Jasmine fool...you know how I feel about your side hustle at Baltimore City Public Schools," John said.

"Side hustle? Where I work full time? You're funny. Anyway, I don't know. I thought we were getting to a good place, you know? Since meeting her and taking her home for Thanksgiving I seriously started thinking about my future."

"What?" John exclaimed, clutching his imaginary pearls.

"Hush boy, I'm trying to be serious here. Assuming we get one shot at this thing called life, I'm thinking that maybe I no longer want to fill it with mindless activity and women I care little about." John stared at me, holding his fork. I ignored his stunned expression. "Ego boost? Yes. But it's always short lived, unlike the innate desire I feel for Jasmine. Our bad days are better than most of my good days with other women you know?" I heard the words coming out of my mouth. To some extent, I was surprised at my own true confession.

"Wow! You know word on the street is you're already off the market."

"What? Who told you that?" I asked a bit shocked.

"You know girls don't have much, or do much, for me but they try like hell to get to you through me."

"You don't say," I said with suspicion and put another bite of tasty salmon tandoori in my mouth.

"Here's what I know to be true," John said, demonstrably pointing his finger at me.

"Oh boy, do I want to hear this?"

"When have I ever asked you for your permission to provide my unvarnished opinion?" I started to answer as John put his hand up. "That's a rhetorical question. You're a great catch Teresa. Always have been ever since I've known you and that's been what?"

"It's been over fifteen years since my first year at SCAD," I answered him.

"And, you know you're a catch." He kept talking, not missing a beat. "So much so, that after Imani broke your heart, you've gone through women like most of us change our undergarments. I think the thought of limiting your options scares you to death."

I stared out the window at nothing in particular listening to John sum up my personal life in a matter of seconds and echoing my mother's words from months earlier. "I also know that I've never seen you so invested in one person...dare I say, happy even, not just content and settling. And out of all the girls I've met, knowing full well that I'm sure I've only met a fraction of them, I really like Jasmine. And I like Jasmine for you."

"Well thank you for that but I thought you liked Sheila?"

"Girl please, I tolerated Sheila. I was so glad when that high maintenance, siddity Negress finally showed her ass one too many times and you cut her loose. Lord only knows why you put up with her for more than two days, let alone two years. She was exhausting!" John finally paused, "T honey, what do you want?"

I contemplated his question a while and finally spoke, "I don't know. I'm not sure about much of anything anymore. Maybe I never was. Jasmine made some comment about me not taking care of the family and..."

"What family?" John interrupted.

"Exactly! That's what *I* said. 'Cause she made it clear that she wasn't trying to start another relationship anytime soon. Then all of a sudden, she's mad because we're not in a relationship. What in the holy hell is that?"

"You know it's been like ten months since you two have been dating right?"

"What?" I exclaimed.

"And although neither of you wants to admit it, you have been in a relationship damn near a year."

"It hasn't been a year." I counted using my fingers, "June, July, August, September...March..."

"T, my damn daffodils have started blooming. Spring is all but here."

That realization hit me square in the face. I knew John was correct, he generally was, which drove me nuts. "Jeez, you're right. Time flies when you're having fun I guess."

"You know I am. That's just it...you're having fun. Admit it. You like her. You want to be with her."

"I do like her," I admitted and smiled.

John held his hand out. "Okay Bitch, turn it in."

"Turn what in?" I asked.

"Your player card."

***

The last quarter of the school year was joyous, and havoc filled. It seemed like every time I turned around, my students' work was on display somewhere around town...City Hall, malls, BWI airport... I was having a hard time keeping up.

Jasmine and I hadn't really found our happy place again— consistently at least—after that bad snowstorm. Our vibe was off. It struck me then that with my schedule, I hadn't seen or talked to her in almost two weeks. And the last time we did talk, you could cut the tension with a knife. The easy flow wasn't there. Our conversations felt distant and forced.

In May, my principal informed me that my seventh-grade students received third place in the National Student Art Consortium. *Nice!* I, along with two students, would represent them and the school at an awards ceremony the first week of June in D.C. I really wanted to celebrate with Jasmine. I wanted her next to me. What was the point of success if you didn't have anyone to share it with? Except, I hadn't spoken to her, and I wasn't sure where we were or how we got there. So, I called. She didn't answer and I left a message. I still had three weeks before the ceremony, I would fill her in to see if she wanted to go.

Two weeks later, Principal Sheldon handed me two awards dinner tickets after a weekly staff meeting. I could feel my heart pounding and suddenly it felt like I was having trouble breathing. Jasmine still hadn't called me back. Shit! Was that season over? It became increasingly apparent that many of my other 'options' were women I no longer wanted to spend time with.

I really didn't want to go alone though so I started making calls. "What's up T?" Tina answered, I could hear Boney James' saxophone in the background.

"You. What's good Ms. Turner?" I used my nickname for her, she had legs like the icon. Legs she used to wrap around me.

"Girl please, I haven't heard from you in damn near a year."

I was confronted by the march of time again. "Ah, it can't be that long, seems like I'm always thinking about you," I replied.

"Save the bullshit, T. What do you want?" Tina cut me off.

Damn! "I wanted to know if you wanted to go out." I stuttered and gripped the phone.

"Out? Like outside of the house?" Tina sounded suspicious.

"Why did you have to say it like that? Yes, outside the house… to an awards dinner. More specifically, my students are getting an award and I wanted you to go," I tried to laugh.

"I wouldn't mind seeing you get a little award and all, but I got me a real girlfriend and we're good," I could hear the smugness.

"Well congratulations and good for you." My response wasn't genuine and sounded dry even to me.

"You should find you somebody T. Like one somebody. I like having someone who wants to be with me, day… night… inside… outside." Tina paused when she said the last four words. I winced; her words cut like a dull knife. I wished her well and hung up. Wow! Tina got a boo and wanted to provide advice to boot.

I called Mariah. We had caught up a bit at TK's family and friends' dinner. But today, she threw lots of shade and suggested I "ask the woman you were with," before hanging up on me. "Ahhhh! I tried to. She won't return my call!" I yelled in the air. I thought about "freak of the week" Jennifer but couldn't go through with the call. Lord only knows what she would show up wearing. I hadn't seen her with a lot of clothes on.

Ugh. I got myself into this mess. Before Jasmine, I was able to come and go as I pleased, remain a mystery, and dictate the flow of whatever quasi-relationship I happened to be in at that moment. Jasmine, however, wasn't trying to hear that. Whenever we went a few days without talking or I told her I had plans for the evening, she instantly got an attitude. This in turn only made me retreat further into my shell but I thought Jasmine was good with how things were. The whole "family" thing completely caught me off guard and now it seemed like Jasmine wanted no part of me.

By the time I called John it was an hour later, and I was slouched on the sofa with my head in my left hand and the phone in my right. I told John about the awards dinner, failing to find a date, and Jasmine disappearing.

"So, now what?" John asked.

"That's all you got? I just sat here and poured my heart out to you, and you ask, 'now what?'"

"Chile please, don't take it out on me. You upset because you just realized you in love with someone and she isn't returning your phone calls."

My face scrunched. There was a sharp pain in the void where my heart should have been. "I left Jasmine another message this evening and had half a mind to ride by her house but talked myself out of that idea," I confessed. "Why don't you go with me?" I asked John.

"Go where?" he asked.

"To the awards dinner. Have you not been listening?"

"Of course, I'm listening, you're just bouncing from thought to thought and I'm having trouble keeping up. Nonetheless, I'm sorry sweetie—Dre and I are heading to LA for a few days to boy watch."

"Fine, I'll figure something out," I pouted.

I knew I was reaching when I called my mother to ask if she wanted to come up and attend the dinner with me. Even my mother was busy! She and her church lady friends had a shopping trip planned to an outlet mall. My father half-jokingly thanked me for asking him second, but said he was staying near the house since Mom would be away. He also said that I must not be working hard enough to get Jasmine to go with me. *Thanks Dad!*

The thought of being without that smart, hyper-sensitive, quirky woman brought tears to my eyes. John said that I was in love. Was I? I hadn't really considered that that was what I was feeling. The question was, did she love me or even still like me? What I did know was that I had left a shit ton of messages that hadn't been returned.

***

The awards dinner was great! My students, and their brilliant talents, were rightfully recognized and I made a few important contacts. But that really didn't matter all that much to me in the broader context, I was there by myself. The people at the table were cordial, but I imagined they secretly pitied me because of the empty chair next to me. Jasmine should have been sitting there looking gorgeous, smiling, and smelling like warm spices and zesty citrus.

She had seeped into my life and into my consciousness. I found myself thinking about her when I woke up, when I was going to bed, working out, painting, eating lunch… basically all the time. I liked being in her space and her in mine. I liked experiencing new things with her but also marinating in life's mundane moments… listening to her breathe, holding her close, kissing her very, very soft lips.

Before I met Jasmine, I thought my life was pretty full and satisfying. Then she and Coco eased into it and my senses became heightened, the world became brighter, like I had been living in a muted impressionist painting and then stepped onto a bright Synthia Saint James book cover. But for some reason now, Jasmine wasn't answering her phone and it seemed as though she disappeared into thin air as quickly as she had appeared, and I missed her.

I drove back from D.C. and headed straight to Jasmine's house. I wanted more out of life. I wanted the steadiness and stability my parents enjoyed. I wanted a partner, and I wanted that partner to be Jasmine.

As I pulled up in front of her house, I noticed an unfamiliar car in the driveway. *Hmmm, maybe it belongs to one of her girls.* After ringing the bell, Coco started barking and I could hear her running to the door, which made me smile. I smiled with anticipation, an anticipation that was building in my chest and making my breathing quicken. When the door opened, my smile vanished, and my heart sank to the pit of my stomach.

"Hey, can I help you?" Toni, Jasmine's ex—I recognized her from the pictures that had since been removed—stood in the doorway.

I felt flush. Words were stuck in my throat. Although my mouth gaped open, I couldn't formulate or voice an intelligible thought out of the hundreds that were swirling in my head. "No, I uh, have the wrong house." I turned around and left before she could see my tears.

{FORTY-SIX}

Jasmine

"Did I hear the doorbell?" I asked, winded from carrying a tote bin up from the basement with stuff that I found in drawers and closets that meant something to Toni at one point. She promised to pick it up a while ago. So, when she called out of the blue saying she wanted to come over because I needed to sign documentation she received from her personnel department, I was suspicious, it was Toni after all.

"Yeah," Toni replied, "someone trying to sell windows and siding."

"This time of night? Did you open the door? I never open the door; anybody can get a shirt with a logo on it." I questioned, going to the door to peek out the living room window. I scanned the street for solicitors.

"It's okay, it was a small guy, I figured I could take him," Toni said laughing.

I laughed too, "Let's get the paperwork finished so you can get going."

"Jasmine," Toni said softly, "when human resources changed our health insurance coverage, it seemed like a good time to update other employee information. It didn't seem right to just remove your name off the beneficiary forms without having another conversation. Do we really need to do this? I know we haven't been together for months…"

"It's been almost a year Toni. And must I remind you that you left? And had somewhere to go when you did?"

"I know Jazz, but this makes it so final," Toni lamented.

"Yes, it does." I felt a surge of emotion, mostly sadness but also nostalgia and my eyes started welling up. I took several deep breaths to gather myself and let out a heavy sigh. "I'm sorry we came to this point after so many good years together," I admitted. We grieved the end of relationships, good, bad or otherwise. I knew she and I had made the right decision about ending our union. We weren't good together anymore. I talked nonstop for the next hour about the relationship overall and highlighted specific events where both of us could have thrown a penalty flag, called a flagrant foul, a technical... something to indicate any given situation was wrong or uncalled for.

Toni protested a few situations I noted but finally acknowledged it didn't matter because I clearly recounted the slow stair step decline of our relationship. From Toni's perspective, she said it just didn't seem that bad and for the life of her, she couldn't say when or why she started acting like she was single.

"Jazz, you were good for me, and all my friends knew it. They remind me all the time," she said.

"Really?" I was surprised, obviously she didn't care what I or they thought.

"Yeah, they've given me the blues for years to my face and behind my back."

I was dumbfounded and didn't know what to say about her revelations.

"Like, we were all at Pat's house this past Memorial Day weekend for a cookout and WNBA game watch party. The '24 Carat Gold Girls' was there doing their thing," she said very soberly. Ahh yes, the popular dancers that frequented private family parties and did freakishly erotic things with their bodies; I don't miss being around that energy.

"I can only imagine," I said, not really wanting to.

"Pat had one too many Jack and Cokes and decided to remind me and everyone else that I was always the first to give any of them tips or move towards the floor when dancers performed," she shared.

"Wow!"

"Then, everyone felt the need to pile on too."

"I'm sorry that happened to you. No one should be treated like that," I said honestly. I didn't tell Toni that Stephanie had already told me about the incident. She also added that Toni tried to shout Pat down and when it became a pile on, Toni got pissed and left. "You know that wasn't out of the ordinary for you, right?" I said to her.

Toni sat with her arms crossed and sulked. She shrugged and responded, "I don't remember being such an asshole."

I kept talking, "Toni please, getting on the floor at Donna and Lisa's commitment ceremony to catch a garter that was supposed to be for single ladies? Mentioning you didn't want to go to the Rehoboth Beach party because bringing me would be like taking sand to the beach? And the best one? You should be able to stay out for the weekend if there are parties on Friday and Saturday, 'cause you didn't want to waste gas going back and forth from Baltimore to D.C. Really?!"

"So, I was wrong. Givin' me another chance is out of the question?" Toni asked with the most loving smile I had seen on her face in forever.

"Yes, you're wrong and giving you another chance is so far out of the question, it's unrecognizable."

"Damn."

"Toni, I'm sorry you didn't listen when I tried to talk to you about what was happening with us. When you moved out, I realized that I had been living single for a long time because it was way too easy to keep my home alone routine going. So, about that paperwork?"

Toni sighed and slowly pulled nondescript forms out of her leather portfolio. HR included post-its and highlighted areas that required my signature acknowledging that I knew my name was being removed from the documentation. I reminded Toni to also update her bank accounts with new payable on death designations to prevent issues with probate.

"Thanks Jazz. See, I know you still love me. You're still looking out for me."

"Girl please! I don't want your people looking at me sideways if something happened to you and my name still on those accounts."

"You right," Toni said laughing again. "Jazz," Toni's voice became more serious. "Are you seeing someone?"

Damn. How do I answer that? I settled on the truth. "Yes, I've been dating." I really wanted to say, "It's complicated." But that didn't do the situation with T justice. Especially since I hadn't returned any of her calls as of late.

"I thought so. You have a lightness to you."

"Thanks," I said and smiled.

"By the way, that may have been who was at the door."

"What are you talking about?"

"There was a woman at the door. I vaguely recognized her from a picture at the Owings Mills exhibit. Coco seemed to know her though," Toni said sarcastically.

"What the hell Toni, why did you lie?"

"I figured I needed to give it one last shot without you knowing *Teresa* showed up," she whined.

"Toni you never cease to amaze me. Sometimes that's NOT a good thing by the way."

"Hey, I'm sorry, can't blame me for trying."

Now I was truly irritated. "Trying? Why didn't you try five years ago, hell five months ago? You've always thought our relationship operated on your time. See, that's what I'm talking about. None of what I've been saying is new. You're only pretending to listen because our breaking up caused what Toni, an inconvenience in your life?" My breathing quickened and I could feel blood rushing to my head. "You had to look at your finances differently? Of course, you didn't have to find a new place to live, that part was already taken care of. I bet you're paying more for rent now. Kind of cuts into your entertainment expenses huh? Chile please, bye! We've signed everything. Go home Toni, this ain't home no more!"

Toni gathered her things, looked around and responded, "I know, it hasn't been home for a long time." I squinted at the door for a long time after she closed it. "Coco, what the hell just happened?"

I was angry. Was that T? I listened to messages that were still in my voicemail and was reminded that T's awards ceremony was tonight. I was happy for her and her students. I wished I could have been there to celebrate with her. I should have had the courage to just say that. Maybe if T would have acknowledged our relationship or whatever the last year had been, I would have been there with bells on and in cocktail attire. I couldn't even get her to answer basic or fun questions that would have given me more insight into who she was. On the other hand, I was so sure I was right and added pressure on T to move whatever this was to another level. Was that fair?

I wearily started my evening routine; made a cup of chamomile tea, let Coco out, turned off lights, and wrapped up with the nightly security check. Hmmm, an unexpected visit, that didn't sound like T. Maybe it wasn't her. I wanted to call to find out, but after being stealth for weeks, what would I say?

I missed T though. I missed her smile and her laugh, her quiet confidence, her alluring eyes. I had been so busy protecting my heart that I may have unintentionally walled it off from what could be an extraordinary relationship. I hadn't called because, because, because, I didn't know why. Check that, I did know why. I was terrified of loving again. Terrified of loving someone who seemingly dropped out of the sky and literally crossed my path. The unlikeliness of it all had tilted my world off its axis.

{FORTY-SEVEN}

T

Perhaps I could have done some things differently. I should have done better. But Jasmine had a role to play too; her indecisiveness was dizzying. Did I really care, or was I salty because Toni was at her house? The real answer was both! John said to me once that 'the one that got away always looked better on someone else's arm.' I didn't know about that 'cause Jasmine looked damn good on *my* arm. I didn't know much though; two more weeks had passed since the awards ceremony and still no word from Jasmine. I left what I considered to be the final message for Jasmine last week. In it, I apologized because I felt it to be appropriate, and wished her well.

School was out for the summer, and I did what was best for me. I turned down my principal's offer to run the summer arts program and instead worked out more consistently, focused on my art, and reconnected with folks I hadn't spoken to in a while.

My parents came up the first week in July. We had a great time visiting museums in D.C., shopping, discovering new restaurants, and enjoying the 4th of July fireworks at the Inner Harbor. They also—in no uncertain terms—let me know they were disappointed they didn't get to see Jasmine. So was I.

When they headed home, I decided to head to the Harbor for a run that very evening. I could feel the extra weight from a week of rich food and sans exercise. As I rounded the curve on the track, I heard a dog barking and a familiar phrase, "Coco, no!" I knew that voice, which made my heart pound harder than it already had been. I looked to my left and saw the ball of white fur heading in my direction. I slowed to a walk and tried my best not to smile as Coco jumped up and down like a little springboard waiting for me to pick her up. I did. Jasmine and another woman were close behind.

"Hey," I said smiling, an inadvertent thing that just happened when I saw Jasmine, "long time."

"Hello Teresa," Jasmine replied. The other woman smiled widely and extended her hand. "T, I don't know if you remember me, we met at Sam's party last year?" She removed her sunglasses. "I'm Paula, I share an office with Jasmine?"

"Yes, yes of course," I replied, slightly relieved now that I could see her face. I wiped my hand on my shorts, shook her hand, and responded, "It's nice to see you again. How's your cousin?"

"She's okay, thank you for asking. As she anticipated, her unit deployed in January. All things considered, she said she was good when we talked a month or so ago." At a loss for words, I just nodded my head and nervously rubbed my sweating hands on my shorts again.

"Good seeing you," Paula said to me and turned towards Jasmine. She smiled and gave her a hug. "I'll see you tomorrow," Paula said waving over her shoulder. Jasmine tried to protest but Paula was already twenty feet away. Jasmine reached out to extract Coco from my arms. I hadn't realized I was still holding the dog. The same dog that I was terribly irritated with last year and so happy to have seen today. "This is a surprise," Jasmine said turning away, "You take care," and proceeded to walk away.

"Oh, hell no Jasmine, I've left you a lot of messages," I yelled.

"Really T, you want to do this here?"

"Yeah. Yeah, I want to do this here considering I haven't talked to you, and you won't return my calls. This is as good a place as any. What's up with that?"

"Okay, yes, you've left me what four messages?"

"Jasmine, you know that works both ways and you know I've called way more than that. It doesn't matter how many times I called; you didn't return any of them." I felt myself getting worked up. My heart was racing again, and it was suddenly harder to breathe.

"At this point it doesn't matter, Ms. Butler you've been clear about maintaining your single status and stand-offishness."

"Is that a word?" I asked, trying not to smile.

"That's beside the point," Jasmine's hands gestured in the air. "You want to be single? Fine. But that doesn't work for me, I'm out."

"Damn it, Jasmine! You're projecting, that's a psychology term right? I never said I wanted to be single."

She rolled her eyes. "Your actions did. I question your actions."

"Jasmine, I'm not sure what actions you're referring to, but it seems like you're overreacting." This conversation wasn't going well, and I felt like Jasmine had already dismissed me. For someone who 'loved love,' as Stephanie put it, Jasmine certainly wasn't acting like it. I wanted to tell her that I wanted to be with her and only her. I wanted to tell her that I chose her. Instead, I was watching Jasmine and Coco walk away, and potentially, out of my life.

"Jasmine! Wait! Please, don't go!" Unfortunately, she kept walking. "Jasmine, I know you hear me, please wait!" She slowed, stopped, and turned around. "What T, what do you need to tell me?" I knew this was quite likely my last shot.

"Jasmine please, can we just talk?" She reluctantly agreed and we sat on the steps bordering the track.

"I've missed being with you. The fact that you've been okay being apart hurts," I said, rubbing my palms on my shorts for the umpteenth time. My foot nervously shaking. She didn't respond.

"Look, I probably have irrational beliefs about how I think relationships stifle individuality and I don't want to be codependent. Those two things may influence my actions. And I've always been a bit headstrong but that's gotten me this far." She cut her eyes at me. I bit my bottom lip and swallowed hard. "I guess I've just been trying to protect myself." She sat there for a bit with her eyes closed, then shook her head from side to side. "Thank you for sharing," she said and stood up.

For someone who wasn't used to working this hard to move a relationship forward, I was undone. I had pleaded and confided only to be told, 'Thanks for sharing?' I was both angry and hurt. It seemed like Jasmine just didn't care.

"I gotta go," she said and picked Coco up. She paused though, "T, I think you're talented beyond measure and good at what you do, in more ways than one," Jasmine said with a shy smile. "But I also think you need to learn how to make space for special people." She started walking away, again.

Jasmine wasn't wrong, although that's what I had been trying to tell her. I yelled over squawking seagulls, "We never finished your twenty questions!" Jasmine turned around. "Really?" Twenty questions? That's what you got? I'm going home T," she said and dismissively waved her hand.

"Twenty questions in ten minutes on that park bench up there." I pointed to the bench on Federal Hill where she and I sat last year. "I don't feel like playing anymore games T," Jasmine yelled back at me.

I ignored her, knowing full well that after our up and down, mostly up, relationship over the past year, Jasmine's natural instinct was pensive cautiousness that was protected by a steely exterior. Perhaps it came from years of not being treated like a queen. But the woman I had come to know was warm, kind, and liked to have fun.

Here goes nothing. I started walking toward her and Coco. "Dogs or cats?"

"Dogs," Jasmine answered when I was standing in front of her again. "But you know that and oh by the way, you don't even like dogs."

"I didn't know I liked dogs until I met your dog," Coco wagged her tail.

"Give me a chance." I placed my hand over my heart. I was nervous, this may be my last chance with Jasmine. "Give us a chance."

"I'll answer the others up there," Jasmine said pointing to the top of the hill and walking away.

***

"If you were on a deserted island, what one person would you want to be there with you?" Jasmine asked.

"You," I answered.

"Me?" She looked wide eyed. "Why me?"

"Because you're rather resourceful. And quite frankly, I need someone who is both easy on the eyes and isn't afraid of a little sweat."

"Uh huh?!" Jasmine gave me the side eye and continued, "what do you value most in a friendship?"

"Honesty, genuineness," I said.

"Why?" Jasmine turned facing me again.

"Because I like real people. And we introverts have to conserve energy; sometimes it can feel like people are sucking the life out of us. Life is too short to have to wade through stuff and read someone's mind. Just tell me what's on your mind."

Jasmine interjected, "We've talked about this, people are way more complicated than that."

"I hear you. But everything and everyone doesn't always have to be. That's why I love John for example. He's a real one... has lots of sauce. I don't have to guess with him, you know?"

"Yeah, that was my experience with him," she said and smiled.

"Guess what?"

"What?"

"He told me I was a fool. And insisted that I stand outside your house every night and beg you to be with me."

"Smart man!" Jasmine agreed. "Ms. Butler, what do you want?"

"Honestly?" I asked.

"Of course, honestly."

I took a deep, long breath and stared out at the Harbor, listening to its rhythms. I slid closer to Jasmine, clasped her hand, and sat there another moment. "Do you remember the snowstorm?"

"How could I forget it?" Jasmine answered, rolling her eyes at me.

"And the Christmas party?" I questioned.

"Ugh!" She shook her head as if to erase the thought.

"I know I pissed you off. I got excited that we were going to be together and should have done a way better job of thinking through the logistics of the whole thing, the snowstorm I mean."

"Right..."

"I don't know if anything could have prepared me for Stephanie though," I pointed out. Jasmine smiled at that fact. "But I've really only been concerned with caring about myself, and my parents of course, in a meaningful way a majority of my adult life. You and Coco have surprised me just as much as I've surprised you." I paused. "I've had to grow a little more and expand my aperture."

Jasmine nodded and raised her eyebrows suggesting that she agreed with me.

"We both have our own stuff Jasmine and that's not necessarily a bad thing in and of itself since we're as human as anyone else. I don't know what the future holds. But what I do know is that I want you to be a part of it," I confessed and stopped talking. I felt like I had already said a lot.

A minute or so passed and I heard Jasmine take a deep breath. "T, did you stop by the house a few weeks ago? After your awards ceremony?" Jasmine probed.

"What? Yes." My eyes stretched wide, then my brow furrowed. "You knew?

She was silent.

"If you knew, you knew I tried to see you. Why didn't you return my calls? Why have you been missing in action? Why didn't you reach out?" I found myself holding my breath waiting for her response. "Jasmine, I stopped by to tell you that I wanted to be with you and your ex-girlfriend answered the door. I felt humiliated."

"T, I'm sorry," Jasmine said just above a whisper.

"What was she doing there? Ya'll back together?" I asked, feeling sick to my stomach and a lump appeared in my throat.

"No, absolutely not," she responded quickly.

"Then why was she there?" I asked, the lump constricting my air flow, threatening to choke the life out of me.

Jasmine sighed. "I needed to sign some paperwork acknowledging I was being taken off as her insurance beneficiary," she said. I stared at her trying to determine if she was telling the truth. She didn't look at me. She stared straight ahead at the city skyline then started speaking ever so slowly. "T, I'm sorry," she said, tears silently running down her cheek. *Damn it,* now she was crying. My stomach can't take this. "I've had a tendency to plan just about everything in my life to a tee, no pun intended," Jasmine smiled.

"Since I didn't plan this, it still scares me even after spending the last year with you."

"Fair enough," I said, unsure of what to make of Jasmine's revelation. I was still stunned that she chose to put distance between us, but I used my index finger to brush her tears away.

"But the fear isn't as palpable as it once was," she said quietly and looking down.

"And that's a good thing, I think?" I said with one eyebrow raised.

Jasmine softly poked me in the side. "Yes silly. I get more excited about us moving to the next chapter than being afraid of the unknown. I know I haven't returned your calls and I'm sorry for that. I had to take some time to think without being unduly influenced by...," she trailed off.

"By what?" I wanted to know.

"You said it, that we humans can overthink things," Jasmine said. "And I probably do that more than the average bear. It's how my brain works, not to mention how I make a living." She snickered a bit. "I'm trying to learn how to get out of my own way," Jasmine paused, "do you know what really scares me?"

"What?" I asked, not sure I wanted to hear the answer.

"When we are in sync, there is an overwhelming sense of peace and joy that I feel when I'm with you." She let the sentiment hang in the air before continuing, "And more than that, what really frightens me is the intense desire that overwhelms me when we aren't together." I listened intently. She continued, "I thought I knew what love was. And I'm sure that I experienced it with Toni in our better years. But this? Sometimes I think this is almost too good to be true, like it's the fairy tale that I've said I wanted, that I've dreamed about. But at some point, I think I'm going to wake up."

"Jasmine," I said before she talked herself into running away.

"Yes?" she answered and fidgeted.

"Number one, breathe," I paused and took my own advice as well, "number two, I feel the same way."

"You do?" She leaned away to look at me fully.

"Yes." I scooted closer and leaned in so our shoulders were touching.

"You never said anything." She smiled.

"Nor have you until this moment." I beamed.

We sat holding hands, sitting shoulder to shoulder, and staring at the activity in the Inner Harbor until the sun sank below the horizon and turned the sky a combination of vibrant pink, orange, and yellow. The last of the water taxis made its way across the harbor carrying what sounded like drunken revelers all the way up here. People going about their daily lives unaware, nor should they have been, of me and Jasmine contemplating if we would take a chance, a chance on ourselves, a chance on each other, a chance at something raw, yet so real.

I leaned in and whispered in Jasmine's ear, "I want you."

"Excuse me?" she exclaimed, the skeptic always lurking just below the surface.

"Earlier. You asked what I wanted," I said, "I want you. I want to be a part of your fairy tale. I want us to be a family. I want *this*." Jasmine slowly nodded her head 'yes' and laid her head on my shoulder. We sat there like that for a while, neither one of us wanting to pierce the stillness. When dusk settled over the park and everything around us, she stood up and reached for my hand. I stood, putting one hand in hers and grabbing Coco's leash with the other. She leaned in, kissed me, and whispered, "I want that too."

BOOK CLUB QUESTIONS

Jasmine mentioned the ebb and flow of her and Toni's relationship. What actions did they both engage in that contributed to the ebb?

Jasmine and T both leaned on friends for support early in their love connection. How have friends supported your decisions related to establishing new relationships?

T bought Jasmine an unusual gift. What was the most unusual gift you've ever given or received?

Relationships require effort. What tips would you suggest to keep a relationship strong?

A key theme in the book is honesty. In what ways do you think Jasmine and T were honest and were not honest or not completely truthful with each other?

What did T need to learn about relationships to allow her to let down her guard, embrace Jasmine, and be open to a committed relationship?

In what ways did unresolved conflict influence Jasmine and T's decision about the future of their relationship?

Were there any characters you felt connected to? Why?

Jasmine hid Toni's gender from coworkers. In what ways do people in same gender relationships have to navigate societal norms?

CONNECT WITH NAOMI

If you would like Naomi Rivers to participate in your online book club, please email Naomi at naomiriversbooks@gmail.com for availability.

Naomi loves to connect with her readers. Subscribe to her newsletter for updates and giveaways at naomiriversbooks.com or visit her on Facebook and Instagram @naomiriversbooks, or Twitter @nrivers_books.

Would you like to be on Naomi's VIP reader team? Visit naomiriversbooks.com We value your privacy and will not sell your information.

ABOUT THE AUTHOR

Naomi Rivers writes lesbian romance and women's fiction. Her first book, *THIS: A Simple, Complex Love Story*, was written while traveling on four continents. She is a retired U.S. military veteran and resides with her wife and rescue dog on the east coast.